CAPITOL PUNISHMENT

ANDY HAYES MYSTERIES

by Andrew Welsh-Huggins

Fourth Down and Out

Slow Burn

Capitol Punishment

CAPITOL PUNISHMENT

AN ANDY HAYES MYSTERY

ANDREW WELSH-HUGGINS

SWALLOW PRESS
OHIO UNIVERSITY PRESS
ATHENS

Swallow Press
An imprint of Ohio University Press, Athens, Ohio 45701
ohioswallow.com

© 2016 by Andrew Welsh-Huggins
All rights reserved

Printed in the United States of America
Swallow Press / Ohio University Press books are printed on acid-free paper ♾ ™

26 25 24 23 22 21 20 19 18 17 16   5 4 3 2 1

Library of Congress Cataloging-in-Publication Data
Names: Welsh-Huggins, Andrew, author.
Title: Capitol punishment : an Andy Hayes mystery / Andrew Welsh-Huggins.
Description: Athens, Ohio : Swallow Press, 2016.
Identifiers: LCCN 2015044711 | ISBN 9780804011716 (hardback) | ISBN
  9780804040716 (pdf)
Subjects: LCSH: Private investigators—Fiction. |
  Murder—Investigation—Fiction. | Columbus (Ohio)—Fiction. | Mystery
  fiction. | BISAC: FICTION / General. | FICTION / Mystery & Detective /
  General.
Classification: LCC PS3623.E4824 C37 2016 | DDC 813/.6—dc23
LC record available at http://lccn.loc.gov/2015044711

For Pam, who knows the difference

between a lorgnette and a lanyard, and

isn't afraid to say so

The town is clean and pretty, and of course is "going to be" much larger. It is the seat of the State legislature of Ohio, and lays claim, in consequence, to some consideration and importance.

—Charles Dickens, describing his
impressions of Columbus in
American Notes

Fear of something is at the root of hate for others, and hate within will eventually destroy the hater.

—George Washington Carver, in a
quote on permanent display at the
Ohio Statehouse

Sad at heart, I answered: "Sleep and my foolish crew brought me harm, but you, my friends, have the power to set all to rights."

—Odysseus, in Homer's *Odyssey*, Book 10

Prologue

I had to bend over to catch my breath when I finally reached the top of the stairs, which is why the bullet missed me and splintered the wall just above my head. I didn't wait for a second shot. I lunged to my right and started counterclockwise around the curved room, away from the origin of the gunfire. A moment later, exhausted by the climb, I stumbled and fell, dropping what I'd been holding and hitting my head on the worn, century-old wooden bench hugging the inner wall. Staggering to my feet, I touched my forehead with my right hand and felt something warm and sticky. I took a breath and listened. The layout of the room, an enclosed circular walkway, made it impossible to see more than a few feet in either direction. Was I being followed from behind or approached from ahead? I was like a knight in a drained moat trying to escape an oncoming dragon. Except that my armor wasn't very shiny and the dragon was more of a snake. The ringing in my ears from the gunshot made it hard to hear above the rock anthem pumping up the crowd outside and far below, and I nearly missed the sound of footsteps. I glanced behind me, reached down, picked up what I'd dropped and, ignoring the popping in my knees, limped away from the noise as fast as possible. I just hoped I'd guessed the right way to go.

"You don't want to do this," I said, trying to make myself heard over the music. "It's over."

"You're right about that," came the reply, in an unnervingly calm voice.

I paused, trying to figure out how far behind me the words were coming from. I heard another voice echoing outside. Authoritative, confident and assuring, the tone of a man who has gazed into your eyes and knows your heart and wants nothing more than to help you.

"That's Governor Hubbard," I said. "The introduction's about to start. You're wasting time."

"I've got plenty."

"I don't think so. We both know you're on deadline."

"Dead is right."

I took another breath and used my left hand to wipe away the blood dripping into my eyes. I put my hand back on the wall to steady myself; the bloody palm print would be a new kind of signature for the room. Outside, the governor's plummy voice rose and fell in the practiced rhythms that had served him well in numerous elections and would again, many hoped, but this time in the biggest contest of all. "*The person I'm about to present to you is no stranger to the great state of Ohio . . .*" the governor said, but stopped, immediately drowned out by another chorus of cheers.

"Almost time," I said.

"Shut up."

"Pick or choose."

"Shut *up*."

"*The best person I know to lead this wonderful country which I love so much . . .*" the governor said, even louder now, and was once again interrupted by yells and applause.

"It's over," I repeated.

I waited in vain for a reply. The only noise came from outside. Maybe I was too late: maybe it really was finished. Just not the way I'd hoped. Then I heard a new sound, of footsteps hitting the wooden floor hard: the sound of someone running toward me, fast, with nothing left to lose.

1

"YOU EXPECTING SOMEONE?" ANNE SAID, looking up from the table at the sound of the doorbell. Memorial Day, almost three weeks earlier.

"Not if they know what's good for them," I said.

I let the spoon I was holding sink into the bowl of pancake batter on the counter and stumped down the hall. To say it was rare to have a morning together with my two sons, my girlfriend, and my girlfriend's daughter was the understatement of the year, and I wasn't in the mood to miss a second of it.

I opened my front door and eyed the man standing before me.

"Yeah?"

"Well, heck, you're not nearly as ugly in person," he said, grinning.

"I gave at the office," I said, and started to close the door in his face. He wouldn't be the first person to track me down at home and attempt a debate over my two-decade-old college foot-ball career. I had no interest in entertaining the latest incarnation, especially so early on a holiday.

"Hang on, Woody," he said. "I'm not stalking you. I just want to talk."

"It's Andy. And why would I want to talk to you?"

"Fine, *Andy*. Let's start over. I'm a paying customer. I want to hire you."

"For what?"

"Personal protection," he said. He was about my height, maybe a few years older, a little heavy around the middle and in his jowls, but with a handsome, clean-shaven face and a relatively full head of trim, gray hair. He wore a blue button-down shirt, tan chinos, a navy sports coat, and penny loafers, which all seemed a bit natty for that time of day but which he also carried off well.

"Protection from what?"

"Someone's been following me."

"Who?"

"I knew, I wouldn't need to hire you." He handed me a card. **Lee Hershey,** *Public Reporting Enterprise.*

"That's you?" I said. He nodded. "So what is this?" I asked.

"My business. I'm a freelance reporter. Worked at a bunch of places and now I'm on my own, online. Future of journalism is digital, in case you hadn't noticed."

"I think I read that in the paper," I said. "You're being followed because you're a reporter?"

"As far as I can tell, given that I'm up to date on my alimony payments. Something we can bond over, if I'm not mistaken."

"And how would you know that?"

"Reporter," he said, grinning again.

I thought about the crowd in my kitchen and the pancakes I needed to make and the fact I don't like to be reminded of my two separate divorce proceedings at any time of the day or night.

"Listen," I said. "Is there some other occasion besides first thing on a holiday morning at my front door we could talk? Maybe you could call and make an appointment like a normal person?"

"Fair enough. I realize it's early and all that. But it happened again last night, and I know of your work, and I figured it might just be faster this way. Plus I'm kind of used to knocking on doors." He pulled out his wallet and retrieved several twenty-dollar bills. "I can pay up front if you need. I'm not trying to blow smoke or anything."

I hesitated, eyeing the money. I'd spent most of the previous day taking pictures of an insurance company honcho walking into the northside condo of a woman not his wife. I'd gotten the money shot, but the fee for that bit of heartbreak would keep gas in my Honda Odyssey and kibble in Hopalong's bowl for a few weeks, max. I had to admit my prospects were otherwise thin at the moment.

"OK," I said. "Just speed it up a bit. You think this is something to do with your job?"

He was about to reply when Anne came up the hall. I introduced them, a little reluctantly, and Hershey shook her hand with a slight bow. It would have been hopelessly pretentious if I tried it, but, like his outfit, he somehow pulled it off.

"A pleasure to meet you," he said to Anne. "You teach science fiction, don't you? At Columbus State?"

"That's right. How did you know that?"

"Big sci-fi buff. I saw you gave a lecture recently on *The Day of the Triffid*. I love the book, though the movie's awesome too."

"They're both great in their own ways," she said, and to my amazement I noticed she was blushing.

"Isn't *The Sparrow* your favorite book?" Hershey continued. "Probably my second favorite, at least science fiction–wise. I went to a Jesuit high school, so I always sort of empathized with the main character. Father—?"

"Emilio Sandoz," she said.

"That's it. We should have coffee some time, when this is all over. Love to pick your brain."

"That sounds good," she said, with more enthusiasm than I cared for. "But what's your first?"

"Sorry?"

"You said *The Sparrow* was your second favorite."

"So I did. I'm a big Philip K. Dick guy. So I have to go with *Do Androids Dream of Electric Sheep?*"

"Love that book," she said. "And if you like that, have you read—"

I cleared my throat. "I don't mean to interrupt," I said, which was not strictly true. "You were saying something about being followed?"

"Of course," Hershey said. "Sorry to get carried away."

"Who's following you?" Anne said, with concern in her voice. Hershey repeated what he had told me.

"And you have no idea who it could be?" I said.

From behind us came what sounded like the beginnings of an argument at the breakfast table. "Excuse me," Anne said. "I have to see to the troops. It was nice meeting you. We'll have to have that coffee."

"It would be my pleasure," Hershey said, doing that bow thing again.

"So," I said, once Anne was gone, trying not to dwell on the way Hershey's eyes followed her progress down the hall.

"OK," he said. "Ever heard of Triple F?" I shook my head.

"It stands for Fair Funding Focus, otherwise known as Governor Hubbard's school-funding plan."

I thought about this. "The acronym is all F's?"

"Leave it to the Democrats. After they realized their mistake, they tried changing the name to 'A Better Collaboration,'—ABC, get it?" he said. "But it was way too late. Serves them right, in my opinion."

"I guess. So what about it?"

"It's the biggest story in the state at the moment. And one I've been kicking ass on, pardon my French."

"It's big because—?"

"Ohio's school-funding system has been ruled unconstitutional so many times it's practically got 'Return to Sender' stamped on the first page. Hubbard thinks he's finally got the numbers right. Enough to appease the state Supreme Court, anyway. Get it declared fit for duty once and for all. That alone would be huge."

"And someone's following you because of this?"

"I'm getting there. The thing is, enacting Triple F into law has another aspect to it."

"Namely?"

"The eensy-weensy, itsy-bitsy side benefit of providing the feather in Hubbard's cap to win over Senator Rodriguez."

"JoAnn Rodriguez? The presidential candidate?"

"One and the same."

"What's she got to do with any of this?"

Hershey winked at me. "You know how, in high school, the prettiest girl, by amazing coincidence, always goes to prom with the quarterback?"

"I couldn't say."

"I bet. So imagine Rodriguez as our cheerleader captain. The hunk she really wants on her arm at prom—her choice for veep, in case I've lost you—is our very own Thomas Huntington Hubbard. They'd make such a cute couple—conservative Democrat from California and a moderate midwestern governor. Rodriguez brings the Latinos and women, Hubbard delivers the unions. Voila!"

"OK, match made in heaven. I get it."

"Hubbard's even got a best-selling book, which no doubt you've read. I know Rodriguez's people have, cover to cover."

"I think my Kindle shorted out that week."

"*Core Convictions*," Hershey said. "Biographies of great American populist politicians. Comes with a nice long personal essay that puts him square in that tradition just in case the allusion to his own career escaped you after seven hundred pages."

"So you've read it?"

"Every word, Woody, every word. Thomas Hubbard, literary lion, and don't you forget it."

"My nightstand awaits."

"It's actually better than you'd imagine. But there's only one problem with Hubbard."

"Which is?"

"Something that you of all people can identify with. He may be governor of the most crucial swing state in the country, with a knockout first lady wife and two adorable kids, not to mention *Core Convictions*, but he needs an extra something before Rodriguez extends the invitation."

"Like what?"

"A win, Woody. A *big* win. We're not talking Big Ten championship crapola. Sugar Bowl, minimum."

I considered this. "Triple F," I said.

"Bingo. Hubbard gets his school-funding law passed, he takes Rodriguez to prom, otherwise known as Rodriguez-Hubbard 2016."

"And if Triple F fails?"

"If Hubbard can't deliver the bill, the governor of Pennsylvania is looking like a mighty fine consolation prize."

"And that's why you think you're being followed? Because of the politics involved?"

"The stakes are pretty high. Objectively speaking, I think some of my stories have annoyed people with a powerful interest in seeing the education bill passed."

"And they're trying to stop you? Or what?"

"Not really sure. Though for starters, I'd guess they're trying to find out who my sources are."

"And who are they?"

"People whose identities I prefer not to divulge for now."

"So I just avert my eyes and look the other way when you're in the parking garage talking to Deep Throat?"

"Don't worry about that part of it," he said. "Just hang with me when I need you. They'll get the message, whoever they are."

"And you really have no idea who it might be?"

He shrugged. "Maybe it's Hubbard's folks. Maybe it's Rodriguez's camp. Maybe President Ryan's people are coming down from Michigan to make sure I'm not being followed by Rodriguez's people. Maybe it's nutso Tea Party types who want us to go back to slide rules and corporal punishment. I don't know. But I care to find out. That's why I came to you."

"Are you worried, or just curious?"

He hesitated. "Normally, I'd say, you know, fuck 'em if they can't take a joke. I mean, it's a free country, First Amendment, Fourth Estate, and all that."

"But?"

"But it's a bit of a scary world right now. A *Charlie Hebdo* world, if you know what I mean."

"That sounds a lot more serious than someone trying to bust your sources."

"For the record, I don't think guys with black masks and daggers are out to behead me. It just seems like an overabundance of caution is the way to go."

"Have you talked to the police?"

He shook his head.

"Why not?"

"I report it, it becomes a public record, someone writes about it. I report news. I've no interest in being the news. So what do you say?"

"How long are we talking?"

"Couple of weeks, tops. They need to pass the bill soon, ostensibly to hit the next budget cycle July 1, but also because Rodriguez is itching to make a choice. Hubbard's on the lawmakers' backs trying to get this done."

"And what do you want me to do, exactly?"

"Tag along on a couple of assignments, act as my eyes and ears if I pick up a tail, provide a little muscle if things get rough."

"Muscle's all you're going to get, since I don't carry a gun."

"That's good, since firearms give me a rash. We have a deal?"

Despite a couple of rough edges I'd picked up on, and despite the way Anne had uncharacteristically swooned for the guy, I agreed that we did. I didn't really have a choice, as my bank account could attest. Hershey handed me several of the twenties as a down payment, and I got his e-mail to send him a contract.

"So what's the first job?"

"You know the Clarmont?"

"The steakhouse, on South High?"

He nodded. "First assignment is having a drink there with me, tomorrow night."

"A drink?"

"Or two. Plus you'd be on the clock."

"Why the Clarmont?"

"Legislature's back in session after Memorial Day with the push on to pass this damn bill. Everyone in town will be there. One-stop shopping for tips. And suspects."

"Half the state's powerbrokers eat and drink at the Clarmont. Like one of them's going to risk making a run at you while you're sipping your gin and tonic?"

"First of all, it's vodka and tonic. Second, how about we just call this 'Department of Better Safe Than Sorry.' Third, like I said, I want to send a message."

"OK. What time?"

"Five o'clock. Pick me up?" He asked for my cell phone number, and texted me the address.

"See you then," I said, starting to close the door. But Anne, coming back up the hall, interrupted.

"Oh, good, you're still here," she said. "I realized I had this with me." She handed Hershey a paperback.

"*The Android's Dream,*" she said. "By John Scalzi. I thought you might like it, you know, because of Philip K. Dick."

"How kind of you," Hershey said, beaming. "I'll get right to it. Then we'll have a perfect excuse for coffee."

"I hope you enjoy it."

"I'm sure I will."

After we said our good-byes and I shut the door, Anne and I walked down the hall to the kitchen.

"Nice guy," she said a little too enthusiastically.

"Right," I replied, focusing on pancake duty. But what I was thinking, my face getting a little warm, was why did Hershey know the title of my girlfriend's favorite science fiction novel, and I didn't?

2

I PICKED HERSHEY UP LATE THE NEXT afternoon at his house in a modest, well-kept subdivision tucked between Hague and Trabue Avenues on the west side. The beige, split-level ranch was a little plain but had prettier landscaping, a neater lawn, and more flowers than I'd ever managed.

"Nice place," I said as he got into my van.

"It's all right. I mainly just eat and sleep here. Most of the time I'm downtown."

"You have an office?"

"The nearest coffee shop. Plus a cubicle in the Statehouse pressroom."

"Family?"

"Do multiple ex-girlfriends count?"

I didn't reply. I drove slowly up the street, checking fore and aft for any company. Unless people walking their dogs while blabbing on their cell phones were considered a threat, we were OK for now.

"Have you been followed out here?"

"Couple times. Someone tailed me last week as I was going to work."

"Get a look at the driver?"

He shook his head.

"Black or white?"

"Couldn't tell."

"Man or woman? Fish or fowl?"

"Sorry."

"No offense, but aren't you supposed to be a trained observer?"

"I've got a blind spot when it comes to people wishing me harm. Which is why I hired you."

"Smart move," I said, doubtfully.

THE CLARMONT SITS JUST south of Sycamore, where the Brewery District with its nice restaurants and well-heeled brick office buildings starts to peter out and the grittier South End begins. "Seafood & Steak," its red-lettered sign advertised. The parking lot was nearly full when we pulled in.

As Hershey held the door for me, I nearly collided with a woman rushing out, head bowed over her phone.

"Excuse me," she said, without looking up.

"Watch yourself, Lauren," Hershey said. "This guy might flag you for an illegal tackle."

She glanced at Hershey and frowned. "What are you doing here?"

"Warning people not to text and walk. Anything good in there?"

He pointed at the thick blue three-ring binder she was holding in her left hand. "Fair Funding Focus," it said on the cover.

"You tell me," she said. "You seem to know all about it." She had short, honey-blond hair, blue eyes that searched and then dismissed me a little too quickly, like a dog groomer snubbing a mutt, and a hint of a southern accent; I was guessing Georgia, or maybe east Texas.

"I've only scratched the surface," Hershey said. "Have you persuaded them to deep-six the charter school amendments yet?"

"Oh, very funny."

"Just a question."

"A dumb one, as usual," she said, and brushed past us.

"Friend of yours?" I said, as we went inside.

"Frenemy, like most of the people I know around here."

"Who is she?"

"Her name's Lauren Atkinson. She's head of the state teachers' union. She came up the hard way, fighting skinflint school boards that insisted on four assistant football coaches but screamed bloody murder if the teachers asked for an extra planning period once a week. We ever meet with *her*, you're going to need reinforcements."

"Her binder said 'Fair Funding Focus.' Didn't you say they realized their mistake and changed the name?"

He laughed, a deep, rich sound that, annoyingly, made you want to laugh right along with him.

"They changed their minds back again after I reported how much it was going to cost taxpayers to reprint all the binders. C'mon."

After we found a couple of seats at the bar, Hershey ordered his vodka and tonic, and on impulse I ordered the most expensive beer they had, a twenty-ounce bottle of Belgian ale I knew I wouldn't like but which I would enjoy watching Hershey pay for. My passive-aggressive way of tweaking him for charming Anne with all that sci-fi talk. I'm a tough guy, like that. Hershey was chatting up the bartender and I was scanning the crowd for dagger-wielding killers when a woman walked up, stopped, and tapped Hershey on the shoulder.

"Hey, asshole," she said.

He turned. "Hello, Kerri. What do you know?"

"I know I'm thirsty as hell."

"*Plus ça change . . .*" Hershey said with that smile of his, and nodded at the bartender. A moment later a glass of white wine materialized, and Hershey handed it to the woman. They clinked glasses, and Hershey turned to me.

"Kerri MacKenzie, Andy Hayes."

"And you are?" she said.

"He's a hired hand making sure people like you don't beat me up," Hershey said, as I handed her my card.

"Bodyguard, huh?" she said. "You'd take a bullet for this guy?"

"Maybe a small one," I said. "If it asked nicely."

She laughed. Hershey said, "Kerri works for the Senate Democrats. She's a 'Senior Democratic Caucus policy analyst,'" he said, making exaggerated air quotes.

"Sounds fancy."

"Not really," Hershey said, winking at MacKenzie. "What it means, since you didn't ask, is donkey blood runs through her veins, she can spell 'Adlai Stevenson' without peeking, and she knows where even more bodies are buried than me, which if I do say so myself is rather impressive."

"And someday one of them will be yours," MacKenzie said, saluting Hershey with a punch in the shoulder with one hand, followed by a toast with the other. But I could tell by her eyes she had enjoyed the compliment.

"Tillman's mad as hell at you," she said.

"Tell me something I don't know. What's his beef this time?"

"As if. Your story about Midwest Testing."

"What about it?"

"They've contributed heavily to his campaign. Big whoop."

"They're the third-biggest school testing company in the country. Tillman's the Senate education chairman. It smells."

"They have a right to let him know how much they value his hard work," she said. She had short, dark hair and a pleasant face with lines around her eyes that looked like she'd earned them the hard way. Midthirties, if I had to guess. No wedding ring.

"I just got here and you've already exceeded my nightly capacity for bullshit," Hershey said. "If Triple F passes," he said, turning to me, "Midwest will be at the front of the line when they start handing out contracts for all the new exams the legislation will mandate. We're talking so much money, they'll have to build new vaults just to hold it."

"Enough with the Triple F. It's 'A Better Collaboration,' now," MacKenzie corrected.

"Spare me," Hershey said.

"So, Midwest," I said, interrupting. "They're greasing the skids with Tillman?"

"Gold star," Hershey said, raising his hand to ward off an objection from MacKenzie. "The distinguished state senator Edmund Tillman. Some donations here, some donations there, an all-expenses-paid trip to Vegas to attend the National Association of Assessment Agencies' winter 'conference.' You get the idea."

"Tillman's pissed because you said he didn't report that trip," MacKenzie said. "But he did."

"Once I started asking questions, he produced back-dated forms that kept him clear of an ethics board investigation by *this* much." Hershey pinched his thumb and forefinger together.

"And which one of our Republican brethren tipped you to that little find?"

"What makes you think it wasn't some GOP sistren?"

"Answer the question."

"As I've been suggesting to Andy here, the names of my sources are between me and my God."

"You're an atheist."

"I'm a Catholic atheist. There's a difference."

"Still love to know who," she said.

"Bet you would."

"But in the meantime," she said, and leaned toward him. He listened, giving me the universal head gesture to shove off for a second. Since every seat was occupied, I stood up and moved to the outer edge of the drinking scrum. I sipped my beer, made a face, and looked over the room of red-backed chairs and white cloth table settings. I recognized a few people, mainly judges and attorneys I'd seen around the courthouse, but most of the faces belonged to strangers.

Hershey waved me back after another minute. "Sorry about that," he said.

"Gotta run. Nice meeting you," MacKenzie said, shaking my hand. It was no-nonsense firm.

"Same." I watched her weave her way through the restaurant, to a booth on the other side of the room where she joined a group of three people.

"She's got a nice ass, but I'm worried she's gaining a little weight," Hershey said, following my gaze.

"I beg your pardon?"

"Don't tell me you weren't thinking the same thing."

"Don't be crude," I said, taking my eyes off MacKenzie, annoyed that he was right. I changed the subject. "Any chance Tillman is having you followed?"

"I've thought about it. Kerri isn't kidding. He's really mad about the Midwest story. He's got a lot riding on Triple F."

"Because he's Senate education chair or whatever?"

"That, and a little bit of monkey move up."

"Meaning?"

"The current Senate president is term-limited. So the caucus is going to need a new leader at the end of the year. Tillman's the perfect guy to replace him."

"Why?"

"Mainly, because he's the governor's man in the Senate on school funding. But also because he can raise money hand over fist thanks to ATM machines like Midwest Testing."

"And he doesn't want any mud on his shoes on the way up."

"You catch on fast, Woody."

"So besides him, anybody else a possible suspect?"

"Like I said, plenty of options. It's a big bill."

"How about, anybody else in this *room*? There's a bunch of people doing a really bad job of pretending they're not watching us right now."

"Tell you what. Let's make some rounds. I do the introductions, you be the judge. Except when we meet an actual judge."

"Now?"

"Why not? That's what I'm paying you the big bucks for."

3

HERSHEY GOT OFF THE STOOL, STRETCHED, grabbed his drink, and started meandering. I took my beer and followed. He stopped at the second table we came to.

"Mind if we join you?" Hershey said.

"Do we have a choice?"

The speaker was a youngish-looking man whose outfit demanded a double take. He was wearing a gray seersucker suit, red suspenders, a red-patterned bow tie that appeared to be the real thing, and tortoiseshell glasses. He looked like Orville Redenbacher on his first day at law school. Hershey grabbed a chair from another table, pushed it toward me, and took the table's lone empty seat.

"Allen Ratliff," he said, nodding at Bow Tie. "Governor Hubbard's chief of staff. But don't hold that against him." Ratliff shook my hand with a grip somewhere between job candidate interview and first meeting of future father-in-law. Hershey turned to the second man, a frowner with a bristly goatee and short-cropped black hair. "Sam Michaels, Education Department's chief number cruncher." Michaels nodded at me.

"Lily Gleason," Hershey said, gesturing at the woman opposite Michaels. "Governor Hubbard's education liaison."

"Nice to meet you," she said with a forced smile.

"And you are?" Ratliff said.

"Andy Hayes," Hershey said, before I could speak. "He's protecting me against the forces of evil. Present company excluded, of course."

I smiled as best I could. I was starting to realize Hershey was like that loud uncle at Thanksgiving ready to embarrass you at the drop of the hat. It was better to sit back and let him do his thing, whatever that was, than risk opening my mouth.

"So what's going on?" Hershey said. "I'm hearing all kinds of stuff."

"You tell us," Ratliff said. "You seem to be the man with the plan."

"I hear Dani Symmes is up in arms about the charter school amendments. Claims 'lack of progress.' True?"

That won a thin smile from Ratliff, a glare from Michaels, and a matronly frown from Gleason.

"I'm sure the Senate will work out something compatible," Ratliff said. He spoke in even, clipped tones, not rushed, not dawdling, like a man who taught himself elocution with a metronome.

"Symmes is Speaker of the House," Hershey said, turning to me. "The House sent the school-funding bill over to the Senate with a bunch of perks for charter schools, which the Republicans love because they're not unionized and they don't have to follow boring 'rules and regulations.'" Hershey was a big one for air quotes, I was gathering. I made a mental note to stop using them so much myself. "The Senate stripped all that charter stuff out, and now they're seeing what they can put back in to placate Symmes without holding their noses so hard they pass out."

"OK," I said, studying the uncomfortable faces of the trio before us. I'd seen wedding crashers on parole more welcome than Hershey appeared to be at the moment.

"So, anything?" he said.

18

Lily Gleason looked despairingly at Ratliff. He looked back at her, though his expression was neutral.

"We'll know more later this week," he said.

"When?"

As though Hershey weren't there, Ratliff leaned back, produced a phone, and popped off a text message as nonchalantly as if he were brushing a crumb from his sleeve. When he looked up he seemed almost surprised to see the reporter still at their table. "Later. And now, if you don't mind, we actually had some business to discuss." He nodded at a thick Triple F binder on the table.

"I'm all ears," Hershey said.

Ratliff sent another text, ignoring him.

"I'll see you around," Hershey said, ending the game and getting up. I stood.

"Nice meeting you," Ratliff said to me.

"Same." Michaels and Gleason nodded but didn't speak.

"So now you can at least say you've met the P-O-D," Hershey said as we made our way across the restaurant.

"P-O-D?"

"Ratliff. The Prince of Dorkness. Can you believe that outfit? He once told me, without the slightest hint of irony, he has a bow tie for every day of the year."

I shrugged. "Some guys look good in them. And some guys think they do. And never the twain shall meet."

Hershey snorted. "You're starting to grow on me, Woody."

"It's Andy."

"Says you."

WITH THAT CLEARED UP, WE WALKED PAST a row of tables, arriving at a booth in the restaurant's far corner. Despite our presence, a woman on one side continued speaking to a man sitting across from her. At last, after an interlude that was starting to feel uncomfortable, she raised her eyes expectantly.

"Yes," she said.

"Hello, Senator," Hershey said. "Just wanted to say hello."

"How kind of you."

"You look familiar," the woman said before Hershey could introduce me. "Have we met? I'm Ottie Kinser."

"I'm not sure," I said, shaking her extended hand as I told her my name. She was black, with four-alarm good looks, dressed in a tailored off-orange suit, wearing gold earrings and a gold necklace.

"My husband, Reggie," she said. I turned and shook the hand of the man across from her. He was wearing a dark suit that looked equally tailored.

"You work for Burke Cunningham," he said.

"That's right."

"Burke and I went to law school together. Weren't you at the banquet last winter?"

"Yes, of course," I said.

How could I forget? Banquet a euphemism for a Rodriguez fundraiser that Burke had organized the night of one of the televised Democratic candidate debates earlier in the year. Burke, the consummate Democrat, and more importantly, my occasional boss as one of Columbus's top defense attorneys. My sister, who was always on me about my lack of interest in politics, had ragged me endlessly after I photobombed a picture of Burke and his wife, Dorothy, posing with the state party chair. A picture inconveniently, at least for me, posted on the Ohio Democratic Party's Facebook page for a couple of days.

"I remember now," Senator Kinser said. "You were with a charming young woman. A runner, as I recall. Such a beautiful girl."

"That's right. Anne Cooper."

"Beautiful is right," Hershey said, much to my annoyance.

"Please give Burke my regards," Reggie said.

"And give Anne mine," Senator Kinser said.

I nodded.

"Senator Kinser is cosponsoring the Fair Funding Focus bill," Hershey said. She waited, patiently, not rising to the Triple F bait. He said, "Any word on the charter schools?"

"We're working diligently on the legislation," she said.

"Any details on that diligence?"

"Perhaps."

"Any you'd care to share?"

"Not tonight. We're just here for dinner." When Hershey didn't respond, she added, "Call me tomorrow. After ten."

"It's a date," Hershey said.

"Sounds like Anne's got a new best friend," Hershey said as we walked away.

"I guess. Don't tell me that the senator is the type to follow you."

"I wouldn't be so sure. Didn't you notice her eyes? She's got a bad case of the 'Ohio Look.'"

"The what?"

We arrived back at the bar and found space in the middle. Hershey cleared his throat dramatically. "The Ohio Look," he said.

"*'The dreamy, far-away expression of a man richly meditating on cheering audiences, landslides, and high office.'* It's an old James Thurber line. You have heard of Thurber?"

I gave him my own look, the one I reserve for people who make fun of me for wearing black socks with sandals.

"OK, OK. But did you know he was a Statehouse reporter here before he went off to the *New Yorker*?"

"As a matter of fact I did. What's any of this got to do with Kinser?"

"Her faraway expression involves a run for state treasurer in two years. She wants a school-funding bill passed as badly as anyone. It'll be at the top of her speech the day she announces."

"Have you written any stories that annoyed *her*?"

"A couple. She's tight with the Planned Parenthood crowd. I've pointed out the proximity of donations from pro-choice folks to her votes on abortion-expansion bills."

"I thought you media elite types were hands-off anything criticizing abortion."

"Couldn't say. I'll write just about anything as long as I've got it first."

"So you're an equal opportunity enemy maker?"

"That may be the nicest thing anyone's ever said to me, Woody."

"I told you, it's Andy—"

"Let's see," he said, ignoring me as he searched the room. "We've done the executive branch and legislative branch. All we need is—." He settled on someone across the restaurant. "Perfect. He's out of the can. Come on."

5

WE WALKED BACK ACROSS the room to the last booth on the other side and stopped in front of an older, white-haired man. He was alone, nursing a tumbler of brown liquid.

"Hello, Justice," Hershey said. "How are things on the bench?"

"Slippery as always," he said.

Uninvited, Hershey moved into the opposite side of the booth, gesturing for me to follow.

"Andy Hayes? Supreme Court Justice William Caldwell Bryan," Hershey said. "Billy to his friends, Bill to his worst enemies, William to his dear departed mother." We shook hands. Whereas Ratliff's grip was tentatively firm and Senator Kinser's professionally warm, Bryan's handshake was an iron grasp. It was like meeting a longshoreman over the bargaining table.

"Justice Bryan wrote the past two decisions finding Ohio's school-funding system unconstitutional," Hershey said. "He is of course watching the Triple F deliberations with great interest."

"A pleasure meeting you, Mr. Hayes," Bryan said, ignoring Hershey. There was something familiar about his voice I couldn't quite place. "I was a fan of yours."

"Thank you," I said. It wasn't the type of comment I was used to hearing from judges.

"You've made an interesting transition. I'd like to hear about it sometime."

"No time like the present," Hershey said.

"But not tonight," Bryan added, lifting his glass toward the reporter. "I know how busy you must be."

"Full house," Hershey said, pretending he hadn't heard as he gestured at the rest of the restaurant. "The governor's chief of staff is here, Ottie Kinser is down at the other end, you're presiding. We could settle school funding right now."

"And ruin a perfectly good steak?" Bryan said as a waiter materialized with a plate.

"A rain check, then," Hershey said. He looked at me, and I slid out of the booth as he followed. Bryan nodded but didn't reply.

"Look at you," Hershey said as we crossed the room. "A personal invite to spill your guts to Billy Bryan. That's impressive."

Our seats at the bar were long gone. The Clarmont had filled up. Hershey made eye contact with the bartender. I gave up on my Belgian ale and ordered a Heineken. The drinks arrived and Hershey started digging for his wallet, but the bartender waved him off, nodding at someone on a stool near the door. Hershey looked in that direction, gave the bartender a thumbs-up, and walked down the bar, drink in hand, with me in close pursuit.

"Thanks for the drink, Jack," Hershey said, coming to a stop.

"You're welcome," the man said. Even I could tell his dark navy suit was the most expensive in the restaurant, which was saying something. He looked like he'd come directly from a Savile Row tailor's shop. "I asked him to spike it with extra rat poison."

"Just how I like it," Hershey said, tipping his drink toward his benefactor as he introduced me.

"Jack Sterling," the man said with a nod. "Why the hell you hanging around this pervert?"

"I'm paying him to," Hershey said. "Just like your 'friends' pay you to be nice to them. What's the latest?"

"First off, screw you. My clients are not my friends. Secondly, not much, as if I'd ever tell you."

"I'm hearing Thursday now, for school-funding amendments."

"Couldn't say."

"Are your people along for the ride?"

"Like I said, wouldn't tell you if they were."

"Are the revenue percentages going down?"

"No comment."

"What's got you so chatty tonight?"

Sterling shrugged. "Barometric pressure's low or something."

"All right then," Hershey said, taking a drink. "Don't be a stranger."

"No stranger than you," Sterling said.

"And that was . . . ?" I said to Hershey a moment later, back at the bar.

"You know that old expression, 'Don't tell my mother I'm a lobbyist, she thinks I'm a piano player in a whorehouse?' "

"Who's he lobby for?"

"He has what they call a diverse portfolio."

"Meaning?"

"Meaning most of what he does is legal."

"Very funny. He's involved in school funding?"

"In a manner of speaking. He represents casinos."

"What do casinos have to do with schools?"

"Damn good question. So right now, a chunk of casino revenue goes to schools. 'Craps for tots,' I like to call it, but it's got an actual name of some kind."

"All right."

"Triple F opens the door for all kinds of shenanigans. In this case, it's Sterling's job to see if he can negotiate down the schools' percentage."

"Why'd he buy you a drink?"

"To put me in his debt, and/or to remind me to slip him something in return down the road. Tit for tat, you know."

"Possible he was just being nice?"

"Around here? Nothing changes hands at the Statehouse without an IOU attached. Don't ever forget that."

Hershey appeared to have run out of people to introduce me to, and so we sat for a few minutes, drinking and watching the room. At last he stood up, nodded at me, threw some bills on the bar, and started to go. The door opened just as we reached it, and Hershey paused to allow a man to step inside. The newcomer stopped short when he saw the reporter.

"What the hell are you doing here?" the man said.

6

"WELL, HELLO, SENATOR," HERSHEY SAID. "Were your ears burning? We were just speechifying about you."

"Yeah? What about?"

"The usual—your district, your taste in suits, your contributions from Midwest Testing. You know my colleague?" Hershey pulled me to his side. "Andy Hayes, meet Senator Ed Tillman."

"You're blocking my way," Tillman said.

"Since we were just leaving, I could say the same about you," Hershey replied. "But as long as we're having a moment, any comment on the ethics board ruling on the Vegas trip?" A smart phone had magically appeared in the reporter's right hand, and I could see it was already recording.

"I told you once, no comment." He had short, brushed-back sandy hair in transition from blond to white, a full face that hinted at too many chicken dinners and not enough time on the treadmill, and a look of controlled anger in his eyes.

"Technically, that was your spokeswoman. What about you?"

"You heard me."

"Seems like you got a pass from the board," Hershey persisted. "They gave you spirit of the law, but not letter."

"I said, no comment—"

"I mean, it would be good to know, good for the people of Ohio to know, whether you're going to repay Midwest for that little jaunt."

The space around us had gone quiet, like that funny pause in conversations at parties that folklore says is supposed to come at twenty minutes after the hour.

"I could have your pass to the Senate floor revoked," Tillman said. "Harassing me like this."

"Whoop-de-doo," Hershey said, holding up his right forefinger and moving it in a circle. "Whole thing's online now. I can watch you on my phone while I'm taking a dump. That is, if I want to bother."

"How dare you."

"I'm just trying to do my job."

"Better enjoy it while it lasts."

"I'm sorry?"

"You heard me."

"I heard you," Hershey said, pushing the phone a little closer. "I'm just not sure I understood."

"What I mean," the senator said, lowering his voice, "is you should enjoy your job. Because if you write one more word about Midwest Testing, one single word more, you're going to be sorry."

"That's your comment?"

"No. That was a threat. This is my comment: Go to hell. Put that on your goddamned website."

The restaurant was now so quiet I could hear the clink of dishes and the chatter of conversation back in the kitchen.

"Go . . . to . . . hell," Hershey said slowly. "OK, got it. Anything else, Senator?"

Tillman's left eye twitched, and for just a moment I thought he was going to lose it. I braced myself, hoping to God I wasn't going to earn my paycheck by restraining a state senator.

Instead, Tillman shouldered past us. "Out of my way," he said.

"Good night," Hershey said to his back. "And all the ships at sea."

7

"WANT TO SEE SOMETHING?" HERSHEY SAID a minute later as I pulled out of the Clarmont parking lot and headed north on High.

"More than that? I don't think so."

"That? That was nothing but a scrimmage. I'll take you to a real game sometime." He gave me instructions for our next destination.

"What are you going to do with that?" I said. "What Tillman just said?"

"Upload the audio, soon as I get home. Then I'll mull it over. Believe it or not, PRE's a family-friendly website. Might have to paraphrase."

We drove in silence past the glowing windows of the block-long Grange Insurance building and started up the hill into downtown. The night had gotten cooler, and it was beginning to rain. We were passing the Justice Center at Mound when I glanced in the rearview mirror and said, "How'm I doing so far?"

"Doing?"

"The bodyguard shtick. You're satisfied?"

"Expectations surpassed."

"In what way?"

"Well, for starters, you resisted the powers of the P-O-D, who may be a nerd but has been known to paralyze battalions of hostile Republicans with that hypnotic voice of his. You had a powerful state senator gushing over what a nice couple you and Dr. Cooper make. To top it off, Justice Bryan was practically ready to invite you squirrel hunting. There's people who've hung out on Capitol Square for thirty years who'd give their left nut for that kind of reception."

"Good to hear."

"Why do you ask?"

"Because assuming you didn't hire someone else to help you out, we've got company."

"What?"

I gestured behind us without taking my eyes off the road.

"Who?"

"SUV, two cars back."

"How can you tell?"

"Educated guess, plus I'm pretty sure I saw it pick us up after we left the restaurant. Can you make out the driver?"

He glanced back. "It's raining too hard."

"OK. Take out your phone."

"I'm not calling the police."

"I figured as much. So how about doing something useful for a change and get ready to take a picture of the license plate?"

"It's too far back and there's cars between us."

"Not the front. The back."

"How?"

"Hang on."

I drove into downtown, past the Statehouse and up toward Broad. At the last second I swung into the left turn lane without signaling, entered the intersection and tapped the brakes. The driver immediately behind us saluted my efforts with an angry horn and shot through the light on my right side. The second car followed, then the tail.

"Now," I said.

"Got it," Hershey said.

I completed the left turn, turned again and parked on Wall, a sliver of street running north-south between High and Front.

"How'd you do?" I said.

"Shitty." He showed me a smeared blur that might have passed for art but definitely not for evidence.

"Next time," I said.

DESPITE THE RAIN, WE got out, ran around the corner, dashed across High and through the glass doors of a small, stone-paneled building on the corner of the Statehouse grounds with "Underground Parking" etched in its façade. I followed Hershey down a flight of steps. A few moments later we emerged in a nearly empty parking garage. We walked past dozens of squat green pillars and a random leftover car or two until we reached a revolving door on the far side. Hershey pulled a key card from his wallet, waved it in front of an electric reader, and entered the door as it began to move. I followed a moment afterward.

"What are we doing?" I said.

"Entering the Statehouse."

"Believe it or not, I figured that out. I mean, where are we going?"

"Up," he said. "Got a treat for you."

Inside, we ascended a steep flight of stairs past the jagged flanks of the building's foundation. At the top, we paused by a glass cabinet holding old Statehouse artifacts. Behind it sat a pile of bricks, commemorating what a placard said was a rodent-infested former state office building dubbed "Rat Row." To the right of the cabinet a sturdy-looking gavel lay atop a gleaming pedestal.

"Fashioned from a two-hundred-year-old oak tree that got hit with lightning last summer in southern Ohio," Hershey said, examining it. "Not far from Justice Bryan's hometown, as a matter of fact. Supposedly a replica of the original Statehouse gavel."

"Where's Bryan from?"

"Little town called Paw Paw Bottoms."

"There's no such place."

"Sure there is. You're the Ohio farm boy, Woody. Look it up."

Hershey reached out and patted the gavel's head. "Hefty bugger. You should show this to Anne."

"Why's that?"

"Perfect weapon if zombies ever make it this far. OK, this way."

I followed Hershey around the corner and into the middle of a large hall. "The Crypt," he said, gesturing.

"The which?"

"What they call the lower level. It feels basement-y, even though it's the ground floor. There's no single space in this building that better epitomizes what goes on around here."

"Oh?"

He pointed down at the floor of alternating mottled white and rust-red ceramic squares. "Below us, floor tiles lifted from the old state lunatic asylum." He looked up. "Above us, a terrific example of a groin vault."

I examined the white, curved ceiling of painted bricks, crisscrossed with sprinkler pipes, and made out interlocking arches that met at a point overhead. I glanced at Hershey, looking for more explanation.

"An architectural design. Where two vaults meet to form a ceiling," Hershey said. "Lunatic asylum floor, a groin arch overhead. Perfect."

"Because—?"

"Because all these crazy people pass through here every day, working on all these lofty laws and resolutions and platforms and other bullshit, but the only thing anybody's really thinking about is their groins."

He laughed that same laugh, low and rich and infectious, and once again I joined in despite myself. He was like that annoying class clown you know you shouldn't humor because you're going to pay for it one way or the other, but you just can't help it.

I ought to know, I reminded myself.

"Over here," Hershey said, walking a few more steps and stopping in front of a green door recessed into the white brick wall. He pulled a jumble of keys from his pants pocket, selected one, looked casually to his left and his right, looked left again, unlocked the door and pushed it open. He gestured for me to enter. I walked into a darkened office illuminated by the light from a computer screen on a desk. Hershey followed behind and quietly pulled the door shut. He crossed the room and unlocked a second, smaller door to the left.

"What are we doing?" I said.

"We're climbing. Hope you've been working out."

I peered into the dark space beyond the newly opened door. Before me, a spiraling flight of stone stairs rose out of sight.

"Two hundred and seven steps," Hershey said.

"No elevator?"

"Where's the challenge in that?"

Less than a minute later, we stopped while Hershey used his cell phone to illuminate a printed phrase on the wall. "Commit No Nuisance," it said.

"What's that supposed to mean?" I said.

"They're not exactly sure. But back in the nineteenth century, this was a big destination for honeymooners. Climb to the top of the Statehouse! See the view!" He looked at me with a grin. "Honeymooners, Woody," he said, winking.

I shook my head and we resumed our ascent. The narrow space, the stone steps, and the bare limestone walls made me feel as if I was really in the 1800s. We kept going, and going, and just when my knees were starting to protest, with my lungs not far behind, we emerged into what looked like a curved hallway bending around an inner, circular wall.

"Top of the Statehouse?" I said, once I'd caught my breath.

"Almost," Hershey said, circling around to a set of stairs on the other side of the room. "This is 1857. We're four years away from the finished product. Up here."

We headed up another set of stairs, this time wooden, with the years of passage visible in the sagging middle of the boards. A minute later we entered a room identical to the one below, except that the limestone floor was replaced with wooden planks.

"Welcome to 1861," Hershey said.

8

I STEPPED INTO THE UPPER ROOM. TALL, narrow windows circled the space and let in just enough of the downtown lights to bathe the room in twilight gray, but it was still difficult to see. I moved away from the stairs and stood at one of the windows and looked out at the statue of William McKinley glistening in the rain at the far western edge of the Statehouse lawn.

"What is this place?"

"Top of the Cupola," Hershey said. "What the original architects went for instead of a dome. It was all about Greek Revival in those days. This is the highest point in the building."

"Impressive."

"Thought you'd think so. A little thank you for helping me out."

I moved to the next window to the right. I said, "Curious how you got a key to this place. I assume they don't hand those out to any old reporter."

"You'd assume correctly."

"So?"

"A lady friend of mine had a copy. We rendezvoused up here a couple of times."

"To do what?"

"To 'commit nuisance,'" Hershey said. "What do you think?"

"Give me a break."

"What can I say? She had a thing for unusual meeting places."

I looked at him, trying to see if he was serious. The glance he returned was inscrutable; boyish and teasing. The class clown.

"How'd this friend happen to have a key to the Statehouse Cupola?"

"Connections."

"Who is it?"

"Next question."

"OK. Is it a source? Or someone who might be following you?"

"No comment on the first count, doubtful on the second."

"This is ridiculous. How am I supposed to find out who's after you if you won't tell me anything?"

"I didn't say it was going to be easy. You'll just have to trust me on this one."

"Why?"

"Because if I gave you the name of every aggrieved woman I'd slept with, we'd be here all night. I'm sure you can identify. C'mere. Check this out."

Before I could protest, he turned and played his cell phone flashlight across the room's whitewashed wall. My eyes widened. I'd missed the sight before me as we'd entered the space. Hundreds of signatures covered the surface, big and small, in blue and red and black pen, some in bold flourishes, some in tiny script, a few with cartoony illustrations, almost all with an accompanying date. Hershey started walking, keeping the light on the names.

"It's a tradition for visitors to sign when they come up here," Hershey said. "Dates back well over a hundred years, although these are all relatively new. When they renovated this place in the 1990s, somebody thought it was a good idea to paint over everything up to that point. Can you imagine what was lost? I mean, Lincoln stopped here once, and not just lying in his casket on the way back to Illinois. But we'll never know if he came up here. These are the only survivors from before."

I followed his gesture. A low rough-hewn bench encircled the wall, names and dates carved into the planks.

"Here's the oldest one I've found," Hershey said, up ahead. He shone his light on the name. *J. Cook, 1870.*

"Any idea who that was?"

"Somebody who liked to commit nuisance, I'm hoping."

We continued along the wall, looking at more names. I made out the signature of a former governor and a couple of reporters I knew, but few others. As we walked, I reminded myself I was supposed to be a bodyguard, not just a tourist. In that moment I realized how difficult it would be to detect an attacker up here. Because the room circled the curved inner wall of signatures, you couldn't see very far in either direction. Anyone from an aggrieved woman to a pissed-off source could be lurking just a few feet away without being detected. I straightened up and started casting glances ahead and behind. I wondered if this had been such a good idea.

We made the full circuit and arrived back where we started. I stood and looked around and listened. Finally, convinced we were assassin-free for the moment, I peered at the wall of signatures again.

"Where's yours?" I said.

"Never signed."

"Why not?"

"Well, for starters, I've never been up here, officially," he said with a grin. "And second, I'm more the observer type, you know? I like to watch, not be watched."

"You don't want to be part of history?" I said, gesturing at the signature of an Ohio State basketball player now in the NBA.

"Kind of like I said before, Woody. I record history. I don't need to be part of it. So listen. You and Dr. Cooper ever want to spice things up . . ." He showed me the key with arched eyebrows.

"I'll keep that in mind," I said.

"I bet you will."

We descended a few minutes later, me leading, easing my way down, feeling the strain on my knees even more than on the way up. Halfway back down to the level where we'd started, Hershey stopped me and led the way through a door into a room filled with desks and metal racks, and then out into a corridor. We climbed down another set of stairs and a minute later found ourselves in an enormous circular hall.

"The Rotunda," Hershey declared. He pointed up, and I stared into what looked like the inside of a giant bell overhead. "We were just walking around the outside of that," he explained. "The outer wall of that dome is what all the signatures are written on."

I nodded, and followed him as he walked slowly around the circumference of the room. On the far side we stopped in front of a marble frieze depicting Confederate generals surrendering to their Union counterparts at the Battle of Vicksburg. At the top, a bust of Lincoln looked out over the room.

I started at the sound of Hershey's echoing voice, reading the inscription. "'Care for him who shall have borne the battle and for his widow and his orphans,'" he said. He stood there a moment longer before walking to the center of the room. He gestured upward at the salmon-colored interior of the dome.

"I love seeing this at night," he said. "Gives you a real sense of reverence."

"Reverence?" I said, skeptically.

"Sure. Can't you feel it? The aura? The vibe? Our founders' hopes and dreams, enshrined in a building it took decades to construct in order to last centuries. We're at ground zero of democracy in Ohio. The home of eight presidents. Count 'em, *eight*. And as they say, as Ohio goes, so goes the nation."

"Help me out here. A minute ago you were cracking wise about lunatics and groins. An hour ago you were stage whispering your contempt for almost everyone we met at the Clarmont, except for your Democratic operative pal who you ogled instead. No offense, but am I missing something?"

"Oh, and you've never made fun of the things you love?"

"I'm just trying to figure out what I've gotten myself into."

"So I'm a hypocrite—congrats on the big reveal. Among other things, it probably puts me in good company with all the people I write about. Satisfied?"

"Not really."

"Open your eyes, then. I mean, look at it." He gazed around the Rotunda, gesturing at the walls. "To paraphrase Obi-Wan Kenobi, 'You will never find a more wretched hive of scum and villainy.' But it's *my* hive, and yours too, and the people's of Ohio. It's all we've got and it's actually something. And I'll be damned if I let the fools who run this place ever forget that."

I followed his gaze, and stared up into the dome again. I lowered my eyes and thought about what he'd said. After a minute I had to admit I saw his point. There was something undeniably majestic about the place, a stateliness that recalled the pillars of Democracy, of ancient Greece and Rome. Glancing about, I half expected to see a crowd of senators in sandals and togas pass by waving parchment rolls at one another in heated debate. I blinked, clearing my head. I looked around again and settled on an enormous oil painting hanging to my left.

"The Battle of Lake Erie," Hershey said. "Turning point in the War of 1812."

I studied the painting, observing a man with wavy, dark hair, his arm outstretched as he commanded a small boat of sailors in the heat of battle.

"Commodore Oliver Hazard Perry," Hershey continued. "He's the 'Don't give up the ship' guy."

"You don't say."

"He commanded the *Lawrence* in the battle. After the British more or less pounded it into oblivion, he got in a rowboat, traveled half a mile through the raging battle to the *Niagara,* fired that ship's do-nothing captain, took control and let the Limeys have it. Unbelievable. They don't build men like that anymore."

"I guess not."

"Afterward, he wrote that famous line to his commander: 'We have met the enemy, and they are ours.'"

"Stirring."

"Maybe. But I prefer Pogo's version," Hershey said.

"Which is?"

"*We have met the enemy and he is us.* Much more appropriate for this place."

We stood a few more minutes, taking in the scene, neither of us talking. Then Hershey turned abruptly, headed down a set of stairs, and used a key to open a door. We stepped inside. "Pressroom," he said, turning on the light and gesturing around the windowless room, consisting of cubicles down the middle and on either side—some empty, some with computer monitors and keyboards, some bulging with reports and books and stacks of paper. At the far end of the room sat a wooden table empty except for the ubiquitous blue Triple F binder. A sign above two TVs bolted to the opposite wall said, "No man's life, liberty or property are safe while the legislature is in session."

"So now you've seen it," Hershey said. "The luxury penthouse of the media elite."

"I always suspected it," I said.

We retreated, crossed the hall, went through another door, descended a set of stairs past a green metal and glass elevator shaft, and arrived back at the Crypt level. I had paused to look at the commemorative gavel again when I heard a sound. I turned and was blinded by a flashlight.

"Put your hands up," a voice squeaked. "Do it now."

9

I WAS STARTING TO COMPLY, DESPITE THE fact the voice sounded like that of a young child or a very old woman, when I heard Hershey say, "Isn't it past your bedtime, Ephraim?"

"Not with miscreants like you sneaking around."

"Pot calling the kettle black, if I'm not mistaken. Kill the klieg light, will you? Want to introduce you to someone."

After a moment the light winked off. I blinked, trying to get my bearings in the partial darkness. When I could see properly, I took in a small, elderly man in a tweed three-piece suit and thin brown tie staring back at me through wire-rimmed glasses. Nearly bald, face lined with age, slightly stooped. He was no Roman senator, but he looked as if he could have strode across the same hall a century ago without raising any eyebrows.

"Ephraim Badger, meet Woody Hayes," Hershey said.

"It's Andy," I said, stepping forward and shaking his hand.

"I know who you are," he said. "Question is, what are you doing with him, this time of night?" He nodded at Hershey.

"We're boning up on legislation," Hershey said.

Badger shook his head and made a clucking sound. "You know you're not supposed to be here this late."

"I was giving Andy a tour," Hershey said. "And technically, you're not supposed to be here either."

"I work here."

"You volunteer here, Ephraim. One of these days you need to learn the difference."

"One of these days I'm not going to be able to cover for you," Badger squeaked.

"Never going to happen."

"I'm serious," Badger said. "You're running a big risk. Patrol catches you—." He slid his finger across his throat.

"I don't think they do that to trespassers anymore," Hershey said. "Anyway, we were just leaving. How about you?"

"I'm waiting for you to leave."

"You're doing a fine job of it. Keep up the good work."

"*Get out*," Badger squeaked.

"Nice meeting you," I said. In response, Badger frowned and turned the flashlight back on, directing it straight into our eyes.

"Who was that?" I said as we headed back to the garage.

"That was the world's most dedicated Statehouse tour guide."

"He gives tours this time of night?"

"At night he prowls. Tours he does during the day. Every day but Sunday, when he's in church an hour or six."

I looked around the garage as we walked, aware that the pillars studding the darkened space could be hiding any number of people wanting to do Hershey harm. Between the Clarmont, the tail we'd picked up on High, and the episode with Badger, I was starting to figure out that the list was long.

"What's his story?"

"Former history teacher. Taught in Columbus public schools for something like forty years. Supposedly he retired on a Friday and starting volunteering here on a Monday."

"Is he the one who taught you so much about this place?"

"One of them. Something I didn't mention earlier was that most of this building was constructed with prison labor. They'd walk the inmates over from the state pen every day."

"Bet the Teamsters loved that."

"Good one," Hershey said, rewarding me with a deep laugh. "Ephraim here claims to be the great-great-grandson of one of those inmates."

"Is he?"

"No reason to doubt him."

"Think he'll turn you in?"

"For what? I've got a legitimate key card and a press pass to boot. People walk through the Statehouse all hours, especially this time of year."

"Not all of them go up to the Cupola, I bet."

"Point conceded."

"So what about his ancestor. The one who helped build the Statehouse?"

"What about him?"

"What was he in prison for?"

"A terrible crime, supposedly."

"Which was?"

Hershey grinned. "He killed a reporter."

10

ANNE AND AMELIA WERE SITTING ON THE porch of a duplex on Crestview in the Clintonville neighborhood north of campus when I drove up the next morning. It was a nice part of town. It was a nice house. It had been painted recently, the windows looked new, and the gutters were as clean and shiny as freshly polished gunwales. Promising.

"The guy's not here yet," Amelia announced when I got out of my Honda Odyssey.

"The guy?"

"The apartment guy."

"How about the other places?" I said.

Anne shook her head. "First place was a dump, second place too expensive."

"Third place just right, Goldilocks?"

"Depends on the cable hookup," she said with a smile. Her face, like her daughter's, was covered in freckles brought out by the spring sun, except for the skin around the white tissue of her scar. She'd pushed her sunglasses up onto her red hair. She looked impossibly beautiful. Amelia was wearing a shirt that said,

"Quiet, Vader Is Coming" and had already buried herself back in a book.

I looked around. "Nice street."

"Not bad."

"Not the suburbs."

"Indeed."

"Not that there's anything wrong with the suburbs," I said.

"Suburbs are people too," she agreed.

A white Ford F-150 pickup truck pulled up along the curb. A man got out, walked around the front of the truck, and approached the steps.

"Anne?" he said.

"That's right," she said, standing up. She shook his hand. "Anne Cooper. This is my daughter, Amelia." A beat later, she added, "And my boyfriend, Andy. But it's just Amelia and me. For the apartment."

"Richard Deckard," he said. "Nice to meet you." He was wearing leather work boots, jeans, and a tucked-in Ohio State golf shirt tight against a big but not huge belly.

He unlocked the door and showed us in. You could see right away it was special. Refinished hardwood floors, repainted walls, new stove and refrigerator in the kitchen. A strip of yard in the back, but surrounded by a new fence. Beyond that, a gravel pad for parking, a nice bonus given the narrow Clintonville streets. A half bath downstairs and a full one up, both clean and smelling of paint and spackle. Two bedrooms, each with decent-sized closets.

I could tell Anne liked it from the way she squeezed my arm as we came back downstairs. Amelia liked it too, especially the size of her proposed bedroom, which was far bigger than the one she lived in at the moment in the self-same suburbs with Anne's parents. Their refuge after Anne's deranged husband tried unsuccessfully to kill Anne but not before disfiguring her, after which he turned his knife on himself. The place was nice enough that Anne's disappointment showed all the more when Deckard told her, almost apologetically, that although the rent was eleven hundred, plus two months down, it would probably go up after a year or so.

"That's probably out of my range," she said. "But could I get back to you?"

"Sure. Just I got a few other folks looking at it today is all."

"I understand."

They shook hands on the porch, and Anne and Amelia went down the steps and headed to the car. I was a couple feet behind them when I heard Deckard say, "Excuse me?"

I turned to look at him.

"Aren't you Woody Hayes?"

I nodded. "I go by Andy now."

"OK. Sorry."

"No problem."

"I saw you on the news. You're a detective."

"Investigator, technically."

"What I meant. You do jobs for people?"

"That's right." I glanced up the street at Anne and Amelia, lingering on the sidewalk next to Anne's red Toyota. The only one in Columbus, at least the only one I'd ever seen, with both "Starfleet Academy" and "13.1" bumper stickers.

"Got a situation I wouldn't mind talking to you about."

"OK."

"Has to do with my daughter."

"Go on."

"Her fiancé, more like it."

"He in trouble?"

"He's not, but his brother is."

"What kind of trouble?"

"The big kind. He raped a four-year-old boy."

I SAID, "WHO WAS the boy?"

"His girlfriend's son."

"Where's the brother now?"

"In jail. Awaiting trial."

"What's his name?"

"Wardley. Derrick Wardley."

I looked up the street at Anne. She tapped her watch. I nodded.

"So how can I help you?"

"Something's not right with Troy. That's my daughter's fiancé. He's gone into shut-down mode, ever since Derrick got arrested. Won't talk to his parents, his friends, anybody. Barely speaks to Bonnie."

"That's your daughter?"

"Yeah."

"Won't talk, meaning what, exactly?"

"I don't mean can't talk, just doesn't. Doesn't do anything, in fact. Lost his job a couple months ago because he stopped going."

"What did he do?"

"Worked in a warehouse. He was a picker, for auto parts. Not the most exciting work, but he was good at it. Good money, too."

"Does Bonnie have a job?"

"Works at FedEx Office. Part-time. She's handy with computers. Used to do some IT work for a company. These days, people hire her freelance to build websites, help them with online genealogy records, things like that."

"They live together?"

"That's right."

"Troy's brother. What'd he do to the boy?"

"Raped him, at night, putting him to bed."

"How'd he get caught?"

"The boy's grandmother noticed something wasn't right. It was a huge shock, gotta tell you. Not like Derrick was any great shakes, but nothing like *that*. Least that's what Bonnie says."

"Where's the boy now?"

"Grandparents. The girlfriend's, not Derrick and Troy's folks."

"So what is it you want me to do, exactly?"

"I'm not sure. Could you talk to Troy?"

"Talk?"

"See what's bugging him. Find out what's going on."

"What's bugging him? You mean, like beyond what's up with his brother?"

"Thing is, they weren't ever that close, at least according to Bonnie. Maybe it's something else."

"Why would he listen to me if he won't talk to his parents or to Bonnie?"

"I don't know. He's an Ohio State nut, like everyone else. Might get a kick out of meeting you. I know it sounds strange, but I'm not sure what else to do. I saw you here, realized who you were, thought I'd ask."

"What about a doctor? A psychiatrist?"

"We tried that. He won't go."

"You must like this guy a lot to want to hire me."

"I'm just trying to do the right thing by Bonnie."

I rolled what Deckard was telling me around in my head. Thought about the irony of someone asking me to play the role of famous Buckeye football player. Like seeing if Lance Armstrong was available for color commentary on the Tour de France. Then I thought about being Hershey's part-time sidekick for a couple of weeks tops. Realized I wasn't flush enough to be picky.

"Sure," I said. "Why not."

"How much do you charge?

I was about to tell him my rates when I glanced up the sidewalk again. Anne was leaning over and reading something Amelia had shown her in the book.

"It's a nice apartment," I said, nodding at the duplex. "You did a good job on it."

"Thanks."

"Wouldn't mind seeing Anne there."

"Guess I wouldn't either. Seems like a nice lady. What's she do?"

"College professor. Columbus State. But she's had some financial issues since her husband died."

"And it's just her? And her daughter?"

"That's right."

"I cut her some slack on the rent, you talk to Troy. Something like that?"

"That's about it."

"How about a hundred a month?"

"I was thinking two hundred."

"I'm losing money at that point."

I shrugged. "Short-term, maybe. But a shrink, if Troy ever agreed to it, won't come cheap. Plus you're not worrying whether Anne's a meth head or a slob or falls asleep smoking."

"You promise you'll make a real run at Troy. Not a knock on the door and you're gone if he dead-eyes you, like he does everyone else?"

"Promise," I said. "I'll get to the bottom of it. One way or the other."

We talked a little more. When we were done I walked up the street and filled Anne in. At first I wasn't sure she'd go for it. Independence means a lot to her, especially after what happened in upstate New York. It had been tough on her staying with her parents, despite the support they'd shown her.

But as she was hesitating, I added, "Speaking of names. You notice the landlord's?"

"His name?"

"Richard Deckard. Like the bounty hunter in that movie *Blade Runner*. Rick Deckard."

"How did you know that?"

"It's your favorite movie, right?"

"True. And how do you know *that*?"

"Lee Hershey isn't the only guy who knows how to work the Googles. It's right on your faculty profile. Based on Hershey's favorite book, right? *Do Androids Dream of Electric Sheep?* I rented it last night. After I got back from the Statehouse."

She sighed. "That was sweet of you."

"So what do you think?"

I gestured down the street where Deckard was studying his phone.

She hesitated a couple moments longer. She glanced at Amelia, who was engrossed in her book. I looked at the title. One in the *Hunger Games* trilogy. Even I'd heard of those.

"All right," she said. "I'll take it. I can build up a little cushion over the year, for when the rent goes up."

"Sounds like a plan."

"Good thing you were here," she said.

"Good thing he's got troubles," I said. "'Good' being a relative term, of course."

11

WE WENT TO NANCY'S ON NORTH HIGH TO celebrate, squeezing ourselves into a booth near the rear. Hershey called me just as my meatloaf arrived.

"I need you again tonight."

"When?"

"Ten o'clock or so."

"Where?"

"Can't say."

Something in his voice sounded different. Flatter, less exuberant. "Why not?"

"Top secret. Plus, I'm not sure yet."

"What's happening at ten?"

"I'm talking to someone."

"Who?"

"Can't tell you that either."

"A source?"

"Just someone."

"But why do you need me?"

A long pause. "It's an uncomfortable conversation I need to have. It's not completely related to what I'm working on, but since you're on my dime, I'd like you along. How's that sound?"

"Strange."

"I can't help it." He sounded tired, and dejected.

"All right. Pick you up again?"

"Sounds good. See you then. Oh, and tell Anne I really enjoyed that book. You can pick it up tonight."

"You finished it?"

"Oh, yeah," he said. "I move fast."

"Right," I said, and cut the connection.

BONNIE AND TROY LIVED in a white story-and-a-half house in Linden on the north side. It looked like another one of Deckard's rehabs, with fresh paint, new siding, and newly poured concrete steps. Someone—I was guessing Bonnie—had done a decent job with flowers out front.

"What?" said the young woman who answered my knock later that afternoon. She stood behind a heavy black-metal screen door. A dog materialized beside her.

I held up my business card, pressing it against the screen so she could see. "Your dad asked me to come by. Check up on Troy."

"He did what?"

I explained my meeting with Deckard.

"Hang on," she said. She disappeared into the house. I made out what sounded like a phone conversation, Bonnie's voice veering from defiant to distraught. It got quiet, and then I heard a murmured conversation in the living room with someone. After another minute Bonnie returned.

"He doesn't want to talk to you," she said. She was big like her dad and strong-looking, with long, auburn hair tied back in the remnants of a French braid and heavily made-up eyes that looked a little shinier than they had a few minutes earlier. An intricate weave of red roses was tattooed down her muscular right shoulder and arm. She was wearing yoga pants and a tight-fitting sleeveless blue shirt that said, "Arch City Roller Girls."

"Did he say why not?"

"Just said he didn't."

"Any chance he could come to the door?"

"No."

"It would only take a minute."

"He doesn't have a minute."

"I'm not here to cause trouble. Your dad asked me to talk to him, and that's it for starters. Shoot the shit about football for a while. Nothing else."

I could see her hesitating. I caught her shiny eyes. She looked away.

"Maybe tomorrow."

"What time?"

"Earlier. Sometime in the morning."

"Ten?"

"Yeah. Something like that."

"I'll come by around then. So, you play?"

"What?"

"Roller Derby. Your shirt."

"Oh. Yeah. I'm on the team."

"How is it?"

"It's good. It keeps me going." She paused, as if realizing she'd said too much.

"Tomorrow."

"OK," she said, starting to shut the door. Then she stopped. "Thanks," she added.

12

I DON'T NORMALLY DRINK BEFORE JOBS, but Roy called me as I headed home, insistent we get a beer. I didn't need much persuading. I had a few hours to kill before picking up Hershey, and Roy made it sound serious, and what's the worst that could happen? Which is how I found myself shortly before eight that night at Heyl's Tavern a couple blocks from my house in German Village, staring at my can of Black Label as I took in the bombshell he had just dropped.

"Closing the church," I said.

"You heard me."

"The soup kitchen too?"

"Afraid so."

"But that's your livelihood. No, more than that. It's what you do. Like in a cosmic sense."

"Yeah, well, cosmic sense ain't paying the bills."

I took a drink of my beer and wrestled with the news. Roy had been single-handedly running the Church of the Holy Apostolic Fire and its accompanying soup kitchen in Franklinton, the tough neighborhood just west of downtown, for as long as I'd known him, which was just after he returned from his second tour of Iraq with a fistful of medals and minus part of one leg. Something had happened over there—to this day he hadn't told me what exactly—that inspired in him a strong desire not to return to his prewar career as a chaplain at a suburban hospital chain.

"Things are that bad?"

"Donations never really came back to prerecession levels," he said. "Been limping by on Sunday collections and grants and the odd hundred-dollar bill some dope boy drops in the gutter by accident. We're mainly living off Lucy's salary, to be honest."

"Could you retire and just play golf?"

"With my handicap?"

"What would you do?"

"Dunno," he said. "St. Clare said they'd take me on full-time, doing outreach work. But I'm not sure I want to work for a hospital again."

"Anything I can do to help?"

"Got any rich uncles?"

"Got one who's a pig farmer. Does that count?"

"Way I'm headed it might."

We were silent for a minute, sipping our beers. Roy was having something dark and hoppy. The Indians were on TV, losing to the Royals.

"Seems like too much at times," Roy said.

"What does?"

"Problems I'm dealing with. We got rid of the pain pills, and now every third skel who comes in is hooked on heroin. And the girls. For every one I get off the street I see two more the next night. And they're hooked too. And meanwhile. . ."

I waited.

"Meanwhile, the city's exploding with growth. It's gone from Cowtown to Boomtown since I got out of college."

"Your point?"

He smiled sadly. "Bright lights, big city, up there." He pointed vaguely north. "Needle tracks, no hope, down here."

"You sure know how to show a guy a good time," I said.

"You remember Theresa?"

"Ex-hooker who helped me out with the missing laptop case. Hard to forget."

"That's former human trafficking victim to you. She's my last employee. Helluva worker. But even she's threatening to quit."

"For what?"

"Second shift at White Castle."

We both took a couple more drinks. Roy asked me about the job I was doing that night.

When I finished, he said, "You're picking this guy up, but you don't know where you're going or who he's meeting?"

"That's about it."

"A little loosey-goosey, even by your standards. Do you trust him?"

"Not a question of trust. I'm supposed to keep him safe. If I don't like the setup, I'll exercise veto power."

"What about the First Amendment?"

I shrugged. "I could give a shit about his story, if that's what you mean. That's not my job."

After a couple more minutes of conversation I excused myself to use the restroom. When I came back Roy was gone. I looked around. The bartender nodded toward the door. I finished my beer, thinking it seemed odd for him to leave like that. But a minute later he came back inside.

"This girl came in and said she'd clipped an Odyssey. Sounded like yours. She was in a rush for someone to see so I went out. Couldn't find any damage."

"Said she hit my van?"

He nodded.

"Where is she?"

"Took off, once it checked out. She seemed upset."

"Crap. OK. I better look at it."

I tugged at my wallet, but Roy stopped me.

"On me. Appreciate you listening. Even though you're still drinking swill. Black Label? Jesus."

"Some people have comfort food. I have comfort swill. Though had I known you were buying, I would have traded up to PBR."

Roy left money on the bar and we walked out together. I made two trips around my van but couldn't see any problems.

"Lucky," Roy said.

"I guess."

"Maybe I'll talk to you tomorrow," he said.

"Sounds good. Hey, wait a second."

"Yeah?"

"You got a favorite science fiction novel?"

"What?"

"You heard me."

"Why do you want to know?"

"It's kind of a marital aid."

"Despite the fact you're not married."

"Humor me."

He reflected. "Three of them, actually. A trilogy, by C. S. Lewis."

"The *Chronicles of Narnia* guy?"

He nodded. I pulled a notebook out of my sports coat pocket. "Shoot."

"*Out of the Silent Planet, Perelandra*, and, ah, *That Hideous Strength*. Last one's probably my favorite."

"What are they about?"

"Earth, Mars, Venus, allegories of good and bad. How long do you have?"

"Not that long."

We shook hands and I watched him walk down the street to his car. I checked the time and saw I still had a few minutes before I had to leave to pick up Hershey. I got into the van and put the key in the ignition. And that's when it hit me. A wave of exhaustion, like heat stroke or one too many bench presses after too many hours at the gym, but all at once, rapidly flooding my limbs. Any desire I'd had to work that night evaporated. I tried to focus, but my eyes were blurring uncontrollably. Suddenly, all I wanted to do was sleep. Something was wrong. I'd only had two beers, and on a full stomach. And swill, at that. I shouldn't be so tired. But I couldn't keep my eyes open. I struggled, tried to make out Roy. The only thing I saw were taillights pulling away. I tried reaching for my phone but couldn't seem to find my pocket. Then I saw nothing but shadows. Then nothing but black.

13

I WAS BROUGHT BACK TO A SEMBLANCE OF consciousness by a rapping noise, and a man's voice, loud and insistent. I tried unsuccessfully to open my eyes. It felt as if someone had glued them shut, thought better of it, and stapled them instead.

"Sir," the voice said. "Open the door."

I tried my eyes again, and made some progress. Glanced to my left. A uniformed Columbus cop was standing outside my van, flashlight in hand. I opened the door. And nearly fell out.

"How much did you have to drink tonight?" the officer asked a minute later, after I righted myself.

"Couple beers."

"Just a couple?"

"That's right."

"Know how many times I've been told that?"

"A couple?"

An ache was building in the back of my head, the kind I knew wasn't going to go away with an aspirin or two. My mouth was dry and tasted like metal, and my eyes were still battling my lids. After a couple of false starts, I dug out my phone and looked at the screen. One-thirty in the morning. I had four missed calls, all from Hershey, followed by two text messages. The first one, at 10:01, said, **Are you coming or not?** The second one said, **Well, geez, tell Anne I said hi,** accompanied by a winking emoticon.

"Asshole," I muttered.

"What was that?" the officer asked.

"Sorry. Someone I was supposed to meet. He can be kind of a jerk."

"You're sure you only had two beers."

"I'm sure. They'll vouch for me. Inside. My friend Roy will, too." The words coming slowly, like coins pulled out of a pocket and examined one at a time.

A sergeant joined our merry band. My name broadcast over police frequencies has that effect.

"How many beers did you have?" he asked. We repeated the drill.

"Why are you here?" I said, my head starting to clear. "I wasn't driving."

"We got a call from a concerned citizen."

"Concerned I was passed out? That's nice."

"Concerned you don't have a residential parking permit for that space."

The night air was cool, and I took a series of deep breaths. The hour at the bar was starting to come back to me. Roy's financial problems. Theresa, the ex–human trafficking victim. The C. S. Lewis trilogy. And something else, a nagging suspicion about what might have happened to me.

It took another twenty minutes or so, but the cops let me go after warning me not to drive. I didn't need persuading. I locked up my van with a promise from the police they wouldn't have it towed, leaned against it, and dialed Hershey's number. It went immediately to voicemail. I left a brief message of apology, then texted him, tapping out the letters as quickly as my fuzzy brain allowed. **Really sorry. Call when you can.** Then I stumbled home. My decision to drink before working was starting to feel like a bad idea. A really bad idea. I wasn't used to disappointing paying clients, even a guy my girlfriend appeared to have a small crush on. When I arrived home fifteen minutes later, I threw Hopalong into the yard, brushed my teeth, drank a tall glass of water, collected the dog from the yard, drank another glass of water and collapsed into bed, fully dressed.

I WAS AWAKENED BY music. I tried to lift my head from the pillow and just as quickly lowered it. I felt as if someone had massaged my cranium with a pair of wood-handled ball-peen hammers. I lay there and tried to identify the song crashing against my skull. Who the hell would play something so loud, so early, so close to my bed? It came to me a couple of moments later. "Jump," by Van Halen. My new cell phone ring tone. I fumbled at my nightstand.

"Yeah," I answered, finally.

"This Andy Hayes?"

"Yeah."

"Lieutenant Mike Hummel, State Highway Patrol. You know a Lee Hershey?"

"Yeah."

"When was the last time you saw him?"

I struggled to think. "Two nights ago," I said after a long pause.

"Did you text him early this morning?"

I forced brain cells to grind together, to form synapses and produce thought. "Yeah," I said.

"How soon can you be at the Statehouse?"

"Why?"

"We need to have a little chat."

"About what?"

"About Hershey. He's dead."

14

I GOT OUT OF BED, STUMBLED INTO THE kitchen, and forced myself to drink a glass of water. Swallowing felt like someone was opening a burlap bag of marbles over my head. I drank to the bottom anyway. And had another. I made coffee and poured it into a chipped Capital University mug and drank it in the shower under water as hot as I could bear, waiting until the warm ran out and it turned icy and so cold I thought I might vomit. Then I vomited. I got out, shaved, got dressed, and poured another cup of coffee. Starting to think a little straighter, I called and left a message for Burke, telling him about Hershey. And me. And my suspicions about what had happened at the bar.

I walked up the street, retrieved my van—the promise not to tow apparently hadn't included a promise not to ticket—and arrived downtown a few minutes later. I circled the Statehouse in vain; all the underground garage entrances were closed. I saw trucks for Channels 4, 7, and 10 parked in front of the Third Street entrance. A knot of reporters clustered around a trooper on the steps. I kept driving, found a space in a surface lot off Main, tucked a five-dollar bill into the parking slot, and walked back. It wasn't even nine.

The press briefing had broken up by the time I got there. It was a hot day and the flags in front of the Capitol—U.S., Ohio pennant, and POW—hung limply from their poles. I pulled my Columbus Clippers cap down tight over my head and strode with as much purpose as I could muster toward the entrance. I'd made it to the first step leading to the Third Street doors when Suzanne Gregory from Channel 7 intercepted me.

"What are you doing here?" she said.

I stopped and looked at her. I realized I was having troubling focusing. It occurred to me I probably shouldn't have driven. I said, slowly, "I can never remember whether Warren G. Harding was the twenty-eighth or twenty-ninth president. Figured some-one inside might know."

"Twenty-eighth, as you know, given how many goddamn times you quizzed me on Ohio presidents. Why were you work-ing for Lee?"

"You look fetching today," I said, stalling. And she did: a sleeveless peach summer dress with a necklace of paste stones and bracelet to match.

"As much as I hate to say this, don't change the subject." She softened her voice a bit. "You look like shit, by the way. Are you OK?"

"Not really."

"What about my outfit?" Kevin Harding said, walking up.

"Very *Front Page*, without the suit, shined shoes, and fedora," I told the *Columbus Dispatch* reporter, trying not to slur my words. Harding was with a thin, brown-haired woman I didn't know. The look on her face, which included red, swollen eyes, warned me off any sartorial observations. A couple other reporters headed our way.

"Why were you working for Lee?" Suzanne repeated.

"No comment."

"That's a bullshit response."

She was right. Right as a reporter, and right as my ex-fiancée, who more than any other journalist in town deserved a better answer.

Instead, I said, "It's all I've got." I was starting to feel worse again, and not just from whatever I suspected had been slipped into my beer. It was starting to dawn on me what I'd done last night—or more to the point, hadn't done. The consequences of going to a bar before a job.

"C'mon, Andy," Harding said. "Lee was our friend. You gotta give us something."

"I wish I could—"

"Andy Hayes," a voice barked from behind us.

I turned and saw a trooper standing at the top of the stairs. He gestured at me to approach.

"Sorry," I said, and turned dizzily in his direction.

"What's going on?" Suzanne said. "Are you being questioned?"

"Andy," I heard Harding say. "Are you a suspect?"

"Let's go," the trooper said, opening the door.

"Thanks for the lifeline," I said, safe inside. "So what's the drill here?"

"Drill is I'm taking you to see Lieutenant Hummel," he said.

He led me up a marble staircase and guided me into a light-filled atrium, which I saw was just across a hall from the Rotunda, where I had listened, somewhat incredulously, as Hershey waxed on about government and democracy and grandeur just a day and a half earlier. Thick, rounded limestone columns rose on that side of the room, the kind you'd see outside an Athenian temple, or a New York investment bank, while enormous floor-to-ceiling windows formed the north and south walls. Just in front of the columns, tables and chairs had been set up, and several patrol officers, uniformed and plainclothes, were at work on laptops or talking on cell phones. Up above, troopers patrolled a pair of brass-railing walkways, eyeing the people below.

"That's Hummel," my guide said, pointing to a dark-haired man on the phone.

There was something familiar about the detective I couldn't place. As we approached, Hummel gave me the once over, nodded, and went back to his conversation.

I stood for three long minutes, looking here and there around the atrium to pass the time, doing my best not to keel over. Besides the horde of officers, there were none of the usual trappings of a crime scene, which meant the evidence technicians had either done their job quickly or Hershey had died elsewhere in the building. I thought about the Clarmont, and about the senator who'd threatened Lee. *"You're going to be sorry."* Our trip to the Cupola, the long march up the steps to the top. *Commit No Nuisance.* Hershey's claim of committing his own nuisance with a lady friend up there. All those signatures, new and old. The odd tour guide whose ancestor supposedly killed a reporter.

Hummel finished his call, put the phone down on the table and immediately started typing on a laptop. I waited a few more seconds, trying not to focus on my headache. Then I said, "Excuse me."

Hummel kept typing.

"Excuse me?"

Nothing.

"You doing an online Dunkin' Donuts order?" I said. It came out louder than I intended. A couple of heads turned. I kept going. "Wouldn't mind a Boston cream. And large coffee, black. No sugar."

Hummel looked up and stared at me.

"Actually, make that two doughnuts. I'm working up quite an appetite, just standing here."

Now Hummel stood up. "I beg your pardon?"

"You heard me." It was all I could do not to squeeze my head between my hands to stop the pounding. "Get yourself a coffee too, if you want, and maybe a bear claw. On me. Unless you've already had one today."

Hummel walked around the table, planted himself dead center in front of me, and stared at me, hard. It was pretty effective, the fact I had a good five inches on him notwithstanding.

"Don't believe I heard you correctly."

"Believe you did."

"Think you're funny?"

"Think I'm here. Like you asked. You're with the patrol?"

"That's right," Hummel said. "And listen carefully. I'm not taking any crap from a rent-a-cop."

"Fine with me."

"Glad to hear it."

"Because I'm not taking any crap from a glorified meter reader," I said, feeling my knees buckle as I sagged, then dropped to the floor.

15

A FEW MINUTES LATER, SITTING ACROSS
from Hummel, holding a bag of ice on my forehead and sipping
a bottle of water, I started to feel like myself again. And what
myself wanted to do was to be someplace, anyplace, but there.

Hummel looked at me. "Gonna live?"

"Possibly."

"Are you hung over?"

"In a manner of speaking."

"What's that supposed to mean?"

I told him about the job I'd been doing for Hershey. Explained
about the bar and my beer and the ruse with the mysterious girl
and my van. I left out Roy and the Church of the Holy Apostolic
Fire and his money woes for now. Roy had a thing about being
dragged into murder investigations.

"You think someone spiked your beer?"

I nodded.

"Any tests run?"

"Not yet. Top of my to-do list after this."

"Hershey texted you. Last activity on his phone."

"OK."

He looked at his notes. "Second one said, 'Well, geez, tell Anne I said hi.' And then it's got that winking face thing. Who's Anne?"

"My girlfriend."

"Why would he mention her?"

"I'm guessing he was implying I had decided to spend time with her instead of picking him up."

"Did you?"

"No. Like I said, I was at Heyl's Tavern. Hershey was a bit of a charmer when it came to women. He was teasing."

"Make you mad, him talking about your girlfriend like that?"

"Don't even try. I was working for Hershey. I have a strict policy against killing clients. Plus, like I said, I was passed out at the time. Call Columbus PD. I'm sure there's a report."

"Who said someone killed him?"

"Give me a break," I said, folding my arms over my chest and glancing at the array of officers scattered through the room. "You're going CSI-Statehouse because he tripped and fell?"

He didn't respond. I said, "So why's the patrol involved? Was Hershey speeding before he died?"

"Very funny. It's the Statehouse. We're the state patrol. It's our jurisdiction. That OK with you?"

"I suppose. Why aren't you wearing one of those Dudley Do-Right hats like the guy who brought me in?"

Hummel just shook his head, like a teacher at the end of his rope. "Hershey didn't tell you who he was meeting last night?"

"No."

"Or where?"

"Correct."

"Strike you as a little odd?"

"Yes and no."

I went over the visit to the steakhouse. Hummel consulted his notes a couple times as I talked. He perked up, as I knew he would, when I got to the end and the part about the tail.

"No idea who it was?"

"It was raining too hard. Hershey figured it had something to do with his reporting on Triple F."

"Stupidest name ever for an education plan," Hummel said. He looked ready to say something else when another detective approached, holding a cell phone as if he'd just fished it out of a toilet. "It's *her*," the man mouthed.

"One sec," Hummel said, lowering his voice.

"She's adamant," the man said.

Hummel glared at me. He looked around the makeshift table, found a yellow legal pad, and pushed it in my direction. "List of names," he said. "Everyone Hershey talked to at the Clarmont."

The detective behind him cleared his throat.

"You're a popular guy," I said.

"Picked up on that, did you?" Hummel said.

"Who's *her*?"

"Her, wise guy, is the patrol superintendent. My boss's boss. And she's calling because the public safety director is leaning on her, because the governor is leaning on *him*, and on, and on." He pointed at the pad of paper. "Everybody in the restaurant, OK?"

"Gonna be a long list," I said.

"Just make sure it's a complete list," Hummel replied.

16

I WROTE FOR FIVE MINUTES, TRYING TO remember everyone I'd run into at the Clarmont. Lauren Atkinson, to start with, the state teachers' union president whose southern accent couldn't hide a sour disposition. Kerri MacKenzie, the Senate Democratic analyst who'd seemed pretty buddy-buddy with Hershey. Was she his Cupola partner? *Nice ass, but I'm worried she's gaining a little weight.* A sexist comment, or a hint? Allen Ratliff, the Prince of Dorkness. Lily Gleason, Hubbard's education liaison, put off immediately by Hershey. Sam Michaels, the brusque Education Department guy with the goatee. Senator Ottie Kinser and her husband, Reggie, the power couple who remembered Anne and me from Burke's fundraiser for Rodriguez. Justice Bryan, the white-haired elder statesman type from Paw Paw Bottoms. If there really was such a place. Jack Sterling, the casino lobbyist with the bespoke tailored suit. *Extra rat poison.* And of course, Ed Tillman, chairman of the Senate Education Committee. *Enjoy your job. Because if you write one more word about Midwest Testing, one single word more, you're going to be sorry.* Had he meant that in the usual, bombastic way people made such idle threats? Or had he had something darker in mind? Finished, I put the pen down, picked it up reluctantly and wrote "Ephraim Badger." It seemed a stretch, since both Hershey and I had towered over the tour guide, who looked like he couldn't weigh much more than a Hopalong and a half, yet I'd seen myself that he wandered the Statehouse late at night. The list was longer than I expected. But did it reveal anything? How many of those were Hershey's sources? Was one of them his killer?

I waved the paper at Hummel, who was still on the phone. He nodded and made a gesture that I could go. I stood up, left the water on the table and the ice on my chair, walked up to a uniformed trooper, and asked for safe passage to the exit on the other side of the Rotunda to avoid the reporters on Third. As we were passing through, my eyes rested on the painting of the Battle of Lake Erie, the one Hershey had lectured me on. And that's when I realized what it was about Hummel. The wavy, dark hair. The sideburns, long for a patrol guy.

The detective, I realized, bore a striking resemblance to Commodore Oliver Hazard Perry. I wondered if anyone had ever told him that. I decided not to find out just then.

LIGHTHEADED BUT STARTING TO feel marginally better, I retrieved my van and a few minutes later walked into my doctor's office on South High just south of Whittier. Cheryl glanced over the counter with a bemused look.

"Don't tell me you've been shot again."

"That was a one-time deal. You make it sound like a hobby."

"You need a hobby," the receptionist said. "And I've been telling you for years I'm available."

"Scorpio and Sagittarius. Would never work."

"Story of my life. What's today's ailment?"

I explained about the beer and my suspicions of a Mickey Finn. I left out the whole murder thing for now.

"That's almost better than getting shot," she said. "Let's see what we can do."

A few minutes and a sore middle finger later, a vial of my blood extracted and headed for a lab, I was back in my van with results promised in a couple of days but no guarantee insurance would cover the full amount of the test. Story of *my* life.

Just as I started the engine my phone buzzed and I saw a Channel 7 news alert pop up—meaning Suzanne—followed by one from the *Dispatch*—meaning Kevin Harding. They both said approximately the same thing:

Sources say Statehouse reporter bludgeoned to death

THREE HOURS LATER, STILL groggy from the nap I'd taken upon returning home after the bloodletting, if nap is what you call collapsing onto a couch and into immediate unconsciousness, I scrolled through news headlines on my phone.

Veteran reporter slain at Statehouse, the *Dispatch* declared at the top of its website.

Police: crusading reporter brutally beaten, screamed Channel 7.

Even the *New York Times* weighed in, intoning: *In Battleground Ohio, Reporter's Dogged Pursuit of Truth Takes Deadly Turn.*

Details were sketchy, with the stories consisting mostly of background on Hershey, but one detail, attributed to multiple sources by each report, stood out. Hershey's body had been found in the center of the Rotunda. *Ground zero of Democracy in Ohio.* Now his own ground zero, I thought.

A few minutes later I left my house and drove north, out of German Village. I went up to Fourth, headed west on Broad and went through downtown. I saw several TV news trucks still parked outside the Statehouse. I crossed over High and Front and drove across the Broad Street bridge. On my right, the new state Veterans Memorial was slowly rising on the site of the old Vets hall, demolished unceremoniously the year before for reasons I still wasn't clear on. All cities grow and change, but Columbus had a penchant for bulldozing its own history, always on the hunt for something bigger and shinier, something to ward off the fear it would never be more than "Cowtown," never lose the "Ohio" appendage tacked on in every reference, never be known for anything but Ohio State football and state government. The irony, I thought, was that the worries persisted even as the city, as Roy had said, had boomed in unimaginable ways since I'd come to town two decades earlier. We were the only big city growing in the Midwest. We were a foodie mecca. We had an NHL team, for God's sake. Yet the hand-wringing continued. We were a metropolis still convinced we hadn't had our Sally Field moment yet: "You like us. You really like us."

Roy's church sat off Grubb Street a couple of blocks farther down on Broad, a long-shuttered cinder-block electronic parts factory he'd wrestled, over several years, into a house of worship and soup kitchen, of sorts. Inside, Theresa Sullivan was sitting at a table in the main hall, filling out forms. Her transformation from drug-addicted prostitute to sober girl Friday for Roy still took some getting used to, starting with a complete set of teeth and a healthy face that no longer looked quite so skeletal.

"The fuck you doing here?" she said, looking up.

"Taking back the nice things I was just thinking about you."

"Like what?"

"Like never mind. Hey, know how many college quarterbacks it takes to screw in a light bulb?"

She shook her head.

"Just one. But you get a whole semester's worth of credit."

She gave a barking laugh someplace between a cackle and a guffaw.

"Thought you'd like that," I said. "Pastor Roy around?"

She nodded toward his office. I headed in that direction, but stopped when she called my name.

"Knock, knock," she said.

"Who's there?"

"Woody."

"Woody who?"

"Woody you got in your pocket, sailor?"

I FILLED ROY IN on the night before, my passing out, my suspicions about the beer. I asked him for more details about the girl who'd walked in and spun the story of hitting my van. I hesitated before getting to the punch line, but it didn't matter. He quickly put what I was telling him together with the news of Hershey's death.

"You were supposed to protect him."

"Stand next to him, anyway. He kept saying it was more about sending a message."

"Sounds like someone sent him one instead."

"Apparently."

"I'm sorry. Oldest trick in the book, and I fell for it."

"Old tricks usually work best."

"What can I do?"

"Don't blame yourself, for starters. We don't have time for that. Maybe write down what you remember about her. What she looked like."

"Young, kind of cute. Blonde. Wearing a Buckeyes ball cap."

"Narrows it down to every other girl under thirty in this town. Probably intentional. Anything else?"

He didn't reply. His face was stoic, and I could tell he was deep in thought. I wondered just for a moment if I should have told him about the beer at all. But I knew it would have been dishonest not to.

"Don't worry," I said. "It'll be fine."

"Sure it will. For everyone except Hershey."

17

ANY CONCERNS I HAD ABOUT ROY'S GUILT over my apparent drugging evaporated as soon as I got back into my van and received a call from Richard Deckard.

"What the hell," he said. "Bonnie said you were supposed to come by this morning."

"Shit. I'm sorry. Something happened."

"Screw sorry. You said you were taking this seriously. Or were you just messing with me to get your girlfriend a cheap place to live?"

"No," I protested. "I just—"

"That's a lot of change I dropped off the rent. On your word. You're supposed to be this big-shot detective now. All that other stuff's in the past. But maybe not? Once a bullshitter, always a bullshitter?"

"Look, I'm sorry. I'm headed there right now."

"You got like one more chance on this," he said. "Then I'm pulling the plug and Anne can live in the projects for all I care."

Dark clouds gathered in my head as I headed north to Bonnie's house. Clouds of anger but mainly of self-recrimination. I had fucked up, and badly. I'd indirectly caused Hershey's death, a first for a client. I'd broken my word with Deckard by missing my appointment with Bonnie, regardless of Hummel's summons—I could have told him to wait, I realized. I wasn't exactly a suspect. Worse, I was in jeopardy of letting Anne down, and not in a small way. I didn't have the money to make up the rent difference if Deckard pulled the plug.

"Shit," I said, pounding the steering wheel as I drove. "Shit, shit, shit."

"YOU SAID THIS MORNING," Bonnie Deckard said, staring through the screen door after I rang the bell a few minutes later. "It's almost five. I'm leaving for work soon."

"I'm really sorry."

"You could have called."

"I know."

She hesitated before letting me in. The door opened into the living room, which looked like a small tornado had swept through on the way to west Kansas. Laundry was piled high on a couch, and dishes and beer bottles littered a coffee table. In a recliner opposite the couch sat a young man I took to be Troy, a video control gizmo in his hands, moving it back and forth as if steering a small boat in a storm. On the TV, computer-animated zombies staggered down a country lane.

"Troy," Bonnie said, raising her voice. "It's the detective. The one I told you about."

He said nothing, eyes locked on the screen.

"My dad wanted you to talk to him."

"I told you, I don't want to."

"It will only take a minute." Bonnie looked at me for confirmation. I nodded.

"Nothing to talk about," Troy said.

"He just wants to help."

"I said no."

"Please?"

"*No.*"

I looked at Bonnie, then at Troy, then back at Bonnie. Thought about Lee Hershey and blown opportunities. I walked over to the recliner, found the remote tucked beside Troy, picked it up, and turned the TV off.

"The hell?" Troy said, staring at me.

"Thing about zombies," I said. "They're the undead. So they're not going anywhere. Just like me."

"Get out," Troy said.

"Soon enough."

"What do you want?"

I turned around, cleared a space on the couch, and sat. The dog from the other day materialized again, looked at me, sniffed my hand, and collapsed beneath the coffee table. I reached out and scratched his ears.

"Nice pooch," I said. "What's his name?"

"Greg," Bonnie said, defensively.

"Greg?"

"He just seemed like a Greg. OK?"

"Greg works," I said. I turned back toward Troy. "Bonnie's dad asked me to talk to you. About Derrick."

He said nothing.

"Said you lost your job recently. That you're upset. About your brother. It's understandable."

"None of your business."

"Something going on he should know about?"

"I said, none of your business."

"Mr. Deckard hired me to make it my business."

"Get lost, OK?" He was schlumpy and pale, with dark hair that looked like it needed washing, wearing red workout shorts and a gray cotton ribbed wife beater with a faded American flag on the front. He had a scraggly beard that sat uncomfortably on his doughy face and a bigger belly than a kid his age should have.

"This what you do all day?" I said. "Play video games?"

"Can you please just leave?"

"Are you any good at them?"

"What?"

"Are you any good at video games?"

"Why are you asking me that?"

"Just curious."

"No," he said. "I'm no good at them. I just like playing them."

"What are you good at?"

He stared at me. "I'm not good at anything," he said.

"Must be something."

He kept his eyes on the blank TV screen, not replying. His mini-outburst seemed to have forced him farther back into himself, like an abused dog frightened by its own barking. I glanced up at Bonnie, who was sitting on the far end of the couch, watching us. I realized she was crying.

I said, "Bonnie's dad said you're a Buckeyes fan."

Troy said nothing.

"What do you think of the kid they recruited for quarterback? Glenville High, out of Cleveland?"

Still nothing.

"Michigan State could be tough this year. Could spoil things. Just like in '98."

Troy flipped me off.

"Maybe you should leave," Bonnie said.

I shook my head. "Your dad hired me to talk to Troy. That's what I'm going to do. What do you think about the special teams—"

Faster than I would have thought possible for a guy in his shape, Troy rose from his chair, walked over to the couch, grabbed my arm, and pulled, hard. "Get the hell out of here, why don't you?"

I yanked my arm free and stood up. "Just calm down, OK?" I said.

Without warning he launched himself at me. I took the full force of the charge and fell back on the couch as he landed heavily. I cursed as the back of my head bounced off the wall. Greg skittered out from under the table and started barking furiously.

"Troy, no," Bonnie said, tugging at him as she started crying again.

Recovering, I wrapped my arms around Troy, folded him into a bear hug, squeezed hard, and lifted him off me as gently as possible. Instead of responding, he lay on the couch where I placed him, breathing hard, not moving.

"I just want to talk," I said.

"There's nothing to talk about," he whimpered.

"Your brother's looking at life in prison. Seems conversation-worthy."

"It's nothing to do with me."

"It's a lot for anybody to deal with. If not me, maybe you should see someone."

"Like who?"

"An expert."

"A shrink."

"Maybe."

"I don't want anybody messing with my head."

"It's not like that," I said. "It's talking with someone trained to listen."

"No."

"OK," I said, changing tactics. "What about your parents?"

"What about them?"

"How about talking to them?"

He shook his head, face still partially buried in the couch.

"Why not?"

Nothing.

I might have left it at that, and gone and told Deckard that I was sorry. Told him that I'd tried but failed, and pursued some alternative payment plan for Anne's rent, like sucking it up and pulling night security duty at Wal-Mart, which I deserved at this point, had Bonnie at that moment not taken a deep, shuddering breath and started crying even harder.

I said, "How about I talk to them?"

"What?" Troy said.

"You heard me. How about I talk to your folks?"

"*No.*"

"Why not?" I looked at Bonnie for help, but she was crying too hard to meet my eyes.

"Because I said so," Troy said.

"Not much of a reason."

"Like I care."

"All right," I said, making a decision. "Change your mind about talking, let me know."

Neither of them replied. Greg had crept back to the edge of the couch, and I reached down, scratched his ears, stood up, and let myself out. Back in my van I pulled out my phone and called Deckard.

"It's Andy Hayes," I said. "I need a number for Troy's parents."

18

AS I HEADED SOUTH ON CLEVELAND AVENUE I turned on 97.1, The Fan, in the hopes of distracting myself with Columbus sports radio chatter as I drove. The Reds' recent drop below .500 had several people up in arms, as did yet another quarterback controversy brewing at Ohio State. I was trying to decide if I had an opinion on any of it when I glanced in my rearview mirror and realized I'd picked up company again. Small, beige SUV two car lengths back. The upper portion of the windshield was tinted and I couldn't make out the driver. I slowed until I saw the light ahead of me turning yellow, then I gunned it through the intersection. I checked a moment later: they'd covered the move.

I turned right at Hudson, drove a few blocks, and took the entrance for 71 South. They stuck with me, a car or two between us, as I merged into traffic. I picked up my phone from the passenger seat and raised it to my right ear as though I were talking to someone. I settled into the middle lane, waited for them to follow, and as they did, I began to slow down, still protected by the buffer of another car. Fifty-five, fifty, forty-five. At forty the car behind me swung around to my left and sped by, exposing the tail. I tilted the phone toward the rearview mirror and blindly pressed the photo button. Then I went back to pretending to talk while glancing occasionally in the mirror. They stayed with me for the next few minutes, always a couple of cars between us, but when I made the turn to exit onto Spring, they kept going. I had a red light at the exit and examined my efforts. The first few were useless, blurry images of my rear window. But the next couple, I saw, had been successful. I had the plate.

I WOKE UP FRIDAY morning just past seven, a late start I treat myself to when trying to shake off being drugged, followed by suffering a minor concussion hitting my head on someone's wall after being tackled. It was so late that Hopalong's normal look of big-eyed pleading for his walk had morphed into a stare he reserved for such ordeals that I dubbed the morose gaze of castigation. I dragged myself out of bed, forced myself to do some push-ups, drank a cup of coffee, changed into running clothes, leashed the dog, and circled Schiller Park four times. Back home, after weights and stretching I started to feel groggy again, but resisted the temptation to return to bed. I ate breakfast, brought my laptop to the kitchen table, and tapped the plate number from the night before into an informational database I could subscribe to as a licensed private eye.

When I saw the results, I wondered if I'd entered the plate wrong. The registration came back to what appeared to be an automotive parts store in Detroit. I double-checked the photo and saw I had it right. I called the number for the store, but it was disconnected. Stumped, I spent the next several minutes reading the long story in the paper about Hershey's murder. Then I went online and found Suzanne's story for Channel 7. I checked other papers that had written their own, looked up the AP article, and cycled through the rest of the TV stations. The facts were bare, and brutal. Lee had apparently been alone in the pressroom when he'd been attacked by someone from behind. He'd been hit hard a couple of times with a blunt object that hadn't been identified, then struck the edge of the pressroom table with his head as he fell. He stumbled out of the room, up the stairs, perhaps looking for help, perhaps dazed and not thinking straight, and stepped into the Rotunda, where he'd collapsed directly in the center and died within minutes of a brain hemorrhage.

I was on a third cup of coffee and trying to decide what to do next—call Anne, go back to Troy and Bonnie's, find another career—when the sound of Van Halen interrupted me.

"The *bodyguard*," the woman's voice said. "You sure as hell blew that assignment."

"Who's calling?"

"It's Kerri MacKenzie. What *happened?*"

It took me a second before remembering who that was. The Senate policy analyst I'd met at the Clarmont. The Democrat. The woman whom Hershey—and yes, yours truly—had set lascivious eyes on.

"That's what I'm trying to find out," I said.

"Weren't you supposed to be protecting him?"

"Yes."

"But you didn't."

"No. Obviously."

"Is that all you have to say?"

"Could we meet?"

"You've got to be kidding."

"For once in my life, no," I said.

AN HOUR LATER WE sat down at an outside table at Cafe Brioso at High and Gay just north of downtown, the aroma of the coffee shop's roasting beans drifting over us. MacKenzie slid her copy of the Triple F binder onto the table. I appeared to be the only person in town without one.

"Sorry," she said. "We had to grab our stuff and get out of there pretty quickly."

"I can imagine."

"Probably not."

"No offense," she said a few minutes later, after I'd given her the short version of what happened before I was supposed to pick up Hershey two nights earlier. "But how do I know you just didn't get shitfaced and pass out in your van and realize after you woke up you needed to cover your ass?"

"You have to take my word for it." I didn't bother telling her about Roy and the cops and the blood test.

"That's convenient."

"I guess, though there's also the fact I'm not in the habit of letting clients die."

"Like that's some big comfort now."

"Lee was supposed to meet someone Wednesday night," I said, trying to change directions. "Was that you?"

"Me? No."

"Do you know who it was?"

"No. Why would I?"

"I'm not sure. I figured it was someone in state government."

"He didn't say who?"

I shook my head.

"Where was the meeting?"

"Don't know that either. He wouldn't tell me. I was just supposed to pick him up and I'd get instructions from there. Of course, now, I'm guessing it was the Statehouse."

"That sounds like Lee. He got into that cloak-and-dagger stuff."

"No idea what he was up to?"

"No."

"Are you one of his sources?"

"I gave him tips from time to time. Who hasn't around here?"

"Just for the heck of it, where were you Wednesday night?"

"I beg your pardon?"

"I told you where I was, not that I'm happy about it. How about you?"

"Now you think *I* killed him?"

"Didn't say that. But the cops are going to ask you the same thing, sooner or later."

"I was home."

"Can anybody vouch for you?"

"You'll just have to take my word for it," she said.

She smiled. I smiled back.

"How'd you get into this stuff?" I said after a moment.

"Stuff?"

"Politics. Whatever it is you do."

"Pretty basic," she said, looking across the street. "Cradle Democrat, dropped out of college to work for Clinton, cried the night Obama was elected. It's in my blood, like Lee said."

"Think a Democrat killed him?"

"I have no idea. I'd like to think not."

"He seemed to make a lot of Democrats angry."

"He made pretty much everyone angry."

"You?"

"Sure. Party first—that's the rule. You heard me complain about Midwest Testing. That story was bullshit."

"So your tips only involve Republicans?"

"Party first," she said.

"The other night, at the Clarmont. You told Lee something. What was it?"

She colored. "Nothing."

"Wrong answer. There's no such thing as nothing now."

"Does it really matter?"

"I won't know unless you tell me. You're the one who called me, by the way. Why was that?"

"I was upset. I wanted to find out what happened."

"As do I. So what about it?"

"It was just a rumor I heard."

"About what?"

"An affair."

"Between who?"

"The governor and someone. Satisfied?"

"The governor and who?"

"I don't know. The rumor was someone in his office."

"Lily Gleason?"

"As if."

"Why do you say that?"

"She's damaged goods because of the scandal, duh."

"What scandal?"

"The kind everyone around here hates," MacKenzie said.

"Which is?"

"The kind that ran with Lee Hershey's byline over it."

SHE WENT OVER THE details, which had something to do with a bloated computer consulting contract signed by the state family services agency with a company owned by Gleason's husband. Gleason had been in the legislature at the time, and the publicity, including a lawsuit against the husband by a company who'd lost the initial contract, ended her career and didn't do any favors for her husband's business. Bankruptcy and a nasty divorce followed. Lee broke the story and had it exclusively for a couple of days before the rest of the press corps caught up.

"Could either of them have been the person Lee was supposed to meet?"

"After what he did to them? Extremely doubtful."

I thought back to the Clarmont and the playful punch MacKenzie had given Hershey, the banter between the two of them. I said, "Lee took me up to the top of the Cupola, Tuesday night."

"He did?"

"It was quite the trip. Have you been?"

"Couple years ago."

"He had a key, which he claimed he got from a woman he used to fool around with up there."

"He said that?"

"Pardon the question, but was that you by any chance?"

"Me?"

"That's right."

"Like, I was messing around with Lee?" She seemed legitimately aggrieved. But she was also blushing.

"Just a question."

"No. It wasn't me."

"Any idea who?"

"None."

"Do you believe him?"

"It sounds like something Lee would have said."

"But not something he did?"

She shrugged. "Hard to tell with him sometimes. He could blow a lot of smoke."

"I got that impression. Back to suspects. That senator, Ed Tillman. Could he have killed Lee?"

"I don't think so."

"Why not? He made a threat about Lee not having a job."

"Tillman had had a long day. He lost his temper."

"Which sometimes leads to mistakes."

"Tillman sold insurance before he got here. He's not exactly an excitable guy. That's the most worked up I've ever seen him, in fact."

"How'd an insurance salesman get to be Senate education chairman?"

She smiled thinly. "He sold policies to school districts. Around here, that passes for expertise."

19

I WALKED HER BACK TO THE STATEHOUSE when we'd finished. They were letting staffers in at the Third Street entrance with appropriate ID, but not the private eyes accompanying them. I thanked her, asked her to stay in touch, and walked around the north side of the building to head back to Front and my van. I was passing one of the Civil War cannons ensconced permanently on the grounds when I saw a familiar figure walking down the path toward High. It was Ephraim Badger, the diminutive, late-night prowling tour guide. I called his name.

He stopped and turned, looked at me with a puzzled expression, turned back around and kept walking.

"Ephraim. Wait."

He reached the corner of Broad and High and crossed without acknowledging me. For a retired history teacher he moved fast. Maybe all that prowling. The light changed, and I had to wait for several cars before I could follow. At last I headed in his direction down High, only to see him pop onto a city bus. I picked up the pace and made it on two passengers behind him.

"Ephraim," I said to his back as he threaded his way down the aisle.

"Ticket," the driver said.

"Just a second," I said. "I need to talk to that guy."

"Ticket or get off. I'm behind schedule."

I pulled out my wallet and peered inside. It held several of Hershey's twenties but no actual dollar bills. Of course. Down the aisle, Badger tucked himself into a window seat.

"Can you give me one second?"

"Off," the driver said.

"Please?"

"*Off.*"

"Ephraim," I said as loudly as I dared. "I need to talk to you."

Badger looked up at me as if seeing me for the first time. "Nothing to talk about," he squeaked.

"Sir," the driver said. "This is the last time."

"Why not?" I said to Badger.

"We," Badger started to say, before a bus rolling past us drowned him out.

"What?"

"*Sir,*" the driver said.

"*We have met the enemy and he is us,*" Badger said.

Someone jabbed me from behind. "Move your ass before I move it for you," a woman said. Casting a last look at Badger, I turned, muttered an apology, and got off. I contemplated a mad dash into a restaurant to buy something to get change, or trying to hail a taxi, but realized after a minute how silly both options were. With a hiss and groan the bus pulled away.

"*We have met the enemy and he is us.*" The same *Pogo* quote Hershey used the night in the Statehouse. But why?

I was back in my van, about to pull out and head to Grove City to see how Anne's packing was getting along, when my phone rang.

"It's Jim Flanagan," the man on the other line said. "*Cleveland Press.*"

"No comment."

"Not looking for comment. I've got some information I want to share."

"About what?"

"About who might have killed Lee Hershey."

20

THE RINGSIDE IS A THROWBACK BAR, occupying the same corner on Pearl Alley downtown in the same small brick building for more than a century even as other structures rose and fell and rose. These decades the bar sat across the alley from the forty-story Rhodes state office building, a skyscraper with about as much charm as a regional department store in Soviet Russia. Flanagan was waiting for me outside a couple of hours later. He grinned as I walked up.

"It's been a while," he said, shaking my hand.

"We've met?"

"I was a sportswriter for the *Lantern* when I was at Ohio State. Covered football my freshman year, your senior season. Don't tell me you don't remember me."

"You were the punk with the pen and the attitude?"

"Always the wise guy. Thanks for coming down on short notice. Let me buy you a beer."

He pulled open the bar's heavy red wooden doors, and we stepped inside. We took the last dark-paneled wooden booth at the back, by the stairs. The after-work crowd was thinning, but the place was still busy. Flanagan ordered a Budweiser. I got a

Rolling Rock, and because I hadn't eaten yet I asked for a burger and onion rings.

"So how's the private detecting business?" he said.

"It's had better years. You've got information about Hershey?"

"Getting right to the point," he said. I couldn't tell if it was a statement or a question and either way didn't respond. He was about my height, with short brown hair, a closely cropped beard, and wire-rimmed glasses, wearing a red shirt and corduroy pants. Our beers arrived, and at Flanagan's instigation we clinked bottles.

"You were at the Clarmont, two nights ago," he said.

"That's right."

"I've heard everybody and their brother was there."

"Their step-cousin too. Though I don't recalling seeing you."

"I was on deadline. Unlike Lee, some of us actually spend time in the office."

"Good for you. You still haven't answered my question."

"Hold onto your pants. You know about Senator Tillman and Midwest Testing and Las Vegas?"

"The almost-but-not-quite unreported junket? A little bit. I also heard Tillman threaten Lee with his job. Pretty much everyone at the Clarmont heard that."

Flanagan nodded. "And you know why Midwest Testing was a story? A good one, I'll give Lee that."

"Besides possible ethics violation involving a trip to Las Vegas?"

"Yeah, there's that. But do you know about the grand jury?"

"No."

Flanagan sat back, a look of satisfaction on his face. He took a long pull on his beer. "County prosecutor's taking another look. He wasn't quite satisfied with Tillman's explanation. That's an angle Hershey didn't have."

"But you do?"

"It's in tomorrow's paper."

"Is your story implying that that gave Tillman a motive to kill Lee?"

"Not in so many words."

"In other words, yes."

He shrugged.

"This is your big tip? Something the whole world will know in twelve hours?"

"I only figured out this afternoon you were involved. I called as soon as I could. I just thought, you know, you'd appreciate knowing beforehand."

"Big of you."

"And that you might remember my largesse down the road if you learn anything about Lee's death you might consider telling *me*."

"Ah," I said. "And now the game's afoot."

He grinned. "As your predecessor, Sherlock Holmes, put it so aptly."

"Shakespeare."

"What?"

"That's Shakespeare, not Sherlock Holmes. *Henry IV*. Common mistake."

"Jesus Christ," Flanagan said, shaking his head.

"Sorry. Flypaper brain."

"It's not that," he said. "It's just the kind of fucking thing Lee would have done. He was always correcting people with shit like that. Is that why he hired you? Obnoxious minds think alike?"

"Not that I'm aware of," I said, feeling uncomfortable. "So what do you want from me, exactly?"

"Same thing I gave you. Information. You game?"

I sighed. I thought about the fact I could have been helping Anne pack boxes at the moment. Should have been. I may not have inflicted my flypaper brain on her as badly as I had with others—Suzanne's crack about President Harding came to mind—but my irregular schedule grated on her, I knew.

I said, "How long have you been a reporter?"

"A while."

"Always with the *Cleveland Press*?"

"Started with AP. Worked for Cincinnati, Dayton, then the *Press*."

"But always here?"

"Cincinnati first, where I'm from. Then the Columbus bureaus of the other papers."

"Why here?"

"Wanted to cover politics. Statehouse press corps was the place to be. Lots of jobs in those days."

"How well did you know Hershey?"

"Pretty well."

"Friends?"

He finished his beer and looked around for our waitress. He caught her eye and she nodded. He turned back to me.

"*Shakespeare*," he said. He shook his head.

"I said I was sorry."

"I know. It's just that Lee and I weren't really friends. More like sworn enemies."

I TOOK A DRINK of my beer and glanced around the restaurant. The Reds were on TV and losing again. At the bar a couple flirted. Above the drinks board I noticed two stained-glass windows, one with a donkey, the other an elephant. I looked back at the couple. A bipartisan affair? I wondered. Was that even possible anymore?

I returned my attention to Flanagan, "Enemies how?"

"Lee had a thing for the ladies," he said. "As many divorces as you, if I'm not mistaken. No offense."

"Plenty taken," I said, recalling Hershey's comment about alimony payments. It's hell having your own Wikipedia page. "So what?"

"So my wife cheated on me with him."

"I'm sorry to hear that."

"You and me both." His beer arrived and he took a long pull, draining half.

"When was this?"

"Last year."

"Did you reconcile?"

He shook his head. "I wanted to, but she refused."

"She wanted to stay with him?"

"I guess," he said, with a sad smile. "Kelly was bipolar. Tended to act on impulse at the worst times."

"Other affairs?"

"Not that I know of. But life could be a little rough when her meds weren't jibing. Late-night binges on Amazon with the credit card, things like that. Not like I was some kind of knight in shining armor. But at least I was open to us, you know, afterward . . ."

"Is she a reporter?"

"Was. She was laid off during the recession and got into PR."

"Was she still with Lee when he—?"

Flanagan shook his head. He turned and looked for the waitress again. But she was good. This time she'd been keeping an eye on him. She was already on the way. I took a swig of my Rolling Rock, taking it to half empty.

"She was killed in a car crash late last year," Flanagan said. "I think it was over between them by then, and she was trying to figure out what to do. Turned me down, like I said. But Lee got tired of his women pretty quickly. Some people struggle with their faith. He struggled with his monogamy, such as it was."

"I'm sorry," I said again.

He drank the shoulders off his third beer and waved the comment away.

The waitress brought my dinner. I reached for an onion ring and took a bite.

"Why are you telling me this?" I said.

"Why not? Lee was a sack of shit. But even I have to admit, he was a damn good reporter. Personally, do I want an inside track to anything you hear about his case? Sure. But I'm also the head of the Statehouse reporters' association, in which Lee was a member in good standing. We want some answers."

"Just for paperwork purposes, plus, I guess, because of your history with him, you have an alibi for that night?"

"I was out of town. Whole day."

"He was killed at night."

"Whole day," he repeated.

"Out of town where?"

"Just out of town."

I nodded uncertainly. "Lee said he had to have an uncomfortable conversation with someone that evening. Any idea who that might have been?"

"Could have been anyone. Unless you were his friend, most conversations with him could be uncomfortable."

"Fair enough," I said, and took a bite of my burger.

"So how about it?" Flanagan said.

"How about what?"

"My proposal."

I took another bite, added an onion ring, chewed and washed both down with a swig of beer. I wasn't ready to reject him altogether. I couldn't see how such an arrangement would benefit me. But it probably wouldn't hurt either, as long as the flow of information was tipped firmly in my balance.

I was about to respond when the door opened and a woman walked in. I recognized her from the crowd of reporters outside the Statehouse the day before. The one with the red eyes. She saw me, did a double take, hesitated, and then walked over. She seemed taken aback when she saw Flanagan sitting across from me.

"Didn't mean to interrupt," she said.

"No interruption," Flanagan said, shifting to his left. "Have a seat. I was just telling Andy here how much I hated Lee's guts."

21

"LIZ BRANTLEY," SHE SAID, STICKING OUT her hand across the table when she was seated.

"Andy Hayes," I said, as we shook.

"I know who you are."

"Usually a bad sign. You're a reporter?"

She nodded. "*Capitol Corner.* It's a Statehouse newsletter."

"You knew Lee?"

"Yes."

"I'm sorry about what happened."

"Thanks. So am I."

The waitress came by. I agreed to a second beer, and Brantley ordered a glass of white wine. Flanagan had another Bud.

"Liz's got a book coming out," Flanagan said.

"Is that so?"

She nodded. "Next month."

"Just in time for the political conventions," Flanagan said. He lowered his voice. "*Swing State Ohio: The State That Crowns Presidents.*"

"Not a great title," Brantley demurred.

"But a great premise," Flanagan said. He turned to me. "No Republican has ever won the White House without winning Ohio. Did you know that?"

I nodded.

"And only two Democrats," he continued. He looked closely at me. "Who?"

I glanced at Brantley, then back at Flanagan. "Kennedy, and Franklin Roosevelt in 1944."

"*Fuck*," Flanagan said. "Just like fucking Lee."

"Jim," Brantley said.

"Flypaper brain," I offered.

"Andy was working for Lee," Flanagan said, ignoring me.

"I know," Brantley said. "Any idea who might have—?"

I shook my head. "You?"

"None."

"Where were *you* Wednesday night?" Flanagan said.

Brantley glared at him. "At home, alone, working on my blog while I watched *House of Cards*. The one with Ian Richardson, not Kevin Spacey. And no, no one but my cat can vouch for me. How about you?"

"Out of town," Flanagan said.

The waitress brought our drinks. Flanagan raised his newest bottle for a toast, and we all clinked glass. He took a long pull on his. Brantley sipped her wine, and I let my beer rest next to my plate while I took another bite of burger.

"Liz and Lee had a history," Flanagan said. He was sweating a bit, and his eyes were shining.

"Thank you, Jim," Brantley said.

"You're welcome. I thought Andy here should know."

"Not exactly a state secret," she said.

Carefully, I said, "Were you together?"

"We dated, a while back. Ancient history."

"Sorry," Flanagan said.

"Too late," Brantley said.

"What can you tell me about your book?" I said, trying to break the tension.

"I can tell you I need a cigarette," she said.

AS BRANTLEY HEADED TO the door, Flanagan apologized again, then excused himself to use the bathroom. I looked at my watch. I took two more bites of my burger, waved at the waitress, handed her a couple of Lee's twenties and told her to keep the change. I asked her to let Flanagan know I'd stepped outside.

Brantley was standing just past the restaurant steps, looking down Pearl Alley to the south, across Broad toward the Statehouse, cigarette in hand. I studied her from behind. *Nice ass*, I said to myself reflexively, remembering too late how Hershey used the same expression about Kerri MacKenzie. I thought about Flanagan's accusation a few minutes earlier: *Just the kind of fucking thing Lee would have done. . . . Obnoxious minds think alike?* I averted my eyes and cleared my head. I stepped a little closer.

"You like to read?" I said.

"Of course."

"Science fiction?"

"Occasionally."

"Have a favorite book?"

She thought about it. "*The Handmaid's Tale*. Margaret Atwood."

"What's it about?"

"A dystopian future where America's become a theocracy."

"Sounds cheery," I said, writing it down.

"You said favorite. Not feel-good-iest. Why do you ask?" I explained about Anne.

"Such a good boyfriend," she teased. "How about you? What's your favorite?"

"I'm still collecting titles. I'm usually more into biographies."

"Oh?"

"Just finished *Showdown*, by Wil Haygood. About Thurgood Marshall?"

"Yeah, great book. Haygood's from Columbus, you know."

I nodded.

"Well, you'll have to send me your list of science fiction books when it's done. I'm always looking for something to read."

"Sounds good."

She took another drag on her cigarette and looked down the alley.

She said, "Lee told me something funny once, about the Statehouse."

"Which was?"

"After they built it they were adding some restrooms and accidentally hooked up the toilet pipes to the air vents."

"Ugh."

"The smell was horrible, as you can imagine. It made people sick—they called it Statehouse malaria."

"That's disgusting."

"What's amazing is how long they tolerated it until somebody discovered the mistake. Afterward, they had to haul out dozens of barrels of accumulated filth."

"That sounds like something Lee would know."

"He used to say, 'It wasn't enough that the lawmakers made each other *eat* shit, they made each other *breathe* it, too.'"

I laughed, partly because she had his intonations down perfectly. But Brantley just stood there, looking at the Statehouse, smoking.

I followed her gaze down the alley. I thought back to my trip to the Cupola with Hershey. I wondered if he'd ever taken Brantley there. Or, come to think of it, Jim Flanagan's wife, Kelly.

"I'm sorry about Jim," she said. "He didn't have to bring up Lee and me."

"I'm sorry for your loss."

"It's OK," she said, taking a puff. She smiled wearily. "I hated Lee's guts, too."

The Ringside doors opened and Flanagan came out, nearly tripping as he missed a step.

"She said you settled up," he said, nodding back at the door. "You didn't have to do that."

"No worries." I decided not to mention it was Lee Hershey's money I'd put down on the table.

"What'd I miss? Liz tell you who really did it?"

Brantley said, "Andy was just asking me what my favorite science fiction novel was."

"What'd you tell him?"

She repeated her choice. "How about you?" she said. But it was my face her eyes watched.

"I'd have to think about it." To me, Flanagan said, "Why do you want to know?"

"Personal edification."

"How noble."

"Time to go, gentlemen," Brantley said, finishing her cigarette. "Sunday's column calls. It'll all be spelled out in there. The real story."

"You wish," Flanagan said.

I looked at Brantley, and she held the glance a moment longer than I was prepared for. After a second she broke off and strode up the alley with a wave.

The real story, I thought. Could there ever be such a thing?

22

IT WAS STILL LIGHT OUT WHEN I GOT TO
Anne's parents' house, providing plenty of illumination for a couple of well-deserved scowls from her and her dad. I made up for it by working to nearly midnight, but truth be told, Anne didn't have a lot of stuff, other than books, which we hauled boxes of out of the basement. She'd sold most of her furniture and bigger belongings after the debacle in upstate New York, when her drunken husband failed in his attempt to stab her to death because of a coffee table that tripped him up and gave her time to dash to a bedroom and lock the door. After a few hours' sleep, I spent most of Saturday morning unloading the truck at Richard Deckard's duplex on Crestview and most of the afternoon helping unpack.

I'd looked up Ephraim Badger's address, and on Sunday morning decided to pay him a visit at home. He lived in a small but well-kept two-story clapboard house on the west side on a side street running south of Sullivant. His block was within walking distance of Camp Chase, the graveyard where nearly two thousand Confederate prisoners of war who died during their Civil War internment were buried. Perfect place for a history buff, I thought.

The driveway was empty, and no one answered when I rang the doorbell. I waited a minute and knocked, with the same result. I remembered what Hershey had told me about Badger and Sundays. *In church an hour or six.* Looking around to see if anyone was watching, I shifted to my right and peered as casually as possible through the living room windows. I took in a couple of chairs, a coffee table with the morning's newspaper stacked neatly in the middle, a fireplace to the right, and on either side floor-to-ceiling bookshelves that appeared completely full, if not overflowing.

I shifted back to the front door and, looking around again, tried the screen. Locked. I left it at that, not willing to test the sensitivity of any alarm system he might have installed. I pulled out a card, scribbled a note on the back asking him to call, and stuck it in the door just above the latch. I looked around once more, went back to my van and drove north. On North High I stopped at Cornerstone Deli, bought a bagful of bagels and some cream cheese, and headed to Anne's apartment.

SHE SEEMED DISTRACTED WHEN I got there, a fact I attributed to everything she'd been through with the move. So I was more than a little surprised when she took my hand while we sat on the couch Sunday afternoon, as we took a breather, and looked meaningfully at me.

"A little late," she said. Or so I thought. I glanced at my watch. "Not too bad," I said.

"Me," she said, shaking her head. "I'm a little late."

"Sorry. Did I forget something?"

"My *period*," she said, both exasperated and nervous. "I'm a little late."

"Oh."

"It's not all that unusual. With my running and everything. I just wanted you to know."

"Thank you," I managed.

"I didn't want to say anything before now, because of, you know, everything with Lee."

"Right."

"You OK?"

"We've been careful," I said. "Protection-wise."

"True. But that rock-star sex, you know. Things happen . . ."

I looked to see if she was joking. She returned my glance with the closest she could come to a leer. I could tell her heart wasn't in it.

"I suppose." My head had started to spin a little.

"Don't worry. I'm sure it'll be fine."

"Which part?"

"What do you mean?"

"It will be fine if you're pregnant, or if you're not?"

"You have a preference?"

I said nothing.

"I shouldn't have brought it up," she said. "It happens a lot."

Maybe, I thought, reflecting that while we'd been together for well over a year, such irregularity was news to me.

"Test?" I said.

"Probably wait a few more days. Like I said, it's not that unusual."

"Ah," I said. She searched my face. I could see she was waiting for me to say something else. I couldn't blame her. I was waiting to say something else too. But no words came. The problem was I had everything to say, and nothing at all.

23

NORMALLY I SPEND MY MORNING JOG WITH Hopalong checking out the female joggers and dog walkers at Schiller Park, comparing myself to the much younger and fitter guys on their own runs, and thinking about breakfast and/or lunch. Today, all I could concentrate on was what Anne had told me. It had even topped my funk over Hershey's death, at least temporarily. *It'll be fine*, she'd assured me. All well and good, except what if it wasn't? I was as close to Anne as any woman ever—closer, really, given how I'd treated the others. She even had a key to my house, which for me these days was practically being engaged. But were we ready for the conversation that would follow the stick turning pink? Or was it blue?

I thought suddenly of diapers, and blushed at the memory of how few I'd changed for either Mike or Joe, a constant source of irritation for both their moms. And rightly so. Once again, dark clouds started to gather. Trying to burn off steam, I picked up the pace until I realized Hopalong was struggling to stay with me. I slowed and walked the rest of the way home.

I was opening the door when my phone rang, and I saw from the caller ID it was Burke.

"You know a guy named Ed Tillman? A state senator?"

"Yes. He's the one who threatened Lee at the Clarmont. Why?"

"How soon can you be at my office? He's just been arrested for killing Hershey."

"I DON'T HAVE LONG," Burke said as I sat down a few minutes later. "I'm meeting Tillman at the jail at noon."

"This guy killed Hershey?" I said. "Over a story about a trip to Vegas?"

"What happened there didn't stay there, allegedly. The patrol arrested him at home an hour ago. Ottie Kinser called and asked me to step in, at least for now."

I shook my head. "Tillman's Senate education chairman. And Hershey told me he's a shoo-in for Senate president. I'm not saying guys like that don't break the law. But murder?"

"Well, anybody's capable of anything, in my experience, background or not. And yeah, the guy might be Ohio Senate president material. But, with all due respect to our home state and its elected officials, that's like saying you're the tallest building in Rochester, New York. It doesn't offer any immunity from lethal intentions."

"So what's the accusation?"

"Apparently Tillman rents a motel room on South High for nights things go late and he has to be back early."

"Where's he from?"

"Southern Ohio. Down by Lucasville someplace. He stayed at the motel Wednesday night, and this morning someone called the patrol and told them to look in the motel Dumpster. They found his copy of the education plan, covered in blood."

"I've seen copies of that," I said. "It could do some damage, with enough force."

"That's great."

"Any idea who called the patrol?"

Burke shook his head and leaned back in his chair. I told him about Triple F and Midwest Testing and more about Tillman's threat at the Clarmont.

"He really said that?" Burke asked.

"Afraid so."

He leaned back again, closing his eyes in thought. I waited, accustomed to his ruminations, taking in the unusual decor of his office, a mix of memorabilia from his and Dorothy's travels to Africa, artifacts from the Jim Crow South—"Swimming Pool Whites Only" hung directly over his head, next to his framed law degree—and dozens of family photos.

"All right," he said, rocking forward. "Let's get to work. Sounds like it was a parade of nations at the Clarmont the other night. Somebody in that crowd has to know something. See what they have to say."

"Everyone I talked to seemed to have a beef with Hershey," I offered. "Even Kinser."

Burke nodded. "Hershey did a story a couple of years ago linking political contributions she'd received to attorneys who did pro bono work for Planned Parenthood. She was not pleased."

"Lee mentioned something about that. So she's pro-choice?"

"Is the pope a product of natural family planning? I've known Ottie a long time. I don't think she's up to bludgeoning reporters. But in fairness, talk to her too."

"Am I looking for mitigation?"

"Until I tell you differently, you're looking for an alternate suspect. Starting with whoever spiked your beer and whoever's been following you."

"That may be a dead end," I said. I told him about the Detroit auto parts store.

"Keep your eyes open anyway." He looked at his watch. "I've got to go. I've got to get the tallest building in Rochester out of the slammer."

24

THE WARDLEYS—TROY'S PARENTS—LIVED in Bridgeport, a small suburb of cookie-cutter split-levels tucked between Gahanna and New Albany on the northeast side of the city. Several of the town's lush lawns, including the well-watered expanse at Troy's parents' house, sported red-and-white campaign signs for a candidate with a familiar last name: "Skip Wardley: Fighting for Your Future."

"Help you?" Grant Wardley said, opening the door after I rang the bell late that afternoon. He examined my business card. The neighborhood was filled with the buzz of lawnmowers and the rasp of weed trimmers. My nose wrinkled at the smell of fertilizer and mulch.

I explained about Troy and Derrick. Wardley's face clouded. He was a big guy, fairly fit, wearing cargo shorts and an Ohio State shirt, in considerably better shape than his schlumpy son. I was guessing weights in the basement, and maybe a treadmill from time to time.

"There's nothing to talk about. That's all in the courts now."

"Could I come in?"

"I was about to mow the lawn."

"Just for a minute."

Reluctantly, he opened the door wider and backed up. I followed inside, and he led me through the carpeted living room, dominated by a comfortable-looking slate-gray couch and matching chair, both angled toward an enormous flat-screen TV, and onto an outside patio. A woman sat there with a glass of wine and a magazine. He introduced his wife, Yvonne. Troy and Derrick's mother. She shook my hand nervously, made inquiries about something to drink, and disappeared inside.

"Skip Wardley," I said, waving in the direction of the front yard after we sat down. "Relative of yours?"

"My brother."

"What's he running for?"

"State rep."

"What are his chances?"

He shrugged. "It's a Republican district, and he's as Republican as they come, so they're pretty good."

"What's he do now?"

"He's the Bridgeport mayor. Listen, I don't really think—"

"Troy's been going through a rough patch since Derrick was arrested. Bonnie's dad thought it would help if I talked to him."

"Why you?"

"He said something about Troy being a Buckeyes fan."

"You're Woody Hayes," Wardley said, recognition dawning.

"I go by Andy now. But, yeah."

"Troy know who you are? I mean, your history?"

"I'm not sure. Does it matter?"

He laughed. "Seems like it would. What you did."

"What I did was two decades ago. Right now, I'm here to ask if you'd be willing to talk to him."

Mrs. Wardley returned with two glasses of water. She set them down, picked up the magazine, and went back into the house.

"I'm not sure what I'd say," Wardley said.

"Are you and Troy estranged?"

The question seemed to startle him. "That's none of your business."

"Just an impression I got."

"From who? Deckard?"

"Just a feeling."

"What's between Troy and me has nothing to do with anybody."

"I'm just trying to help him. Seems like a good kid. But kind of lost."

"He is lost," Wardley said. "But he's also a grown man, not a kid."

"Even grown men need their fathers."

"And you're some kind of parenting expert?"

"No more than anybody else."

He stood up. "I've got better things to do than sit here and take this crap. Especially from a guy like you."

"Football," I said. "Video games. Bonnie. Their dog. The weather. Anything. I just think he needs to talk."

He gestured with his right hand in the direction of the door. He trailed me as I reentered the house. His wife was standing over the sink as I passed the kitchen. I called out to her, thanking her for the water, which sat outside, untouched. She turned and smiled distractedly and told me I was most welcome.

"Please don't come here again," Wardley said as I stepped outside.

"Think about talking to Troy?"

"Good-bye," he said, and shut the door.

25

I WALKED BACK INTO BURKE'S OFFICE AT nine the next morning. Ed Tillman was already there in a chair across from Burke's desk. I took the opposite seat, and a moment later accepted coffee from Burke's office assistant, LaTasha. It was generally not a good idea to refuse. Tillman's cup sat untouched on the edge of Burke's desk.

"You were there the other night," Tillman said, sitting up. "At the Clarmont."

I acknowledged it. He took my hand reluctantly.

"I didn't kill that fucking asshole reporter," he said. He looked exhausted, the circles under his eyes like spoonfuls of bruised fruit.

"Watch the language," Burke said. "The patrol doesn't need any more reasons to suspect you."

"But it's the truth—"

"Wednesday night," Burke said. "Where were you?"

"At the motel. I told you."

"Before that."

"At the Statehouse. My committee went late. Lot of testimony about the education bill."

"What time did you finish?"

"It was past six. Maybe later. My office would know."

"Dinner?"

"G. Michael's."

"What'd you have?"

"I don't remember. Chicken, I think."

"Tasty. Anyone with you?"

"Couple other lawmakers staying the night."

"I'll need names," Burke said. "What time did you leave?"

"I'm not sure. Eight, maybe. Eight-thirty?"

"Then what?"

"Then I went to the motel."

"Anybody see you there?"

Tillman shook his head. "I parked and went straight to my room."

"Any idea how your Triple F binder ended up in that Dumpster?"

"No. None. And it's the ABC Initiative, by the way."

"Did you know the binder was missing?"

"We noticed it was gone on Saturday, right after we got started."

"The committee met Saturday?"

"Special session. We had no choice, after they shut down the Statehouse Thursday because of, you know, it. We're on deadline with the schools bill."

"Strike you as odd that the binder was missing?"

"Not really. Sometimes the aides forget to set it out. There were extras, anyway."

"But not extras with your fingerprints all over them."

"I told you—"

Burke cut him off. "Did you see Hershey at the Statehouse Wednesday night, after committee?"

"No."

"Did you kill him?"

"*No.*"

"But you told him he'd be sorry if he wrote anything more about Midwest Testing." Burke looked at me and I nodded.

"I was upset. I shouldn't have said that. He was provoking me, asking me questions at the restaurant like that. But I didn't do anything to him."

Burke turned to me. "Did Hershey record that, or just take notes?"

"He used his phone."

"I've heard it's not on there."

"He said he stored everything in the cloud. Maybe he deleted it."

"Do we know where he stored it?"

I shook my head.

Burke turned back to Tillman. "Why were you so angry? That can't be the first negative story anyone's written about you."

"It's the first one that put me in front of a grand jury. Which is another bunch of bullshit."

"So you were angry at Lee because of his reporting on Midwest."

"Hardly a secret."

"But enough to threaten him?"

"I was taken aback when I saw him. It'd been a long day. And a long couple of months. And it wasn't just the Midwest stories. Hershey was really hard on the school-funding plan. First the Robin Hood memo, then Midwest. I was sick of it."

"Robin Hood memo?" Burke said.

"Something the governor dreamed up early on. Very preliminary."

"What did it have to do with Robin Hood?"

"Nothing. That's what the Republicans called it. Officially, it was the Education Quality Unitary Income Taxability proposal."

"EQUITY," I said after a moment. "That's almost worse than Triple F."

"This memo," Burke continued. "What did it say?"

"The idea was to pool property taxes across the state. Take a portion from better-off districts and use a formula to redistribute it to lower-income schools. Even out the playing field."

"Steal from the rich and give to the poor," I said. "Robin Hood."

"That's a gross oversimplification of what it would have done," Tillman said. "That attitude is why we can't ever fix schools in Ohio."

"I thought that's what Triple F is supposed to do," Burke said.

"That's what the ABC Initiative *is* going to do, if we can ever get it passed," Tillman said.

"All right, all right. So, the memo."

"Someone leaked Lee a draft copy right away, and Hubbard spent the next two weeks backpedaling when he should have been moving forward."

I said, "Any idea who leaked it?"

"I've got some theories."

"Who?"

"A Republican."

"Big surprise," Burke said. "Which one?"

"Does it matter?"

"Of course it matters," I interjected. "Hershey was meeting someone the night he died. We find that person, we're a step closer to figuring out what happened."

"I'd rather it not get back to me."

"You've got a lot bigger problems than worrying about party gossip," Burke said.

"I'm just saying—"

"Name," Burke said.

"Fine. I assume it was Dani Symmes."

"The House Speaker," Burke said.

"That's right."

"Why would she leak it?"

"She hated the idea. '*Robin Hood and His Merry Marxists*,' she called it."

I thought back to what Hershey had said about Symmes, her insistence that the education bill contain something for charter schools. I mentioned this to Burke. Tillman nodded in agreement.

"You think she was Hershey's source for the memo?" Burke said.

"I have no proof, but yes," Tillman said. "And I'm not the only one."

"Is the Senate keeping the charter school amendments in the bill?" I asked.

"We're exploring our options."

"You have to, don't you?" I said. "If you want House Republicans to stay on board."

"I'm not here to discuss our legislative strategy."

"Easy, Senator," Burke said. "Andy's not the one I just bonded out of jail for murder."

"I only meant—"

"When's the last time you saw Hershey?" Burke said.

"At the Clarmont," Tillman said. He glared at me. "With *him*."

"You're sure?"

"Yes."

I said, "Someone was following Hershey. Was that you?"

"Following him? No."

"Positive?"

"Yes. Of course. I wouldn't—"

"You know who it was?"

"No."

"He was supposed to meet someone that night. It wasn't you?"

"He's the last person in the world I'd talk to."

"Maybe you lured him to the Statehouse on some pretext to get revenge," I said. "Snuck in on him in the pressroom when he wasn't looking."

"Don't be ridiculous." Tillman sat back, defiant. Even with the strain showing from what he'd been through in the past twenty-four hours, the senator didn't look the murderous sort; I'd give him that. But then, who did? Gang bangers, maybe. But plenty of killers also wore suits.

"I'd like to go home," Tillman said. "I'm tired. Are we finished?"

Burke looked at the notes he'd been taking, glanced first at me and then at the senator. "I'll be in touch soon about the next step," he said. "Go home and stay home. Don't talk to anyone other than your wife and your kids and the dog. Especially reporters. Understood?"

"Not a problem," Tillman said. "They're nothing but vultures, anyway. Some days I just want to—"

"Do me a favor, Senator," Burke interrupted. "Don't finish that sentence."

26

I SET UP TEMPORARY SHOP IN BURKE'S conference room and, after matching phone numbers with names, started making calls. I was transferred a couple of times when I tried Symmes's office to schedule an appointment with the Speaker. Eventually, I was forced to leave a message. I felt bad when I hung up. I was guessing I'd just sentenced a voicemail to die.

Next, I called the governor's office and tried to reach Allen Ratliff, the bowtie-wearing chief of staff. Soon I'd sent a second voicemail to the gallows. I missed the old days when actual people took the messages that would never be returned. On a whim, I called back and asked for Lily Gleason. To my surprise, I found myself speaking to the governor's education liaison—whatever that was—less than a minute later. She sounded as thrilled as a single mom at work hearing from a truant officer.

"You remember me from the Clarmont?"

"Yes."

I told her why I was calling.

"Why would I meet with you?" she said.

"Hopefully to help Senator Tillman."

"What could I possibly do?"

"I won't know until we have a chance to talk. Do you have time now?"

"Now?"

"I could swing by your office."

"*No.* You can't come here."

"Someplace else?"

"Not during work. I have meetings all afternoon."

"After work, then. It won't take long. I promise."

The line went quiet for a moment. "I don't want to be seen. Do you have an office?"

"It's my kitchen table. What about your place?"

"Absolutely not."

After three tries—out-of-the-way restaurants I thought would be perfect—I gave up and suggested Burke's office. I had a key and I knew he wouldn't mind. We settled on six.

WHEN I OPENED THE door and let Gleason in a few hours later, she came inside hurriedly without looking behind. A bit overweight and frazzled, she was wearing a navy suit, gold earrings, glasses hanging from a beaded lanyard, and blond-streaked brown hair in a slightly messy bun. I put her in her late forties. She declined an offer of coffee but accepted a bottle of water.

"OK. I'm here," she said, as soon as we settled at the table.

"You're the governor's education liaison," I said. "Is that right?"

"Yes."

"Can you tell me a little bit about what you do?"

"It's pretty basic. I work with all the education stakeholders at the Statehouse. I hear their concerns and relay them to the governor. I also keep them up to speed on what we're doing."

"Stakeholders like who?"

"In this case, anybody with an interest in legislation dealing with schools. OK? School boards, treasurers, teachers, the Education Department. They all have associations that I work with."

"Lobbyists?"

"That's right."

"Thank you," I said. On my notepad I wrote: *Stakeholder =
jargon*. Next, I gave her my list of questions about Hershey and his
sources and the meeting the night he died.

When I was finished, she said, "I wasn't following him, and
I'm sorry he's dead. And that's about it."

"So no idea who he was supposed to meet that night?"

She shook her head.

"And no idea what he was working on?"

"Hardly."

"Is there something big happening with the education bill?
Something he might have been close to revealing?"

"Nothing I'd tell you."

"It'll get out eventually, if there was."

"We're trying to pass a complicated plan, with a lot of moving parts. There's your big scoop."

I told her the suspicion that the House Speaker had leaked the
Robin Hood memo.

"That's probably right. Not that it matters. Not that I know
for sure, either," she added, quickly.

"Were you in the committee hearing Wednesday? The one
that went late?"

"For a while."

"Was Lee there?"

"On and off. People came in and out. A lot of the testimony
was repetitive."

"Mind if I ask where you were later that night?"

"Yes."

"I'm asking anyway."

"How is it your business?"

"It's my business because the lawyer I work for is trying to
defend Ed Tillman, who says he's innocent. But it's also my business because someone killed the guy who hired me to look after
him, and I'm not too happy about it. And like I said, it'll get out

eventually. It's a murder investigation. The patrol's not going to be nearly this polite."

"My daughter had a soccer game. I got there in time for the second half."

"How'd she do?"

"They lost."

"Then what?"

"I went back to the office."

"Your daughter was at home?"

"At her father's," she said. I remembered Kerri MacKenzie's story, the divorce following the scandal that Hershey had revealed.

"How long were you at the office?"

"A couple hours. Then I went home," she said firmly. "I was tired."

"Straight home?"

"Yes."

"You didn't meet Lee along the way?"

"God, no."

"I hate to ask this—"

"Then don't."

"But there wasn't a lot of love lost, was there? Between you and Lee?"

"Not much."

"He broke the story about your husband. The scandal over the computer contract."

Anger flashed across her face. "Ex-husband. And everyone knows about that."

"Would it be accurate to say that story led to your divorce?"

"I don't see what that has to do—"

"There's angry at someone because they wrote a story about an improper state contract. And then there's angry because they wrecked your marriage."

She sat back, cheeks burning. "You're asking if I had a motive to kill Lee? Is that it? Is that why I'm here?"

"It's a question I have to ask. One the patrol will ask too."

"Go to hell."

"I'll take that as a no. What about your ex?"

"What about him?"

"Lee's story cost him a big contract and led to bankruptcy. Seems like a motive to me."

"For murder? Come on."

"There's no judging what makes people angry."

She shook her head. "He was mad. Who wouldn't be? But he wasn't vengeful. And what difference would it make? He was home all night last Wednesday."

"With your daughter."

"And our son. And Jesse."

"Who's Jesse?"

"His two-month-old baby with his new wife."

"OK," I SAID, a moment later. "What happens now? With Triple F? Sorry," I said, seeing the expression on her face. "*ABC.*"

"We hope to hell the Senate passes it by the end of next week."

"Without Tillman."

"He resigned as committee chairman this morning. That's a formality. The Senate president would have forced him off in a day anyway."

"Who's taking his place?"

"Ottie Kinser."

"And then?"

"Then it goes back to the House for them to look at any changes that got made. There's plenty."

"What about charter schools?"

"What about them?"

"There has to be something for them, for the House to pass the bill. Right?"

"Unfortunately."

"Why do you say that?"

"Because I'm opposed to charter schools."

"Why?"

"Because they take money away from real schools."

"They're not real?"

"No. Not most of them, anyway."

"So some are real?"

"The ones that work, yes. But most are just flimsy excuses for filching state dollars in the name of education."

"Either way, you can't pass ABC without them, because Republicans control the House. And they like charter schools, right?"

"That's right. And yes, it appears we need charter schools in the bill."

"What's that mean?"

"The House is a fifty-four to forty-five GOP majority," she said, a hint of condescension in her voice. "It means that Dani Symmes has got the votes, but barely."

"Can you sway any Republicans?"

"Gosh. We hadn't thought of that."

"So assuming the House approves it, and the governor signs it?"

She waited, looking bored.

"Then school funding is fixed in Ohio forever and ever?"

Gleason smiled thinly. "It's fixed for a year or so, until the Supreme Court takes a look, to see if it passes muster. They review it, hold arguments, make a decision. Then school funding is fixed, or not, and we're back to the drawing board."

"So after everything the legislature does, it all comes down to the court?"

"Not the court," she said. "One person."

"Who?"

"Billy Bryan."

"The justice?" I thought back to him nursing his whiskey alone at the Clarmont.

"That's right. He's the swing vote. He's literally got the future of Ohio schoolchildren in his hands."

27

I STOPPED AT HAPPY DRAGON ON LIVINGSTON on the way home and picked up a large Hunan beef, hot-and-sour soup, and two spring rolls. Back at my house, I checked in with Anne, who chatted for a few minutes about her day. She'd taught two summer classes and done research for a paper on zombies in movies. I might have been biased, but I felt this was academic research the world actually needed. I mentioned the Statehouse gavel from Paw Paw Bottoms, and Hershey's quip about its usefulness in case of an invasion. I updated my progress on the case. She didn't bring up the blue—or was it pink?—elephant in the room, and I didn't ask. When I hung up I called Bonnie. She was at FedEx on an evening shift. She had nothing new to report about Troy. I thought about taking the dog on a late-night walk, or about renting a movie. Or just reading *The Sparrow*, which I'd picked up from the Book Loft up the street over the weekend. Instead, thinking about Lee's and my tail and the mysterious license plate, I decided to make one more call.

"Jay?" I said, a minute later.

"Andrew," came the reply. "Long time no talk to."

"Hope it's not too late."

"Perfect timing. I'm sitting on a house, trying not to fall asleep."

"What's the job?"

"It's a Cohab 101, with a twist."

"Which is?"

"Well, the guy's a nurse, and for some reason known only to his God and his shrink he decided to leave his hot, six-figure-earning doctor of a wife for a lab tech with a tramp stamp. Now the ex-wife, who's damn tired of paying alimony, thinks he's shacked up permanently with the techie. In a few minutes or so I'm hoping to prove it. So what's up?"

I pictured Jay Scott, a fellow private eye I'd met years ago on a case involving warring Ohio State and Michigan fans, crouched low in the front seat of the fake HVAC panel truck he drove around Ann Arbor for cover. Proving cohabitation was standard fare for him, and, from the sounds of this job, lucrative to boot. I explained about Hershey's murder and our follower and the license plate that hit a dead end at a Detroit auto parts store.

"Detroit, huh? Long trip. Plus I hear it's kind of dangerous over there."

"It's forty-two miles from Ann Arbor, which I know because I Googled it. And it's probably less dangerous since you left. Also, it's a paying gig."

"Who's paying?"

"I am."

"Consider my rate doubled. How soon do you need it?"

"How soon can you do it?"

"I'm working two extra security jobs right now, and I just picked up a missing persons case, plus this guy. Give me a few days."

I texted him the address, went to the kitchen for my dinner, grabbed a Columbus Brewing Company pale ale from the fridge—take that, Roy—sat down on the couch, opened up *The Sparrow*, and started reading. I'd spent worse evenings.

28

AT EIGHT THE NEXT MORNING I MADE another round of calls, first to Dani Symmes's office, then to the Prince of Dorkness, and then, on the spur of the moment, to Justice Bryan's chambers. Voicemails meeting their maker all around. Finally, right before eight-thirty, I reached someone with Senator Ottie Kinser and—probably thanks to her connections with Burke—was granted an appointment.

It was just past ten when I walked into the Statehouse. There was an entirely different feel to the building compared to the last time I'd been there. Today, well-dressed men and women strode down corridors holding power conversations, fiddled on their cell phones in practically every spare corner, and canvassed in secretive huddles on stairwells. The Rotunda was open again, and I walked past a class of elementary schoolchildren on a tour gazing up into the interior of the Cupola's dome. "It looks like Barbie's Dreamhouse," a little girl exclaimed. So much for Roman grandeur. I examined the vertical salmon-colored panels running up to the stained-glass cap and tried to picture it. I'd have to bring Anne's daughter here for independent verification.

Down a flight of stairs, at the entrance to the Atrium, I stopped abruptly. Gone were the folding tables and chairs and tangle of electrical cords where Hummel and his officers had set up operations the day Hershey's body had been discovered, almost a week ago now. In their place, dozens of people sat at round, white cloth–covered tables that were set with silverware and glasses and breadbaskets. As servers in black shirts and pants distributed plates table by table, the audience listened to a man speaking on a small stage by the north-facing windows. "New model of accountability," I heard him say. I looked across the hall to the Senate side, calculating how long it would take me to go back outside, or down into the Crypt, to reach my destination another way. As I mulled escape routes I noticed for the first time a pigeon sitting above the far door on a ledge in a triangular stone lintel.

"Lost in space?" a voice said. I glanced over and saw Jim Flanagan, from the *Cleveland Press*. He had a reporter's rectangular notebook in his right hand and a camera around his neck.

"Didn't realize this place was booked," I whispered. "I was just trying to cross."

"It's open. Follow me."

He walked straight ahead. I paused, uncertain, and proceeded a moment later as he turned and beckoned. I looked around, expecting angry glances, but we were roundly ignored. "A paradigm of educational excellence," the man at the podium said to applause.

"Thanks," I said, when we reached the opposite side. "You allowed to do that?"

"It's always open. It's 'The People's House,'" Flanagan said, making air quotes à la Hershey. "Where you headed?"

"Ottie Kinser's office."

"She a suspect now?" Flanagan said, his eyes lighting up.

"Not that I know of. I'm just crossing my t's."

"We have a deal, right? You'll keep me informed?"

"As much as I can."

"It's a two-way street, remember. I hear something, I'll let you know."

"What would you tell me you wouldn't put in the paper first?"

"You'll just have to be surprised."

"I'm not holding my breath. Who's the entertainment?" I said, gesturing at the podium.

"That's Dani Symmes's boyfriend."

"I'm sorry?"

"Bad joke. That's Phil Williams. He runs Little Red Schoolhouse. It's a charter school management company. Symmes is in bed with him, just not in the biblical sense."

"What's he doing here?"

"It's lobbying day. Come to the Statehouse, have lunch, hear a charter school bigwig, then hit the halls to bend some lawmakers' ears and arms. Maybe sit in on a committee hearing. Glamorous as watching paint dry, in my opinion, but some people really get off on it."

"So Symmes and Williams are tight?"

"Like money in a wallet."

"Why?"

"She's head of the Republican majority in the House, and they love charter schools because they're not unionized. So that's attractive to Williams."

"I've heard she barely has the votes for Triple F. Is she still going to get her charter school amendments from the governor?"

"Most of the time votes around here are like being pregnant—there's no such thing as barely. It's close, but she's got them, period. And assuming it stays that way, Williams will keep giving her big-time campaign donations in return. Marital bliss, Statehouse style. Gotta run. Good luck with Kinser. Down the hall, third office on the right."

"All right. Thanks. Hey, before you go. Why's there a pigeon up there?"

Flanagan turned and gestured at the Atrium. "That whole space out there used to be open to the elements, years ago. Tons of pigeons flying around, and so tons of pigeon crap. It was so bad they had umbrellas on either side that people could pick up to protect themselves as they crossed."

"You're kidding."

"God's truth. When they renovated, they put a stuffed bird up there to commemorate it all. Perfect gesture, I've always said."

"Why's that?"

"It's a reminder of how full of shit this place is," he said with a laugh.

"HOW'S THAT LADY FRIEND of yours doing?" Ottie Kinser said as I sat down in her office a few minutes later.

"She's doing well, Senator. Thanks for asking." *Also, she may be pregnant, and not just barely, and I have no idea what will happen if she is, and there's a possibility I may inadvertently get her evicted. But other than that, she's great.*

"Call me Ottie. Please."

"All right."

"So what can I do for you?" She leaned forward at her desk, clasping her hands, giving me her full attention. She was wearing a dark red jacket, a white pearl necklace, and thick gold hoop earrings. I realized again how attractive she was. It was hard not to give her my full attention in return.

"Senator Tillman. Could he have killed Lee Hershey?"

"I'd like to think not. I truly would."

I asked her the same questions I was posing to everyone.

"I wasn't his school-funding source, I can promise you that, and I wasn't meeting him that night," she said, firmly.

"Could I ask where you were?"

"You can look at my calendar if you want. Our committee went late, I worked for an hour or two here afterward, then joined Reggie for supper. He's preparing for a trial, so he was working late as well."

"Where did you eat?"

"Barcelona. In German Village. Around the corner from where we live. We're neighbors, I think."

I nodded. Real estate in German Village, the tony neighborhood of brick homes and brick streets south of downtown, was notoriously pricy. The only reason I could afford to rent there was gratitude from my landlord for extricating his heroin-addicted daughter from a South End pimp a few years back. I was guessing the Kinsers lived a couple blocks and a couple hundred thousand dollars from me.

"You're the chairwoman of the education committee now," I said.

"Temporarily."

"Can the school-funding bill still pass? After what's happened?"

"It has to. We have no choice."

"Why?"

"To help the students of Ohio, of course. And, as you probably know, because it's Governor Hubbard's signature initiative."

"One that could boost his vice-presidential chances if passed, or so I hear."

She smiled. "A secondary consideration. But yes, that's true."

"And Lee's reporting hampered the bill."

"He didn't do us any favors."

"Could someone have killed him to stop another story coming out?"

"That's quite an allegation."

"It's just a question."

"It seems unlikely, doesn't it? But it is true that Lee made life difficult for a lot of people."

"Like who?"

"Who else have you talked to?"

Without divulging details, I told her about Kerri MacKenzie and Lily Gleason, and my attempts to reach Hubbard's chief of staff, the House Speaker, and Justice Bryan.

"Lily," she said, shaking her head. "We served together, you know. Before everything happened with her husband."

I nodded.

"The whole story is ugly. Very ugly. Especially their divorce."

"I can imagine."

She looked at me meaningfully. "I hope you can." I bristled just a touch: was she inferring something about my own marital history?

I said, "Everyone seems to think that Dani Symmes leaked the Robin Hood memo to Lee."

"I'd have no reason to disagree with that."

"But do you know for sure?"

"No."

"Could she have been the person he was meeting with the night he was killed?"

"Symmes? Now that's a stretch."

She seemed poised to say something else when someone knocked on her door. A young woman stepped inside from the outer office and said, apologetically, "The Senate president is on the phone."

She nodded. "Excuse me," she said to me. The phone rang a moment later. She picked it up, listened for a minute, interrupting with an occasional "Yes," and hung up.

"I'm sorry, Andy. There's an emergency caucus. The Republicans are sticking an abortion amendment into the school-funding plan. I've got to go."

"Abortion amendment? In an education bill?"

Her eyes flashed angrily. "It's something they tried earlier this year as stand-alone legislation. Girls under eighteen would be required to submit an ultrasound photo to a pharmacist before obtaining the morning-after pill."

"What's that have to do with school funding?"

"Nothing, of course, but the fact that most of those girls are in high school gives them the entrée, such as it is."

"That doesn't sound very constitutional."

"That's usually the last consideration in these matters," she said drily. "I need to excuse myself. Did I answer all your questions?"

On a whim, I said, "Have you ever been to the Cupola?"

"The what?"

I pointed upward. "The top of the Statehouse. You can get tours up there. There's a circular wall, the outer part of the Rotunda, where people sign their names."

"Yes, of course. I didn't follow at first. I never have, actually. I keep meaning to. Why?"

"No reason," I said, studying her face, which showed no signs of embarrassment or concern at my question. "Just curious. Thanks for your time."

"Don't hesitate to call again. Give Burke my regards. And Anne."

"I will," I said, and left the office.

29

I WALKED BACK INTO THE ATRIUM, BUT instead of crossing through I stepped inside and to the right, where I leaned against the wall, following the lead of a couple other observers.

"Excuse me," I whispered to a young man next to me. "Is Dani Symmes here?"

He looked at me, looked again, recognition dawning—I'm used to it, after all these years—then pointed.

"There," he said. "To the right of the podium, one table back."

"Thanks."

The Speaker of the Ohio House looked to be midfifties, with a trim, athletic build and short gray hair, wearing a blue power suit and a noncommittal expression as she listened to Williams. I thought about what Flanagan had said. In bed with the guy, though not in the biblical sense. As I looked, Symmes turned and caught my glance. She held it for a long moment, studying me, before directing her attention back to the podium.

I left and reentered the Senate side of the building, planning to head downstairs and out, when I saw Flanagan walking up the marble steps on the left in conversation with someone. The man turned to the reporter to make a point, and I saw it was Jack Sterling, the dressed-to-the-nines rat poison lobbyist. On a whim, I decided to follow. At the top of the stairs they turned left, walked slowly down the hall, turned left again, and disappeared into a room. After a moment of hesitation, I stuck my head inside. It was some kind of hearing room, with a long, raised court-like bench at the front. Sterling had taken a seat at the back, where someone was leaning toward him, whispering. After a moment I recognized him as Sam Michaels, the Education Department official I'd met at the Clarmont sitting with Gleason and Ratliff. Two rows up from them, tapping vigorously away on a tablet, sat Lauren Atkinson, the no-nonsense teachers' union president who'd nearly plowed me over leaving the restaurant. Up front, Flanagan was at the bench chatting with a young woman I recognized as the aide who had interrupted my conversation with Senator Kinser a few minutes earlier.

I walked in and sat down beside Atkinson. She looked up, glanced at me noncommittally and without recognition, and looked back down at her tablet. She was wearing a dark suit with a conservative cut. A pile of documents rested on the chair beside her, topped with her very own Triple F binder, the one I'd seen at the Clarmont. I noticed a name hand printed and circled in black ink in the top left corner. It reminded me of my middle school days; all that was missing was fat hearts and smiley faces.

"Frank Washington," I said, reading the name. "Is he the deciding vote?"

She looked up quickly and stared at me. "I'm sorry?"

I held out my hand. "Andy Hayes. We met at the Clarmont. The day before Lee . . ."

"I remember." She ignored my hand, reached out and in a single motion turned the binder over.

I took a new tack, and handed her my card. I said, "I happened to stop in and saw you sitting here."

"That's nice," she said, uncomfortably. I remembered what Lee had said, how she'd come up the hard way battling school boards.

I explained about Burke being asked to represent Tillman. "I'd be interested in talking to you about that night," I said.

"What about it?"

"There was a lot of anger in the restaurant, from what I could tell. Anger at Lee. I'd be interested in your take on that."

"I don't think so," Atkinson said. There it was again, that southern lilt. Under a different set of circumstances I might have found it attractive.

"I wouldn't need long. We could meet anywhere you'd like."

"As I said—"

"I gather the teachers' union has a big stake in the school-funding bill."

"That's obvious."

"But perhaps you're not thrilled about the charter school amendments."

"I don't think this is an appropriate place to discuss that."

"Do you have time for coffee later? I'm just trying to get the lay of the land."

"I think you have it," she said. "We have a big stake in the bill. And we're not happy about the amendments, as we've said publicly numerous times. And, as you've probably guessed, we weren't happy with Lee's reporting, although of course we're terribly saddened by his death. Now, if you'll excuse me, the hearing is about to begin."

Several lawmakers filed in and seated themselves. The abortion caucus must have ended. Flanagan had shifted down the bench and was now talking to a male lawmaker I didn't recognize.

"You didn't answer my first question," I said.

"I'm sorry?"

"Frank Washington. The name written on your binder. Is he the tiebreaker?" I smiled, trying to show her I wasn't serious.

"I don't appreciate your snooping," she said.

"I meant no offense." I was about to add an apology when I heard a sharp crack from the front of the room. I looked and saw Ottie Kinser with a gavel in her hand. She called the hearing to order.

"Sorry," I whispered as I stood up. Atkinson, furiously scrolling through e-mail on her tablet, ignored me.

I left the room, went back down the stairs, and was headed down a second set of steps to the Crypt when I found my way blocked by a man who bore an uncanny resemblance to Commodore Oliver Hazard Perry.

"Well, well," said Lieutenant Mike Hummel. "Look what the cat barfed up."

30

"YOU'VE BEEN A CHATTY CATHY AROUND here, what I'm told," Hummel said.

"That's my job."

"No, that's *my* job. Your job is to keep the hell away from state police business."

We were sitting across from each other in a small, windowless room off the patrol communications center in a part of the Crypt the tour guides don't tell you about. Hummel was flipping through a red notebook, pausing occasionally to read something that seemed to bother him, as if encountering superfluous items on a grocery list. Finally, he reached the end and looked up.

"Doing all these interviews," he said. "I could have you charged with obstruction."

"Sorry—are you doing good cop or bad cop right now?"

"You think this is a game? Murder mystery at the Statehouse? Like dinner theater except with real blood?"

I said nothing.

"I talked to Hershey's parents. They're devastated. He may not have had the world's biggest fan club, but he was still somebody's son."

"Thanks. That hadn't occurred to me."

"Listen, Andy," Hummel said, leaning across the table. "I need to know the names of everyone you've talked to. Or I'm going to have to get serious. I'm not kidding."

I unfolded my hands and rubbed them on my thighs. I said, "You have a favorite science fiction novel?"

"Quit kidding around."

"Who's kidding? It's a real question."

"So's mine. But I'm the one with arrest authority. And that's bad cop, all right?"

I sighed. "All right," I said. "Ready?"

"YOU LOST ME SOMEWHERE with the Christopher Robin thing," Hummel said, a few minutes later.

"Robin Hood," I said. I went over it again.

"You think this mystery person Hershey was meeting, the person you were supposed to protect him from, is our guy?"

"Or gal."

"Suit yourself."

I shrugged. "He said it was going to be an uncomfortable conversation. I'm not sure what that means, but it obviously didn't go well."

"You think?"

"I think the Robin Hood memo was a huge embarrassment for the Democrats, and it set them back a couple of weeks on the bill."

"And people are saying Dani Symmes leaked it?"

"That's the consensus."

"Which means the suspect, whoever it is, is probably a Democrat, since Lee's reporting pissed them off so much," Hummel said.

"True, unless he was about to break a story having something to do with charter schools that might honk off the GOP. Hershey took a bipartisan approach to his reporting, as far as I could tell. He said he only cared about getting things first. So I'm not sure focusing on party is the way to go. But figuring out who he was supposed to meet with might explain a lot, even if he, or she, didn't actually do it."

Hummel stifled a yawn. I realized he looked exhausted. I guess even commodores get worn out.

"I agree," he said after a moment. "But given that we can't even find a calendar on the guy's phone, we're not going to get very far."

"You're not going to find one, I'm guessing."

"Why not?"

"He kept everything in the cloud."

"The cloud?"

"An online storage account of some kind."

"Which one?"

"I was hoping you'd know that."

He made a note on a piece of legal paper but said nothing.

"So what about the book?" I said.

He looked up. "Book?"

"Your favorite sci-fi novel."

"You're a real pain in the ass, you know that?"

"It's been mentioned. I'm waiting."

"Fine. My wife reads this one lady."

"Who?"

"Joan Slonczewski. She's a biology professor, over at Kenyon College, writes books on the side."

"Know any titles?"

He shook his head. "She has them all, I think. She really likes them. Satisfied?"

"I guess," I said, retrieving my notebook. I made Hummel spell the name, which endeared me to him all the more.

"Now get lost," he said, standing. "I've got work to do."

I rose and turned to go. "Wait a minute," he said.

He left the room, and I heard him stride down the hall, heels clicking almost ladylike on the floor. A moment later he returned with a paperback book.

"Speaking of science fiction. We found this on Hershey's kitchen counter, with a Post-It note with your name on it."

I took it from him. *The Android's Dream.* The book Anne had so enthusiastically recommended to Hershey the morning he stopped by. The book he'd finished in a day.

"It's got a key in it. How come?"

I opened the book to a gap in its pages and pulled out a brass key on a thick piece of string. The other end was taped to a folded-over piece of white notecard with the name *J. Cook* on it, and the initials CN below, underlined twice. It took me a minute.

CN. *Commit Nuisance.*

"Just a bookmark," I said.

"What's the key for?"

"Key to . . . reading," I said. "Inside joke. Hershey was a huge reader. Loved books."

"So I gather. Must have been a dozen just by his bedside."

I left Hummel's office a minute later, fully intending to find Ephraim Badger and present him with the key, no questions asked. I walked around the corner and found myself in a room whose floor consisted of a giant map of Ohio divided into the eighty-eight counties. To the right sat a woman at a desk above a sign promoting daily Statehouse tours on the hour. I approached and asked if Badger was giving any soon. Concern knitting her brow, the woman told me he had called in ill and did I mind a different guide. I thanked her and said another time.

Still holding the book, I walked back under the groin vault and was heading to the stairs when a woman's voice distracted me. I looked and saw Dani Symmes stride past. She was with Phil Williams, the charter school guy, and the young man who'd pointed her out in the Atrium. I turned around and studied an illuminated sign on the wall. "'The virtue of justice consists in moderation, as regulated by wisdom.' Aristotle, Greek Philosopher." Good to know. A moment later I turned back around and followed Symmes and her coterie. Keeping a discreet distance, I tracked them as they went past the commemorative gavel from Paw Paw Bottoms and the display of Rat Row bricks, down the stairs and through the parking garage. They wove their way past

cars and green pillars as they crossed to a building entrance on
the other side. They stopped and Symmes and Williams spoke
quietly for a couple minutes while I stayed out of sight behind
a pillar. Then they laughed, shook hands, and Williams headed
back toward the Statehouse, while Symmes and the young man
walked down a tunnel into the next building.

Hanging back as unobtrusively as possible, I followed Symmes
and the assistant into the lobby of the Riffe Center and toward a
set of escalators. The building was newer than the grim Rhodes
Tower around the corner, lighter and airier-looking, a mix of
brown stone and green-tinted windows with its planed corners
reducing the skyscraper's monolithic feel. It left the impression
of perestroika having come to Capitol Square. We rode up an
escalator, and as I got off I glanced at the bronze sculpture of the
building's namesake, a predecessor of Symmes—*Riffe* rhyming
with *knife*, I thought grimly. Maybe it was my mood, but what I
focused on was not the steely look of determination in the sculpture's bronze eyes but the fearsome, oversized gavel in its hands.

After ascending a second escalator, I followed Symmes and
her companion until they stopped at a row of automatic security
turnstiles in front of a bank of elevators. They used electronic key
cards to pass through. I halted, unable to follow. I was weighing
my options when Symmes turned around.

"Is there something you needed, Mr. Hayes?" she said. "Or do
I need to call my sergeant-at-arms?"

I LOOKED AT HER from across the turnstiles. "Is it possible we could speak in private?"

"No. Matt said you were asking about me in the Atrium. Why?"

I looked at the young man. He reddened, and avoided eye
contact by turning toward his boss.

"I work for a law firm representing Senator Tillman. I was
hoping I could talk to you."

"This law firm. It doesn't have a budget for phones?"

"I've left two messages."

"I didn't receive them."

"I can recommend an excellent secretarial pool."

"That won't be necessary."

"In that case, could I ask a couple of questions now?"

"About what?"

"Triple F. The Robin Hood memo. Charter schools. And Lee Hershey."

"Is that all?"

"While I'm at it, I was wondering if you have a favorite science fiction novel."

"What a fascinating question," she said. "Perhaps someday we could discuss that and other topics. In the meantime, I have no comment, and while this is a public building and I can't force you to leave, my sergeant-at-arms can be very persuasive. Good luck to you."

"How did you know my name?" I said.

"Matt told me."

"And you're . . . ?" I said to him.

"Good-bye," Symmes said, turning toward the elevators.

I WAS PASSING THE gavel-wielding statue on my way down when my phone rang. My doctor, Donald Frank, was calling.

"Golf course flooded?" I said. "I'm surprised to hear from you directly."

"One of my BMWs is in the shop. One of the red ones, I think. I have some time to kill. You were right. You were drugged."

"What I was afraid of. With what?"

"It's hard to tell the exact medication, but there were traces of benzodiazepines."

"Which is?"

"Tranquilizers. Valium, Xanax, that kind of thing. Some kind of roofie."

"Like the date-rape drug?"

"That's an overused phrase, but yes, that's the general idea."

"No way to be more specific?"

"What do you mean?"

"To track it somehow, I guess. Where it came from."

"Guy in sunglasses in Walgreens at midnight?"

"Something like that."

"Unfortunately not. It's like that line from *Spinal Tap*," Dr. Frank said. "'You can't really dust for vomit.' It could be a variety of drugs. Benzodiazepines is as good as it's going to get."

Or as bad, I thought.

"OK. Thanks for getting back to me."

"Sure thing. Come by and say hello when it doesn't involve bodily harm."

"At this point, it might be a while."

"Be careful, all right?"

"I'm trying, doc," I said, unconvincingly.

31

BACK IN THE VAN I THREW THE PAPERBACK
into the glove compartment, the "bookmark" still inside. When I
got home, I typed up notes on my conversations with Ottie Kinser and Lauren Atkinson, summarized my encounter with the
House Speaker and "Matt," and sat back, despondent. A week
had passed since Hershey's death and I wasn't getting anywhere.
For all I knew, I might have passed his killer in the crowded Statehouse halls just now and never realized it.

Trying to push the gathering clouds away, I logged onto the
Franklin County court website and pulled up the rape indictment and the bill of particulars for Derrick Wardley, the brother
of Bonnie Deckard's untalkative boyfriend. He was charged with
assaulting his girlfriend's four-year-old son on at least five occa-
sions. He was also charged with beating his girlfriend up, and
with obstruction of justice for threatening the boy if he told anyone. The threat was dangling the boy's kitten over a pot of boil-
ing water and promising to drop it in if the boy said anything. I
saved the pertinent documents to a hard-drive folder and took a
breath. I'd seen worse, I told myself. I'd investigated worse. But it
didn't make reading it any easier.

Because I didn't have anything better to do, I looked up his brother's name as well. Turned out Troy Wardley had marijuana possession charges against him two years ago, when he was barely over twenty-one. He'd spent thirty days in jail for one, with probation for the other. I kept searching, and to my surprise found a couple of misdemeanor forgeries for Bonnie. Both resolved with fines and probation. I turned next to Richard Deckard, and immediately pulled up three speeding tickets and a drunken-driving arrest four years back. For the heck of it, I ran Troy's parents and his uncle, "Skip Wardley: Fighting for Your Future." I saved the results, and pondered them. In the messed-up world Richard Deckard had introduced me to, it appeared only the grown-up Wardleys lacked rap sheets.

BY NOON THE NEXT day I had only one return call, from Jack Sterling, the casino lobbyist, who sounded as thrilled as everyone else to hear from me but nonetheless agreed to meet me for a drink late in the day. I split the afternoon between Roy's church, helping clean up after lunch and going over his books with him, and taking Hopalong for a romp in the Park of Roses in Clintonville with Anne and Amelia after Anne's second summersession class let out. In a moment alone I asked her about the "situation," as I'd dubbed it, but got only a smile and a reassuring squeeze of my hand. What was the protocol, I thought, for insisting on a pregnancy test at a time like this? I decided, for just a little bit longer, not to find out.

THE MARBLE-LINED LOBBY of the Westin Hotel on South High was busy when I walked in shortly before six. Replace the guests' casual clothes with three-piece suits and long dresses with puffed sleeves and you could have been in the same soaring space a hundred years earlier without changing much. Keeping an eye out for doughboys and Bolsheviks, I went around the corner and walked into the Thurber Bar and sat down beside Sterling. Framed prints of cartoons by the Columbus humorist hung on the wall. I recalled what Hershey had said about Thurber and the Ohio Look.

"How's the rat poison here?" I said. "Is it as good as everyone says?"

He turned and studied me. "Fresh squeezed," he said.

I caught the bartender's eye. Sterling was drinking bourbon. I had a draft Yuengling. The ubiquitous Triple F binder sat on the bar stool beside him. He was wearing a different suit than the night at the Clarmont, but it looked just as top-of-the-line. The lobbying business must be very good.

"So in case it's not obvious," Sterling said, "I was kidding about poison."

"I kinda figured. But for the heck of it, where were you the night Lee was killed?"

"Late drinks with clients, then home."

"Where were the drinks?"

"Out on the town."

"What part?"

"The part where my clients don't care for other people to know I've been with them."

"OK. Any theories on who killed Lee?"

"No."

"Were you supposed to meet him the night he died?"

He shook his head.

"Do you know who was?"

"No. Why?"

I explained the fuzzy assignment I was supposed to be on that night.

"That sounds like Hershey."

"Were you one of his sources?"

"Maybe. He talked to a lot of people."

Our drinks arrived and we tipped our glasses at each other.

"You represent the casinos on school funding," I said, gesturing at the binder.

"That's right."

"They're trying to renegotiate their revenue-sharing deal."

"They're protecting their financial interests while supporting education in Ohio."

"Good line."

He frowned. "Without casinos, Ohio would be just shy of $2 billion poorer every year, with that money evenly split among the surrounding states that already have them. But they're an expensive operation, and the margins can be tough. Anything that affects their bottom line could mean less money for the schoolkids they're trying to help."

"Just casinos? Or horse tracks too?" All seven tracks in Ohio had converted to "racinos" in recent years, cramming hundreds of slot machines into their buildings for extra revenue.

"Just casinos," he said, giving me a funny look. "Racinos aren't covered by the education thing."

"And it's your job to lower the percentage of casino revenue going to schools."

"Bluntly put, but yes."

"And if Triple F tanks, that's not going to happen."

"True."

"And Lee's reporting endangered that bill a couple times."

He took a drink. "I get it. I've got a motive to kill Lee because he was fucking up the bill my people need to pass."

"You said it."

"That's the kind of boneheaded allegation I'd expect from someone like you. Hit your head a few too many times on the playing field?"

"Is it true?"

"Yes," he said. "I beat Lee to death with a one-armed bandit handle. Jesus, Hayes."

"Next question. Can Ottie Kinser get the bill passed? Taking over as chairwoman of the committee like that at the last second?"

"I don't know. I suppose. What choice does she have?"

"None, I guess."

"Have you talked to her?"

I told him about my meeting.

"How'd she seem?"

"Preoccupied."

"Do you blame her?"

"It wasn't just the bill. She had to deal with some abortion amendment. Something the Republicans are pushing again."

"The ultrasound deal. You have to give them credit for ingenuity."

"It'll never pass the Senate, though, right? Or even make it out of committee? So what's the big fuss?"

"The fuss is there's a lot riding on everything right now, as you would know, having just accused me of murdering a reporter to cover my ass."

"I only—"

"Too late. Anyway, that kind of amendment's normally like a twenty-four-hour bug. It arrives, makes a helluva big mess, and then disappears with no trace other than a lingering stench."

"But?"

"But the more votes the Senate president can send Triple F over to the House with, Republican and Democratic votes, the better it looks. The count's close in the House, but not so much in the Senate. The Republicans know this, which is why they decided to push the abortion amendment."

I thought about it. "In exchange for Democratic support for the morning-after-pill restriction, Senate Republicans vote for school funding."

"That's about it. If the amendment gets shit-canned, they don't give their votes. It doesn't matter on paper, since the Democrats have the juice in the Senate to pass Triple F without them. But Hubbard's pushing hard for a bipartisan bill."

"Because of the schoolkids. And JoAnn Rodriguez."

"Smart man. I take it back about your head. Mostly."

"Will it pass? This abortion plan?"

"Hard to say. Same thing happened a couple months ago when the Republicans tried it as its own bill. They got close. Even got people like Tillman to vote for it."

"Tillman voted for a bill limiting abortions?"

"The vote trading was going on even then over school funding. Plus, what did he have to lose? He's from southern Ohio, so he's more or less pro-life, even as a Democrat. He knew it would never pass, and Hubbard would veto it if by some crazy chance it actually made it to his desk. No blood, no foul. So to speak."

"Seems like a ruthless way to get things done."

"You get used to it, hanging around here. Making sausage and all that."

"So now it's back as an amendment."

"With the added benefit of even more pressure on Senate Democrats."

"Why's that?"

"Because the last thing they want before Rodriguez gets here is the school-funding equivalent of Obamacare, with no Republican voting for it."

"Rodriguez is coming here? Like Columbus?"

"Here, like the Statehouse. She's giving a speech next weekend."

"About what?"

"Does it matter? Global warming? Immigration? Homeland Security? Who cares? Whatever she talks about, it's pretty obvious she's going to conclude by announcing her running mate. Hubbard *has* to get that bill passed by next week. His political career depends on it."

32

STERLING EXCUSED HIMSELF, SAYING HE had clients to meet. I ordered a second beer and thought about the problems I faced. My responsibility for Hershey's death. Tillman's pending indictment. Indictments, if you counted Midwest Testing and the grand jury. The person following me. Troy Wardley's silence and self-isolation after his brother's arrest. And of course, Anne and the "situation."

The clouds started to gather again. Rationally, I knew I shouldn't blame myself for what happened to Hershey. I'd been shanghaied, pure and simple. But conversely, what had I been doing at a bar before a job, anyway? Roy's personal problems be damned—it was stupid and careless, and I knew it. Like so many other things I did from day to day. But unlike other screw-ups, I couldn't take this one back. That led me to Anne, and the absurdity of not knowing something that simple chemistry could answer. Why was she being this way? Was it a test? To see if I'd scoot at the first sign of trouble? No, I thought, trying to calm down. She wasn't like that. She had the most forgiving heart of anyone I knew, a miracle given what she'd been through. But still. My face getting hot, I decided to insist on a pregnancy kit. Wasn't that the manly thing to do? The stand-up thing? I'd pay for it, of course. And—I paused—I'd accept the consequences. Whatever that meant.

Mind made up, I finished my beer in two long pulls, got out my phone, unlocked it, and started to dial Anne. As I did, a call came through from a blocked number.

"Yes," I said, sharply.

"Andy Hayes?"

"That's right."

"The private investigator?"

"Yes. Who is this?"

"Tom Hubbard," the governor of Ohio said.

33

AT FIVE MINUTES TO TEN THE NEXT morning, I handed my card to the state trooper manning a wooden counter in a lobby on the thirtieth floor of the Riffe Center and explained my business. He nodded and made a call.

After he hung up, I said, "Do you know Lieutenant Mike Hummel?"

"I know who he is," the trooper said.

"Do you think he looks like Commodore Oliver Hazard Perry? The guy who won the Battle of Lake Erie? There's a painting of him in the Statehouse."

"I couldn't say, sir."

"It's the sideburns," I said. He didn't reply. I cooled my heels and hummed and examined the ceiling for a long couple of minutes until a glass door to the right of the trooper's station opened and a young woman stepped into the lobby.

"Mr. Hayes?"

"That's me."

"Could you come with me?"

I nodded at the trooper as I followed the woman through the door. She was midtwenties, with short, black hair, pretty, wearing a white blouse and a dark skirt with a slit in the back that in her case invited a second glance. She was carrying a copy of my favorite blue binder.

"Nice day," I said, as we walked.

"Yes," she said, not turning around.

We walked a few steps farther and stopped in front of an open door. "Here you go," she said. I turned to thank her, but she was already retreating down the hall.

I entered an outer office, where I presented myself to a woman whose frown at my appearance I didn't understand until I noticed the Ohio State coffee mug, pen, and mouse pad on her desk. Some people just can't let it go. She stood up, knocked on the door behind her, and a moment later I found myself inside and shaking hands with Hubbard. He looked like a governor, fit and hale and hearty, with a full head of perfectly arranged brown hair and blue eyes and a cleft chin made for leading people into battle, even if the fight involved budget spreadsheets and not actual bullets.

"Thanks for coming by," he said, looking me right in the eye, as if I'd shown up unexpectedly for his birthday party and not to ask him whether he'd arranged to have a reporter's head bashed in. For just a minute I felt as if he and I were alone in the room.

"No problem," I said. "I was in the neighborhood anyway."

This won a slightly too loud laugh. "And you know Allen?" he said.

I nodded and shook the chief of staff's hand as he stood from the couch to the right of the desk. The P-O-D was in full regalia, down to a yellow bow tie and matching suspenders.

"We met at the Clarmont," Ratliff said somberly.

"Have a seat, Andy," the governor said, glancing at Ratliff as he gestured at the couch. I sat. The governor took a chair opposite a small coffee table that held several travel books about Ohio. I looked around. Thick binders, including Triple F, filled shelves on a credenza behind Hubbard's desk. Out the expansive windows the Scioto flowed past. Across the room, dozens of names covered a whiteboard on the wall, with check marks beside several. I recognized Symmes's name and a few other lawmakers. Behind us stood floor-to-ceiling bookshelves lined with fat doorstops, including *The Decline and Fall of the Roman Empire*, Churchill's histories of World War II, and Robert Caro's biographies of Lyndon Johnson. On a separate shelf sat framed photographs of Hubbard with every famous Democrat going back to Jimmy Carter and including, by my count, Tip O'Neill, Bill and Hillary Clinton, Barack Obama, Joe Biden, Nancy Pelosi, and Ohio's own John Glenn. Beside those sat Hubbard's book, *Core Convictions,* tucked not so subtly between Obama's *The Audacity of Hope* and Hillary Clinton's *Hard Choices*. No science fiction novels that I could see. Hershey's quip came back to me: "Thomas Hubbard, literary lion." I'd gone so far as to swing by the Book Loft on my way home from the Thurber Bar the previous night, after Hubbard called, to buy a copy of *Core Convictions*. I'd made it through a couple of chapters and checked out some online reviews. Some writers thought his saccharine apology in the introduction for "clunky prose written honestly from my heart" a little difficult to stomach but gave him credit, in a back-handed compliment kind of way, for insisting on penning the thing himself.

"So," Hubbard said. "A private detective. Like Spenser. Abigail devours mysteries."

"I'm not as good a cook as Spenser."

"Of course," the governor said, vaguely. "I know your background, but where are you from originally? Ohio?"

I nodded. "I grew up in Homer. Little town east of here."

Ratliff perked up. "Homer? Interested in the classics, by any chance?"

"I'm partial to *Led Zeppelin IV* and the B side of *Abbey Road*."

"Where did you go to college?" Ratliff said, unfazed.

The governor of Ohio and I exchanged glances.

"Ohio State," I said. "Yourself?"

"Ohio Wesleyan," he said, a hint of derision in his voice. The liberal arts school was just up the road in Delaware.

"Delaware is where Rutherford B. Hayes is from," I said.

"Very good," Ratliff said, in a voice that sounded as if he meant the opposite. "I'm actually a bit of a Hayes buff."

"I understand you had some questions for us," Hubbard interrupted. "I know you're working with Senator Tillman. I really appreciate that, by the way."

"He's retained the lawyer I work for."

"What would you say your strategy is?" Ratliff said. "For the Tillman scenario."

"The Tillman scenario?"

"That's right."

"It depends," I said. "Are you referring to the scenario in which he took bribes from Midwest Testing, which hoped to win a big fat state contract, or the scenario in which he's alleged to have killed the reporter who broke that story?"

Silence settled over the room. The governor frowned, but Ratliff, to his credit, looked unperturbed.

"We understand the gravity of the situation that Senator Tillman faces," he said. "The reason I ask is that we could be of use to you."

"Use?"

"What Allen means," Hubbard said, "is that we're interested in seeing Senator Tillman treated fairly. No one here is pretending we don't have a vested interest in what happens to him. He's our guiding light in the Senate when it comes to the ABC Initiative. Given these events, it will be difficult to move forward. But we don't want any of that to overshadow the tragedy with Lee." I noted his deliberate use of Hershey's first name.

"That's why Allen was asking about strategy," Hubbard continued. "To make sure you know what our priorities are. You, personally."

He did that Bill Clinton thing again, looking at me like I was the only person in the universe he cared about just then. In response, something that might have been irritation flickered over

Ratliff's face, but it was gone so quickly, like the shadow of a door moving across a room as it's closed, that it was hard to tell.

"Why did you want to talk to me?" Ratliff said.

"Lee was supposed to meet someone the night he died. I was supposed to be with him. I was wondering if it was you."

"It was not."

"Any idea who?"

"None."

"Any idea who killed him?"

"I have no idea, other than I'm sure it wasn't Senator Tillman."

"Why do you say that?"

Hubbard cleared his throat before Ratliff could speak. "It's not in his nature," the governor said. "Perhaps Senator Tillman has made mistakes, but he's not a man who would take a life, for goodness' sake."

"Anger makes people do unusual things," I said, wondering if he were putting me on with a phrase like *for goodness' sake*. "Things that just a few moments or minutes later seem completely out of character. I don't have to remind you the senator threatened Lee."

"A slip of the tongue brought on by stress," Ratliff said, reasserting himself. "And not to blame the victim, in any fashion, but Lee Hershey made many people angry with his reporting."

"But only one said he'd be sorry if he kept it up."

"You're taking an unusually prosecutorial view when it comes to your client," Ratliff said. "I thought you were looking for alternate suspects. That's your strategy, I assume?"

"I prefer devil's advocate," I said. "It sounds more lawyerish. And as I said, I'm not here to discuss my, *our*, strategy."

"I wish we could be more help," the governor said.

"I understand Senator Rodriguez is coming to the Statehouse next weekend," I said.

"That's right," Hubbard said.

"With an important announcement."

"That's not related to any of this," Ratliff interjected.

"Perhaps."

"What's that supposed to mean?" Ratliff said.

"It's no secret that passing Triple F carries political as well as legislative importance," I said, looking at the governor. I held up my hand before Ratliff could object to the acronym. "If Lee was working on another school-funding story, and if that story had the potential to harm the legislation, a reasonable person might interpret that as a motive for his death."

"Who's suggesting that?" Hubbard said, but his chief of staff cut him off.

"That's absurd," Ratliff said. "I've never heard anything so ridiculous in my life. It borders on slander."

"Fair Funding Focus is key to your political future," I continued, looking at Hubbard.

"The ABC Initiative," Ratliff said.

"Lee kept throwing up roadblocks with his reporting," I said. "You can't have been pleased about that. Not this year."

"That's enough," Ratliff said. "You're impugning the governor and making a mockery of our invitation to you, which, believe me, went against my better judgment."

"It's all right, Allen," Hubbard said.

"No, it's not," he said, but Hubbard cut him off. Ratliff was beginning to strike me as a functionary with limited usefulness who might not make the A Team if Hubbard's fortunes went national.

"I think it is," Hubbard said. "Andy can't be the first person thinking that, given the gossip around this place. But you can be assured"—he went Bill Clinton on me again—"that we never attempted to interfere with his reporting."

"What about the Rodriguez campaign? They couldn't have been happy either."

"Why don't you ask them yourself, if you think it's relevant?" Ratliff said.

"I just thought I'd ask you first."

"I'm afraid that's all the time we have." Ratliff stood and gestured at the door.

"*Washington Post* interview," Hubbard said, apologetically. "Some kind of profile. I can hardly keep track of them right now."

"Exciting times," I said.

"Thanks for stopping by," the governor said. "I'm sorry we couldn't hear more from you. About ways to help Senator Tillman."

"I'm sorry too," I said.

We shook hands, and Ratliff walked me out and back to the door to the elevator lobby. I felt a twinge of disappointment. I'd been hoping, purely for investigative purposes, to have another stroll with the pretty intern who'd escorted me in.

"I would suggest you watch yourself," Ratliff said, as we arrived at the outer door.

"I'm sorry?"

"You were close to saying things back there to the governor you might regret."

"Are you threatening me?"

"I'm just offering some advice."

I leaned in. "Rutherford B. Hayes is an odd choice for a Democrat to study. He killed Reconstruction."

"A common misinterpretation of what happened in Louisiana and South Carolina," Ratliff said. "He made tough decisions when the country, the entire country, needed them."

"That's what draws you to him? He was an appeaser?"

"You're back to saying things you could regret."

"You're back to threatening me."

"That's not my intention," Ratliff said. "Thank you for stopping by."

"You ever read any sci-fi?" I asked.

"I'm not big into fiction," he said.

"Sure about that?"

34

RIDING THE ELEVATOR DOWNSTAIRS, I WENT over the meeting. Hubbard and Ratliff were clearly at odds with each other over what to tell me, what they knew about Hershey and Tillman, and, at a more basic level, why I'd even been invited up. They were right about one thing, though. I needed to talk to someone in Rodriguez's campaign.

That proved to be a prickly assignment, as I discovered thirty minutes later as I stood in the lobby of the "Rodriguez 2016" Ohio headquarters on East Town, arguing with a tall, thin woman named Regan with short, spiky hair and wearing designer jeans, a light-blue blouse, and a trim navy blue jacket.

"Regan," I said, trying to lighten things up. "Kind of ironic."

"Congratulations on being the millionth person to think so."

"Sorry. I just thought—"

"We have nothing to do with any of this. Lee Hershey, Ed Tillman, ABC. Nothing."

"Are you speaking for Senator Rodriguez?"

"Of course."

"You've talked to her directly about this?"

"What I talk to the senator about is none of your business. I'm telling you we have nothing to share with you."

"On a purely hypothetical basis, you'd agree the campaign would have an interest in Lee Hershey no longer poking holes in Governor Hubbard's signature legislation?"

"If you're implying what I think you're—"

"Hypothetically," I said. "Conjecturally. Just between us girls."

"We're finished here. You'll be hearing from our lawyers."

"About what?"

"Your underhanded attempts to assail Senator Rodriguez."

"Assail? I'm barely at insinuate. Give me a few minutes to get warmed up."

That appeared to be what's known in my trade as the last straw. A minute later I was back on Town, and three minutes after that the sounds of Van Halen emitted from my pocket. It was Burke Cunningham.

"Were you just speaking to someone named Regan?"

"It's possible."

"Did you accuse the Rodriguez campaign of orchestrating Lee Hershey's death?"

"Not exactly."

"But maybe a little bit?"

I acknowledged it. I said, "How did you find out so quickly, if I may ask?"

"Did she tell you they were going to call their lawyers?"

"She mentioned something along those lines."

"I'm on retainer for them in Columbus."

After talking for a couple of minutes, I agreed to inform Burke if I were planning to tread any deeper into campaign-type waters in my investigation. For his part, he concurred with my observation that having a Democratic presidential campaign staffer whose name was pronounced like that of the former president was both cute and a little weird. I filled him in on my interviews so far. As expected, he was particularly interested in what Ottie Kinser had had to say. I assured him I didn't think she was behind Lee's death.

But after I hung up and began walking back to the Statehouse garage to retrieve my van, I started thinking about Kinser. It might have been my innate lustfulness, my awareness of the senator's beauty. Beauty I had no doubt Lee admired as well. The late reporter and I appeared to be peas in a pod, as far as I could tell, at least according to Jim Flanagan. But also based on my own observations, as painful as it was to admit it. Hershey's outer charm and inner, less charming drive. Something I could identify with, at least once upon a time.

As I came to Columbus Commons and began to walk across the park, I recalled what Kinser had said about Lily Gleason. About her divorce after the scandal Lee reported on.

The whole story is ugly. Very ugly.

I can imagine.

I hope you can.

I had taken the phrase as a dig at my marital follies. But was it possible she'd been trying to tell me something else instead? Surely she would have known I could imagine what an ugly divorce looked like. Given her connection to Burke, it wasn't much of a stretch to believe that at some point he had filled her in on my past, personal and professional—at least the parts that hadn't been slapped across the tops of newspapers or blogged to death over the years. So what had she meant? Was it a hint? A suggestion? A clue?

I stopped, reversed direction, and walked to the bottom of the park. I stepped up to the window at Tortilla, ordered three softshell chorizo tacos and a Mexican lime soda, found a table and sat down, and stuffed the first taco into my mouth. As I chewed, I scrolled through my phone contacts until I found the number I was looking for. Gabby Donatelli picked up after the third ring.

"Are you eating?"

I apologized, explaining where I was and what I had in my mouth.

"You bastard. I'm starving and it's barely eleven thirty. What do you want?"

"A guy can't ring up his favorite probate lawyer just to say hi?"

"Ordinary guys, yes. You, no. Start groveling for the favor you need before I come down and yank those tacos out of your mitts."

"OK, OK. Ever heard of Lily Gleason?"

"No. Should I?"

I gave her the short version, how Lee's story exposed a fishy state contract, leading eventually to divorce.

I said, "Is it possible to get details on a divorce filing like that?"

"Sometimes. Depends if it's sealed. What are you looking for?"

"I'm not sure, exactly. I'd just like to know a little bit more. And the involved party's not going to tell me."

"You can check. But that kind of thing's not online. You're going to have to do the whole gumshoe thing and go down to probate court. Ask for the file and see what's in it."

"OK," I said. She explained the process. When she was done I thanked her. "How's married life?" I said.

"Relatively blissful. Karen's got a pretty heavy caseload right now. Oddly enough, the good economy hasn't resulted in less crime."

"Job security, I guess." Gabby's wife was a criminal defense attorney a couple rungs down the ladder from Burke.

"I suppose. That'll all change soon, though."

"Why's that?"

"Didn't you hear?"

I confessed that I hadn't.

"We're expecting. That is, *I'm* expecting. Which is why I'm starving, thank you very much. But the plan now is Karen will take the parental leave."

"Congratulations. That's great news. Your families must be happy?"

"Very."

"Your, ah, parents included?"

"I have to say, it's been amazing."

"In what way?"

"Do you remember what you told me last year? When my folks were so upset we were getting married?"

"I believe I mentioned something about the healing power of grandchildren."

"Well, the swag started arriving within three days of posting our ultrasound on Instagram. My mom's already registered us at IKEA."

"Tricky devils, those babies."

"Let me know how it works out with Gleason's case file."

AFTER I FINISHED MY tacos I walked up to South High, turned left, and headed to the court complex. I rode the elevator to the twenty-second floor, walked into the probate court office, and explained my situation to the woman behind the desk. She nodded as though it were the most natural thing in the world for a complete stranger to ask to see a divorce file. I felt my spirits rising as she checked her computer, only to feel them plunge when she informed me the file had indeed been sealed.

"So there's no way to find out what happened?"

"Not unless one of the parties tells you. And of course, most of the time . . ."

"Right."

"Were there children involved? They're often sealed because of that."

"Yes. But the whole thing started with a lawsuit."

"A lawsuit?"

I explained in broad terms about the computer contract scandal.

"Have you read the depositions?"

"In the lawsuit?"

"Maybe there's something useful there. If the lawsuit led to the divorce, as you said."

I thanked her and hiked over to the clerk of court's office in the next building. The young man at the desk found the complaint against Lily Gleason's husband with relative ease. Though a great deal of information in the court had been placed online in recent years, the documents in this particular suit were not among them. But he said it wouldn't be a problem to print them out. My spirits were rising again as I waited for him to return, then sank for the second time that day as he arrived with a stack of paper almost two inches high, each page holding four miniaturized pages of transcription.

"Please tell me there's an index at the end," I said.

He turned the pile over and checked.

"Um," he said, shaking his head apologetically. "Maybe it's interesting reading?"

I HAD CONSIGNED MYSELF TO A LOST WEEKEND of fine print when to my surprise one of my voicemail messages was returned.

"You wanted to talk to me," said the male voice with a hint of southern Ohio at the edges. "Why?"

"Who's calling?"

"Billy Bryan."

"Justice Bryan?"

"It ain't Judge Judy."

"I was hoping you might have some insights into Lee Hershey," I said, scrambling. "Who might have wanted to hurt him. Or who might profit from his death."

"You mean besides me?"

"Well, I wasn't—"

"I've got time this afternoon. Come to my chambers."

"Your chambers? Aren't you, I don't know, afraid of being seen with me?"

He made a sound like someone trying to catch his breath after a sock to the stomach, except I took it he was laughing. "Couldn't give a damn," he said. "Give the people in this limestone pile something to talk about besides themselves and their gold-plated law degrees for a change. Four o'clock work?"

THE SUPREME COURT BUILDING sits between Front and Civic Center Drive on the west side of downtown. A Depression-era monument, it had been a dumpy state office building housing a variety of dumpy state agencies for years, until the justices got tired of their cramped space across Capitol Square in the Rhodes Tower, that paean to Soviet architecture, and loosened the legislature's purse strings to the tune of eighty-five million for a top-to-bottom renovation that they now called home.

"Nice office," I said a few minutes later, after surviving the security gauntlet and taking the elevator to the eighth floor, admiring the view as I looked out the window at the confluence of the Scioto and Olentangy Rivers. A nicer prospect than the governor's, I noted.

"It's like one of Saddam's palaces, without the torture chambers," Bryan said, directing me to a leather couch in front of a wall full of law books. "Unless you're not having a good day before us in the courtroom, in which case it's hard to tell the difference. So you want to know if I killed that sonofabitch reporter."

"Make my job a lot easier if you did."

"And what is your job?"

I explained about Tillman, the mysterious person Hershey was supposed to meet that night, and all the rest of it.

"So how'd a second-rate college quarterback get into this kind of work, anyway?" Bryan interrupted. "You got a thing for lost causes?"

"Not to be one of those guys who's always correcting people, but I was a first-rate quarterback and a second-rate criminal. It's hard to tell the difference sometimes, especially in this town."

Bryan made that socked-in-the-stomach sound again as he laughed. "You didn't answer my question."

"Long story."

"Sum up."

So I summed up, giving the SparkNotes version of a prison stint for point shaving, a truncated comeback with the Browns, a lost decade of marriages, divorces, and broken engagements and indulging in too much of just about everything except responsibility until my pig-farming uncle—I really did have one—beat some sense into me one long, hot summer back in Knox County, not all that far from Homer, after which an ex–Ohio State football team manager turned defense attorney named Burke Cunningham hired me to canvass murder witnesses in a violent eastside neighborhood for minimum wage and a case of Black Label.

"Tamworth man, myself," Bryan said.

"I'm sorry?"

"Tamworth hogs. What I raise, when I'm not wearing a robe."

"You raise hogs?"

"Got thirty acres back home."

"Which is?"

"Paw Paw Bottoms, and don't bother with the jokes. I've heard them all."

"Righto." So it did exist. For once Hershey had been serious.

"Tamworth are an Old English breed," Bryan continued. "Tasty as hell. What'd your uncle have?"

"He had pigs."

"What breed?"

"Big. And mean."

"So you're a second-rate criminal and a third-rate farmer," Bryan said. "All right, ask me a question. But I'll save you one: I didn't kill Lee Hershey."

"OK. What about Triple F?"

"Worst name ever for a school-funding plan. What about it?"

"You're the swing vote."

"I *was* the swing vote, last two times they sent us a plan. We haven't seen the new legislation yet, obviously."

"Will it pass muster? From what you know of it?"

"It's in better shape than it was six months ago."

"What will it take for you to vote for it?"

He leaned back and studied me. I was struck by his patrician bearing, and how, under a different set of circumstances, you could imagine him with his longish white hair and lined face peering out through the flaps of a tent on a Civil War battlefield.

"First of all, I have an election to win this fall. And it's not going to be easy."

"Why's that?"

"My opponent is a Cleveland municipal court judge who couldn't referee a pumpkin-carving contest without someone holding his hand. But he's got one thing I don't have."

"Which is?"

"The last name of O'Malley, which puts him up five points in the polls before he gets out of bed. More than one person has suggested to me, without irony, that I change my name to O'Bryan just for the election."

"So you have to win before you can think about school funding."

"I think about it all the time. But I can't do much about it if I'm not sitting on the bench."

"Assuming all that, would you find this bill constitutional?"

"You know how many people on Capitol Square are dying to know that?" he snapped.

"At least one," I replied.

He looked startled. "I suppose that came out the wrong way."

"Honest mistake."

"Son," he said, after a moment. "Do you understand how school funding works in this state?"

"Not really. Something to do with local property taxes."

"Where you live depends on what you get. And we're the same as any other place in the country. You've got your Grosse Pointes and your Detroits. Your Evanstons and your Chicagos. Here you've got your Shaker Heightses and your Clevelands, and then farther south throw in all the Appalachian hollers."

"So there's economic disparity. Hasn't that always been the case?"

"Sure it has. But that doesn't make it right. And here's the problem. How do you fix it? Crank up the state money machine? Give the schools better buildings and cross your fingers? Change the entire funding formula?"

"Like the Robin Hood memo suggested."

"In extreme terms, but yes."

"A memo that Dani Symmes leaked to Hershey, giving Democrats more reason to hate him and her," I said.

"So they say."

"So to repeat the question, what will it take for you to support Triple F?"

"With apologies again for my slip of the tongue a moment ago—if I told you that, I'd have to kill you."

"How about a hint?"

He looked at me. For just a moment, he appeared much older and frailer.

"There are many competing factors going into my legal reasoning."

"Such as?"

"Things I wouldn't expect you to understand."

"Try me."

He shook his head. "I can't."

"Why not?"

"Judge O'Malley," he said. "A difficult election."

"That sounds mysterious."

"The law's mysterious," he said, and stood and showed me the door.

36

I HAD DINNER AT ANNE'S PARENTS' HOUSE that night, along with her brother and his family, and between the two of us driving there separately and me playing with Amelia and her niece and nephew and talking baseball with Anne's dad, there wasn't much time to discuss the situation. At the end of the night, I mentioned the test and she read my face and said it would be fine with her if I brought it by in the next day or so. I spent the rest of the evening at home, alternately dozing over Lily Gleason's depositions and reading *The Sparrow*. I called it quits by eleven.

First thing Saturday morning, after jogging with the dog and eating breakfast, I drove to the downtown CVS and bought a pregnancy kit. It took me longer than expected, since the options for testing for human chorionic gonadotropin were frustratingly bountiful. It was worse than trying to buy a simple jar of peanut butter in the age of low-fat, no-fat, organic, and all-natural. I settled on the one with the prettiest packaging and left, feeling less relieved than I thought I would.

Anne was hosting a brunch for her weekend running girl-friends that morning, and it seemed impolitic at the least to interrupt with my purchase. Instead, I drove to Linden, parked, and knocked on Bonnie's door.

"You really upset Troy the other day," she said when she appeared. "You need to leave us alone."

"I talked to Troy's dad."

She stiffened. "So?"

"I told him he should talk to Troy."

"What'd he say?"

"He wasn't interested. Told me to get lost, basically."

"Good advice."

"Why?"

"He's not interested in Troy. Can't you see that?"

"I got that part, yes."

"Listen, I'm kind of busy right now. In the middle of a project. I need to go."

"Mind if I come in?"

"I just said—"

"You and Troy both have records."

"What?"

"Criminal records. I looked you up. It's all online. Everything is. Well, you would know that, in your business."

"Who cares? That's old news. We took care of it."

"Is Troy dealing? Is that what this is about?"

"No," she said, sharply. "Did his father tell you that? Or my dad?"

I shook my head. "I'm just trying to find out what's wrong here. Something's bugging him. I know a good lawyer, if either of you are in trouble. There are ways to work things out."

"There's nothing to work out."

"Why doesn't Troy get another job?"

"He just can't right now. That's all. It's none of your business, or my dad's or anybody's."

"Is it Grant's business? His father's?"

"Please go away," she said. "Please. Just leave us the fuck alone."

The door behind the screen slammed shut, and I heard her shoot a deadbolt. Inside the house Greg barked. I walked down the steps, got back in my van, and drove around the corner. I wanted to test a theory. When I circled back, I parked down the street from their house, behind a pickup truck with a cab and a ladder lashed to the top. I reached onto the seat beside me and picked up *The Sparrow* and started reading. I wasn't surprised that Anne liked it, with its alternating locales of Cleveland and Rome and a newly discovered planet where a cruel but fascinating symbiosis played out between kangarooey-looking carnivores and herbivores, and its sweeping themes of religion and science and love and marriage. But the fact Hershey said he liked it—if he were telling the truth—was giving me additional insight into him. *I* liked it, for that matter.

Not more than twenty-five minutes had passed when a car turned into the street and parked in front of Troy and Bonnie's. I kept reading, careful to avoid any sudden change in behavior—the typical death of the stakeout—but raised my eyes slightly above the top of the book. Well, well. Grant Wardley got out and approached the house and knocked loudly. A few moments later the door opened and he stepped inside. I kept reading for another minute, looked again, reached next to me, lifted my camera from the seat, and clicked off five frames of Wardley's car, making sure the license plate was visible. I put the camera down as casually as if I took pictures of people's cars in semirough neighborhoods all the time and went back to reading. Ten minutes later, Wardley left the house without a backward glance and drove away in a hurry. It might have been my imagination, but I thought I saw a curtain at the front of the house shift slightly as he departed. I waited five more minutes, started the van and drove away myself.

37

WARDLEY FROWNED AS HE OPENED HIS door fifteen minutes later. "I told you to leave me alone."

"You did a nice job on your lawn. It's very trimmy."

"Did you hear me?"

"I'd go easy on the fertilizer, though. If the temperature gets any warmer, it could burn the shit out of the grass."

"Listen—"

"You were at Troy and Bonnie's just now. Just a few minutes after I asked Bonnie about their criminal records. Why?"

"How do you know that? Did Bonnie—"

"Bonnie didn't say anything. I know because I watched you. I also took pictures in case you want any mementos of your trip. Answer the question."

"You photographed me?"

A man walked up from behind and joined Wardley at the door. He might have been Wardley's slightly less fit twin. I was betting on his politician brother.

"Skip Wardley, Fighting for Your Future?" I said.

As if by reflex, he grinned and pushed out his right hand. I took it. It was like holding a recently thawed chicken breast. "Have we met?" he said.

"This is him," Grant Wardley interrupted. "The detective."

Skip drew his hand back quickly. "What are you doing here?"

"I was just asking your brother why he showed up at Troy and Bonnie's house after I asked them about their criminal records."

"It's none of your business," Grant said.

"You made it clear the other day you weren't interested in talking to Troy. Yet there you were, right after I came by. How come?"

"I told you, this is none of your business. Now you either leave or I call the police."

"The obvious suggestion is that having a nephew in jail for raping a kid isn't the best thing for a political campaign." I kept my eye on the mayor as I spoke. He met my gaze, then broke off to look at his brother. "You got them on a leash of some kind? Making sure they don't embarrass Hizzoner here?"

"That's a bunch of bullshit," Skip said, but before he said anything else his brother produced a cell phone from his back pocket and started dialing. My gut told me he was bluffing, that he didn't want a cop on his doorstep on a Saturday morning any more than I did, especially with the publicity-conscious mayor next to him. But it wasn't a risk I was willing to take, especially in the suburbs, where the cops had less to do and more time to do it in and weren't exactly full of good nature toward private detectives from across the line in Columbus.

I took a couple steps to go, and stopped.

I said, "At least I can tell Richard Deckard I got someone to talk to Troy."

38

I HAD ONE MORE THING TO DO BEFORE I swung by Anne's apartment. I was hoping it would take me a while, given my dread of that particular errand.

To my disappointment, no one answered when I knocked on Ephraim Badger's door half an hour later. I was pulling out my notebook and getting ready to leave him a more detailed message than a business card jammed into the door—a business card that was missing, I noticed, which was something, anyway—when I glanced through the front window and saw that one of the shelves of books was partly empty. It left the impression of missing teeth from a formerly perfect smile. I bent a little closer, peered in, and saw books on the floor. I kept looking and noticed an overturned chair. I started to get a bad feeling. I knocked on the door again, and turned the knob. To my surprise it was unlocked and opened easily.

"Ephraim?" I called. No answer. I stepped inside and repeated his name. My stomach fell. The front room was in shambles. Several shelves had been emptied of books, now lying on the floor like wooden shingles ripped from a wall. The pillows on the couch were flipped over or lying askew on the floor. Newspapers were scattered everywhere. I walked farther in, my hand reaching for my phone.

"Ephraim?"

The dining room, which also contained two tall bookcases, was similarly disturbed, with fat volumes of European and Central Asian history ripped off the shelves. Shards of a smashed drinking glass speckled the floor. More newspapers lay torn and scattered on the dining room table. Someone had been looking for something. But had they found it? And where was Badger?

I checked the kitchen, and then a back study, whose ransacked file drawers and shelves emptied of Greek and Roman histories showed signs of similar chaos. On the floor beside a chair sat a half-empty coffee cup, resting on a collection of *Pogo* cartoons. I pulled out my handkerchief, picked the cup up carefully, and set it on a coffee table. As I did, I heard a sound. I froze. A moment later, I heard it again.

I left the study, rounded the corner, and took the wooden stairs two at a time to the second floor. One bedroom was turned inside out from chest of drawers to closet; another, filled with more books, most of them on the floor, was in similar disarray. In the third bedroom, curled up on the floor as if asleep, lay Badger, blood pooling away from his head like a viscous cloud of escaping thought. A heavy leather-bound book lay beside him, blood staining a corner of the cover. I bent over and saw a red bubble form on Badger's lips, followed by the sound I'd heard, someplace between a groan and his familiar squeak.

"Ephraim," I said, leaning over.

For a moment his eyes opened. They studied my face as if he'd been expecting me. Then his lids closed again. Another red bubble formed on his lips, and I heard him speak.

"What?" I said, tapping out 911 on my phone.

"*He is us,*" he said.

AN HOUR LATER I was sitting in the rear passenger seat of an unmarked Ford Explorer parked on the street beside three Columbus PD cruisers. Crime scene technicians were inside, and yellow tape ringed the yard, keeping back the gawking neighbors. Lieutenant Mike Hummel was sitting in the driver's seat, listening to me recount my discovery of Badger. Beside him sat Columbus homicide detective Henry Fielding, who, with his tall, thin frame and billiard-cue baldness, bore as close a resemblance to Lord Voldemort as Hummel did to Commodore Perry. I pointed this out to neither.

Hummel said, "So no idea what someone might have been looking for?"

"None. All I know is this thing he quoted to me a couple of times."

"What thing?"

I explained about the Battle of Lake Erie and Perry's famous summation and the *Pogo* version.

"'We have met the enemy and he is us?'" Hummel said. "Makes no sense."

"Sure it does. He was trying to say whoever killed Hershey knew him. Hershey said the same thing the night he took me through the Statehouse. The *Pogo* quote must have been some kind of private joke they shared."

"Victims know their killers in almost all homicides," Hummel said. "Big help."

"Just to clear up any confusion," Fielding said, "where were you this morning, before you came here?"

I hesitated a moment, then explained about Grant Wardley and my job for Deckard.

Fielding furrowed his brow until his eyes nearly shut. "This guy is paying you to talk to the rapist's brother?"

"That's right."

"He feels the family hasn't been through enough already?"

"I'm just answering your question."

"That'll be a first," Fielding said.

For the third time, he ran me through my arrival at the house, my entry through the front door, my search and discovery.

"You said you left your card, the other day?"

"That's right."

"But he never called."

"No."

Before he could say anything else, I turned to Hummel. "Did you talk to Badger, after Lee died?"

"Why should I tell you?"

"Seems like he might have known something. Getting nearly beaten to death and all."

Hummel made a face that would have struck fear into the hearts of British naval forces, had there been any in Ohio at the moment. He glanced out the Explorer's window at the porch of Badger's house, where a uniformed Columbus police officer stood guard.

"He was a check on a list for us, regards to Hershey. He wasn't at the Statehouse that night."

"Where was he?"

"He was at church, followed by a regular ice cream sundae run. He's got a dozen Baptists for an alibi."

"Was he there the next day?"

"I'd have to check. Anybody that came in had to be accompanied."

"Was anything missing?" I said, gesturing at the house.

"Nothing besides the obvious," Hummel said. "We're still waiting for his kids to get here. The closest lives in Mansfield. They're going to have to go through everything, and who knows how familiar they were with his stuff at this point."

"What do you mean by the obvious?"

"The one thing his son told us about right away. In the bedroom, where you found him, top drawer of the bureau. Where he may have been making for whenever this happened."

"What was in there?"

Hummel glanced at Fielding. "A gun," he said. "And it's definitely gone."

39

IT WAS NEARLY THREE BY THE TIME I GOT to Anne's apartment. Since she wasn't answering her phone or responding to texts, I'd been half dreading to find the remnants of her brunch guests still there. What I wasn't expecting was to walk inside and see my younger son, Joe, sitting on the couch next to Amelia, each of them engrossed in a book.

"Ah—" I said.

"I'm sorry," Anne said with a smile. "It happened sort of fast. Joe's mom said she couldn't reach you and got ahold of me instead. She said Joe had been asking to play with Amelia. It sounded good to me. She's sweet, by the way."

"Who?"

"Crystal. Joe's mom."

"Sweet?" I said. "Crystal?"

"Sweet," Anne said.

"Sweet it is," I said, doubtfully.

"They did a Harry Potter board game for a couple hours. They get along so well. I think they're just taking a break. What'd you bring me?" She looked inquiringly at the bag.

"For the situation," I said, lowering my voice.

"Right," she said, and I saw something in her eyes I couldn't quite decipher. Not disappointment, exactly. Resignation? But then it was gone. "I'll just take that. Maybe now's not the best time"— she glanced at the kids—"but later?"

"Sure," I said.

In the end, the best time didn't come that day. The play date turned into a play dinner, and then a play movie night—*Mutant Ninja Turtles*—and then a play sleepover with a quick ride home to fetch the dog first.

"Tomorrow," Anne said, kissing me goodnight as I pulled a sleeping bag over me on her couch.

"Tomorrow," I said.

AT FIVE THE NEXT morning I jolted awake, remembering something about Dani Symmes I'd discovered earlier in the week, trying to find a better phone number for her. A TV interview that explained a little bit about her drive, not to mention her athletic figure. I sat up, found my phone, got on the Internet, and located the segment again. I thought about the mechanics of making this happen. It was a long shot, but I needed some answers, especially after what happened to Badger.

I got up, dressed quietly, left Anne a note, marshaled Hopalong, and went outside. Twenty minutes later I was pulling up in front of my house. I took Hopalong inside, changed into workout clothes, collected my bike, loaded it into the van, and made for the highway. Half an hour later, wondering if I was on a fool's errand, I started riding the trail at Highbanks Metro Park on the far northern side of the city. The park where Symmes, who turned out to be an accomplished age-group marathoner, always did her Sunday long runs—at least according to the interview she'd given Channel 4 last year. It was just past six thirty, the sun up, a few birds still singing. Nice day for a bike ride.

I was starting to worry about the suspicious glances I was getting from the female runners I stared at one by one as I rode past them when I spied the Ohio House Speaker ahead of me at a turn in the path. To my surprise, Matt, the younger guy from her office, was a few yards behind her, looking as if he was struggling to keep up. I chimed the little bell on my bike handlebars and slowly rolled past them on the left. When I was even with Symmes, I braked and glanced over at her. After a moment, realizing I was keeping pace with her and not passing, she returned the look. It took another moment for my face to register.

"You."

"Me."

"What do you want?"

"Five minutes of your time."

"Out of the question. Do yourself a favor and keep riding."

"Public trail."

"You realize I make one phone call and twenty cops are here."

"Assuming they're Republicans."

"I won't dignify that comment with a response. How'd you find me?"

I told her about the Channel 4 segment.

"Dumbest interview I ever did," Symmes said, keeping her eyes on the path. She had a comfortable, rhythmic stride with only the slightest hitch in her left arm.

"I'll get right to it," I said. "Was Lee Hershey supposed to meet with you the night he was killed?"

"What?"

I gave her the whole spiel. She listened, and glanced back at Matt. He returned an inquiring gaze. She shook her head.

"Absolutely not."

"Do you know who it was?"

"No."

"Were you his source for the latest Triple F story he was working on?"

"Don't be absurd."

"Why do you say that? You leaked him the Robin Hood memo."

"Who told you that?"

"Lots of people."

She shook her head and kept running.

"What about Phil Williams?" I said. Her face stayed neutral at the reference to the Little Red Schoolhouse charter school bigwig I'd seen her strolling with after his speech at the Statehouse.

"What about him?"

"Did he meet with Lee? He's got just as big an interest in the education bill as you."

"Not that I would ever tell you if I knew, but since I don't, I'll say that I strongly doubt it."

"Is there anything you know about what happened to Lee that might help exonerate Ed Tillman?"

"I really am going to call the police now, Mr. Hayes. Partly because you're on the verge of harassing me, and partly because in another few minutes we're planning to pick up the pace and I need to concentrate."

I looked doubtfully back at Matt.

Symmes said, "He's got the phone, in case you thought I was bluffing."

"I'm just trying to get answers about Lee. I was hoping you'd be able to help me with that. I'm really not trying to create any problems."

"You should want answers, since from everything I hear you're at least indirectly responsible for his death. But I have nothing to tell you, other than to heed a final warning to get lost."

"I'm sorry you feel that way."

"Good-bye."

I'd pushed my luck as far as it would go. I had no doubt the Speaker of the Ohio House could summon more than a little firepower if needed, even if the responders were all Democrats. Reluctantly, I stood up on the bike and started to pedal away.

"Mr. Hayes?"

I looked back. Symmes had pulled a little farther ahead of Matt. I slowed.

"Yes?" I said.

"Since you seem to be wrong about almost everything, I'll add one more to the list."

"Oh, goody."

"I'm not the one who leaked the Robin Hood memo."

"You're not?"

"I would have, believe me, if I'd had it. It was the most outrageous proposal I'd ever heard of—an unprecedented shakedown of hardworking taxpayers whose only sin is they happen to be affluent. But whoever gave it to Lee, and they have my eternal praise, it wasn't me."

40

I CALLED ANNE ON THE WAY HOME FROM the park. She was understandably put out by my disappearance. My suggestion that I swing by and take everyone out for brunch seemed to make things worse. Instead, she told me she'd make arrangements with Crystal to get Joe home, and if she needed my help she'd let me know and maybe I could come by later. She didn't mention the situation. I didn't bring it up.

Back home I took Hopalong to Schiller Park and mulled over what Symmes had told me, which wasn't much, other than the declaration—if it was true—that she hadn't leaked the memo. I felt like I was back to square one, since presumably the list of people who'd want that document publicized, presumably Republicans, would have been long.

After a shower and breakfast I sat on the couch and got back to reading the unindexed copy of Lily Gleason's lawsuit deposition. Periodically, after my eyes began to swim, I got up, poured more coffee, did push-ups, splashed water on my face, let the dog in and out and in and out, and poured yet more coffee.

Noon came and went, with no word from Anne about Joe and his mom. I put the papers down, made myself a cheese sandwich, and opened my laptop. I found a number for the Bridgeport mayor's office, called, and not surprisingly, given that it was a Sunday, got voicemail. I left a message for Skip Wardley, asking for him to call. I looked in vain for a home or cell number on all the usual free sites, then logged onto Nexis, using Burke's password. It located what looked like a current address, but no number. Smart. What politician wants to be bothered by plebeians reaching him at home? I scrolled down to see if I could find older numbers. He'd moved around a lot over the years, I saw, both houses and apartments. The longest he had lived anywhere was an address he'd occupied more than fifteen years ago. I was about to give up and see if I could find an e-mail when I looked at the location again. I'd been there, just a day earlier. His brother's house. He'd lived there, from what I could see, nearly three years. From age twenty-two to twenty-five. Right out of college? Made sense. Would have been around the time of the post-9/11 recession. Saving money by living with his older, more successful brother. Not unlike what I did with my uncle, in a way. I looked a little further, poked around here and there, and finally found what appeared to be a legitimate Gmail address. I sent him a note, saying I'd like to talk to him. Figured it couldn't hurt. And maybe it would tweak his brother a bit, light a fire under him.

I closed the computer, poured some more coffee, read a chapter of *The Sparrow*, reluctantly put the book down and picked up the deposition. I promised myself I would only read ten more pages and then call it quits and do something, anything, even if it were reading my uncle's dog-eared copy of *Pilgrim's Progress*.

I sat up two pages later.

Q: Mrs. Gleason, you provided Lee Hershey with information about the invoices that your husband altered, correct?

A: Yes. But I—

Q: Did you give him copies?

A: No.

Interesting. This was the first I'd heard about Gleason helping Hershey with his investigation.

Q: Did you e-mail him electronic copies? Something like that?
A: No. Not exactly.
Q: What's that supposed to mean?
A: I might have e-mailed him a few things afterward. But not at first.
Q: Then how did you provide the information?
A: I told him.
Q: You told him? When?
A: Does it really matter?
Q: Yes. Please answer the question.
Q: (Mrs. Gleason to attorney): Do I have to?
A: Under these circumstances, yes.
A: (Mrs. Gleason): I told him after.
Q: After what?
A: After we—
Q: After you what?
A: (Pause. Inaudible.)
Q: Please speak up, Mrs. Gleason. After you what?
A: After we made love. (Crying.)

I stopped, squeezed my eyes shut, opened them, and read the exchange again. And a third time, to be sure. I took a breath and continued.

Q: You had sexual relations with Lee Hershey. Did I hear that correctly?
A: Yes.
Q: When?
A: I don't remember. Not exactly. I was still in office.
Q: Where?
A: Where what?

Q: Where were you when you told him about the altered invoices?

A: In his . . . At his house.

Q: You were having an affair?

A: Yes.

I digested what I was reading. Hershey had gotten the tip that led to a scandal for Gleason's husband, not to mention the end of their marriage, from pillow talk with Gleason herself.

Q: Did you know what Lee Hershey planned to do with the information you gave him?

A: No. Not at first.

Q: No? Even though he's a well-known reporter?

A: That's right.

Q: Excuse me, but that doesn't seem entirely credible.

Gleason's lawyer objected to the other attorney's tone. After a moment's back-and-forth deliberation, the questioning continued.

Q: When did he tell you?

A: He called me, later.

Q: What did he say?

A: He told me about the story he was doing. He said it was a courtesy call. He said he was sorry.

Q: Did you try to dissuade him?

A: Yes. Of course.

Q: How?

A: I begged him not to. I told him he had betrayed me. That I'd trusted him.

Q: How did he respond?

A: He apologized. Said he had no choice.

Q: No choice?

A: He said it was bigger than me. Than us.

Bigger than us. I tried to imagine the call. Hershey's apology. I wondered how he could have justified such a betrayal.

Q: When you first mentioned the invoices, you had no expectation that he would act on what you told him?

A: No.

Q: No?

A: I mean, I don't know. I was scared. I knew my husband had done something wrong. I thought maybe Lee could help me. Offer some suggestions.

Q: Was that the first time?

A: Was what?

Q: The night you told him about the invoices? Was that the first time you made love?

A: No.

Q: How long had it been going on at that point?

A: A few weeks, I think.

Q: You had had sex before?

A: Yes.

Q: Where?

A: Mostly his house. Except—

Q: Except?

A: Except the first time. (Crying.)

Q: And where was that?

A: In the Statehouse.

Q: The Statehouse?

A: (Crying.) In the Cupola.

41

LILY GLEASON HADN'T GIVEN ME HER CELL phone, and there was no answer at her house or office. I called Burke to fill him in, and then called and left a message for Liz Brantley, the only person I felt I could ask about Hershey and Gleason—Jim Flanagan was out because of Hershey and his late wife. Finally, I called Grant Hospital, where, after convincing a nursing supervisor I didn't represent a threat to national security, I wrenched free the information that Ephraim Badger remained in critical condition and hadn't regained consciousness. I had just reclined on the couch and shut my eyes when Brantley called back. She agreed without hesitation to meet me at Luck Bros' coffee house in Grandview, not far from her place.

"Lee and Lily," she said, after I explained what I'd found. "I'm not surprised. Disappointed, but not surprised."

"I'm sorry to have to ask this. But you didn't know—"

"That he had an affair with a sitting state senator? No."

"Were you and he—?"

"Yes. We were together then."

"I'm sorry."

"It's OK. I don't think she was the only one. It's the price you paid with Lee."

"Do you think Gleason—"

"Could have killed Lee?" she said. "I don't know. I'm not taking anything for granted about this situation anymore."

"Tell me about it," I said. I explained about Dani Symmes and her denial that she'd leaked the Robin Hood memo.

"You really tracked her down with your bike like that?" she said, admiringly. "Kind of thing Lee would have done, you know."

"I'm not sure how to take that."

"In this case, as a compliment," she said, reaching out and touching my arm. "So, do you believe her?"

"I don't know. It would help if we knew where Lee kept his notes on all this."

"He uploaded everything. To the cloud."

"I know. Any idea what site?"

"Cumulonimbus."

"I beg your pardon?"

"Cumulonimbus Cloud Storage. He moved everything there after his iCloud account got hacked."

I pulled out my notebook and wrote it down. "Happen to know the password?"

"I have no idea. Maybe try, 'I'm A Fucking Asshole.'"

I laughed in spite of myself. "How about you? Do you believe Symmes is telling the truth?"

"I'm like you. I'm not sure."

"Could she or Phil Williams have been Lee's source on his latest story?"

"Seems unlikely. They have a lot at stake with Triple F."

"Why?"

"Williams's company. Little Red Schoolhouse? It stands to make a lot of money if the charter school amendments that Hubbard agreed to go through. They don't want anything to screw it up."

"Little Red Schoolhouse. That's a charter school?"

Brantley shook her head. "It's a management company. It provides teachers and equipment and books and all that, through contracts with the schools."

"You make money at that?"

"Don't be fooled by the cutesy name. It's big business. Williams has pulled down millions over the years."

"Shit. It's all so confusing."

"What is?"

"The governor, school funding, who the charter school amendments benefit, or don't. All of it. I don't know how you keep up with everything going on over there. It's like you can't tell whose side anybody is really on."

She nodded. "It's like Teddy Roosevelt said."

"Oh?"

"He said, 'I think there is only one thing in the world I can't understand, and that is Ohio politics.' "

"I like it. Is that in the book?"

She started. "What?"

"Your book. *Swing State Ohio*?"

After a moment she relaxed. "Right. Yeah, I think I mention it."

"So. Phil Williams. Could he have had something to do with Lee's death?"

"I dunno. He's a fundamentalist Christian on top of everything else. Squeaky clean."

"I have lots of fundamentalist Christians in my family I wouldn't turn my back on."

"You know what I mean. So Symmes didn't tell you anything else?"

"No. She's kind of grumpy, especially when private detectives interrupt her Sunday morning run."

"I bet. She was probably chomping at the bit for her guy to call the police."

"I got that impression. It's champing, by the way."

"What?"

"It's champing at the bit. Not chomping. Common mistake."

"Christ."

"What?"

"That's exactly the kind of smart-ass thing Lee would have done. Insult you and correct you at the same time. I take back the compliment."

"I'm sorry. Jim Flanagan pointed the same thing out to me, at the Ringside."

"We're both a little sensitive about Lee, in case you hadn't noticed."

"No, I think I got that part. Jim got touchy when I asked him where he'd been the day Lee was killed."

"'*Out of town*'?" she said.

"Yeah."

"No big mystery. He got nailed for drunk driving in Cincinnati about six months ago. Veered off a street and hit a tree. On his way back from seeing his mom. Right after Kelly, you know . . ."

"After the accident?"

"He was devastated, obviously. His drinking got worse."

"Did they have kids?"

She shook her head. "They'd been trying, without luck. The judge gave him a ton of community service hours on top of three days in jail and a fine."

"Service hours doing what?"

"Janitorial stuff at a recovery center down there. Real grunt work—mopping floors, cleaning toilets, washing people's vomit-encrusted shirts. Jim asked if he could serve the time up here on the weekends, but the judge was a hard-ass about it. He has to go every Wednesday. Same day as the accident. Doesn't get home until late."

"Which was where he was when Lee died. Which was why he didn't want to tell me."

"Probably."

"Thanks for the insight."

"Don't thank me. It's my revenge for him spilling Lee's and my past to you at the bar."

"I'm sorry he felt he had to do that."

"Me too."

"Listen," she said, a moment later. "I have to go. Ask you a favor?"

"Sure."

"I walked. Any chance you could give me a ride home? It's just around the corner."

Brantley lived in a modest one-story white frame house that needed a new coat of paint, not to mention gutters and window shingles. After I parked, she unbuckled but didn't make a move to get out. Staring ahead, through the windshield, she said, "It's the sense of humor."

"What's that?"

"You and Lee. What you have in common. Your jokes. What's the word? Mordant?"

"Wasn't she the evil sorceress in King Arthur?"

She smiled. "I rest my case."

"Didn't mean to be flip."

"Didn't think you were trying," she said. She glanced at her house. "Fancy another cup of coffee? I grind it myself."

"I'm pretty buzzed at the moment, thanks."

"Sure about that?"

Before I could respond she turned and looked at me, put her hand on my thigh, leaned over, and kissed me. I didn't reciprocate, much, but I didn't push her away, either. She tasted like coffee and nicotine and something sweet, like candy, or a hint of booze. It was a taste I'd had before. A taste I realized I missed.

"Pretty buzzed, huh?" she said, pulling back and looking at me, her face close, her eyes wide. I returned the look, seeing in her expression an aggressive desire, which was having an unwelcome effect on me. But also something else. Not fear, exactly, but anxiety of some kind.

"I'm not sure—"

"Not sure what?"

"I'm not sure it's, ah, the smartest idea, given what I'm working on. And also, I'm with someone right now."

"Of course. The sci-fi girl. I like how you mentioned her second."

"I didn't—"

"It's too bad," she said, removing her hand from my thigh. "Or is it just because I'm old?"

"Old?"

"Single and fifty. The world's most desperate fuck. Is that it?"

"No. I have no idea how old you are. And you're very good-looking."

"Jesus. *Very good-looking.* You sound like you're trying to say something nice about a Buick."

"Liz," I said. I looked at her. Her eyes had filled with tears. But her expression was more angry than sorrowful.

She said, "You know one of the things Lee said to me when he dumped me?"

"It's none of my business."

"He said I took too long to come. OK? Said he was tired of the effort. Couldn't take all the drama in bed. What do you think of that?"

I said nothing. I sat and looked out the window. I rolled her words around in my head and tried to reconcile them with the little I really knew of Lee Hershey. Was it just a case of a wolf in sheep's clothing? A charmer with a cruel streak once you got to know him? In a way it didn't matter. Because the truth was, the real problem with Brantley's remark was how close to home it hit, on top of the fact that Hershey and I apparently shared the same propensity for wiseass quips and showing off our knowledge of obscure facts. I knew in my heart what Hershey had told Brantley was the kind of thing I might have said, in the years before the summer on the pig farm. I reached out and took Brantley's left hand and held it for a moment. I listened to her cry a little. But the tears didn't last long.

She opened the door. She turned to me and said, "You really do remind me of him. I was hoping in good ways. But you're probably just the same. Who needs all that effort, huh? You probably like 'em quick and loud. Just like Lee."

I tried to think of something to say, but the dozen responses that flitted through my head all fell flat. She looked at me, waiting, and when I didn't reply she clicked her tongue, got out, and shut the door hard. She took a few steps up the walk and stopped. Her shoulders rose and fell twice. She took another step and dug into her purse. I waited until she put the key in her door and opened it and disappeared inside. Then I placed the van in drive and pulled away.

It was almost, but not quite, the most destructive part of a day steadily going downhill. That came an hour later, back home, when Lily Gleason returned my call and I told her what I'd found. I expected tears but got swearing instead, then silence, and then she hung up. I called her back to make sure she was OK. But all I could do was leave a message.

42

"ANYBODY HOME?" ANNE SAID, A FEW HOURS later, as we sat on the couch after pizza and salad. Amelia had disappeared into her bedroom with a book.

"Sorry," I said, clearing my head. "What was that?"

"I was just saying how you always have some catchy phrase handy, you know? Some witticism."

Just like Hershey, I thought.

"You're like Danny Glover in that one *Lethal Weapon* movie," she continued. "The one where he kills the guy with the nail gun, and then says, '*Nailed* him.'"

"It's two guys. And the line is, 'Nailed 'em both.'"

"See?"

"Sorry."

"It's OK," she said, laughing. "It's kind of endearing, most of the time. Anyway, I was just pointing out I don't have anything snappy or witty to say. Something funny to break the tension."

"I don't think I'm following."

"I just wanted to tell you I'm not pregnant. I got my period today."

"Ah," I said.

"This is probably where you would say something like, 'So the rose bloomed after all, eh?'"

I said nothing.

"Are you OK?" she said after a moment.

"Yes. No."

"Did you want a different report?"

"Same answer."

"Really?"

I cleared my throat. "The result didn't matter. It wouldn't have changed anything. Anything about us."

"You sure?"

"Yes."

"Crystal said you got upset when she told you she was pregnant with Joe."

"She said that?"

"And some other things."

"Like what?"

"Things," Anne said.

"Joe means the world to me. Mike does too. And so do you. Whatever happened between Crystal and me, well—"

"It's OK. I get it. Frankly, I was less worried about your reaction to the situation than I was about mine. I just didn't do a good job of expressing it."

"And how do you feel now?"

"Relieved. I think."

"You think?"

She nodded.

"'Relieved, I think,'" I said. "Funny—that's how I feel too."

ALMOST TWO HOURS LATER, close to eleven, I was turning left onto High Street, feeling more relaxed than I had in days, despite everything that was happening, when I looked in my rearview mirror and realized I'd picked up the tail again. "You've got to be kidding me," I thought.

They were three cars back but doing a good job sticking with me as I passed through the Clintonville neighborhood mishmash of antique shops and coffee joints and a couple remaining old-time bars. A few blocks south I entered the campus area, nearly dead this time of night and this point in the early summer. Just south of campus, I took a hard left onto Seventh without using my turn signal, made a full, slow circuit around the Kroger parking lot before going back up to Seventh and turning right. A block later I turned on Summit and headed south toward downtown. About a minute later I spied the car again, behind a panel truck. Pretty good.

I couldn't see the harm in just heading home, because someone that skilled probably already knew where I lived, and was more interested in where I'd been than where I was going. But why? It angered me that I'd been followed from Anne's, since I had no desire to entangle her in my day job, as difficult as that was at times. I got an idea and decided to keep driving. I followed the Third Street bridge into downtown, past the Abbott labs complex on my left, then maneuvered to the right and turned onto Spring. I headed west, crossing over High, and continued past the Courtyard hotel at Front and then left onto Marconi. I drove slowly past police headquarters on the left and the federal building with its giant anti–truck bomb barriers on the right and pulled up to the light at Broad.

They made me at every turn and lane change, but now, downtown on a Sunday evening, they were more exposed. When the light changed, I paused a full count of five, then slowly crossed over and started down Civic Center Drive, creeping past the Scioto Mile walkway with its swings and benches and plant boxes. Just as I pulled even with the western side of the Supreme Court building where I met Justice Bryan a few days earlier, I slammed on the brakes, turned hard to the left, pulled forward and positioned my Odyssey across the street's dividing line, blocking both directions. I heard the squeal of brakes, and saw the bounce of flashing headlights as the SUV stopped to avoid a collision. I was out of the van fast and started running toward the car. I saw a look of panic in the driver's eyes, heard the engine gunning and tires squealing. The K-turn was spot on. I watched until I saw the SUV turn right at Broad and disappear going east. None of that really surprised me, though I was suitably impressed with the maneuver.

What caught my attention was that the driver was a woman. And I'd seen her before.

43

I TOOK MY USUAL JOG WITH HOPALONG THE next morning, came back, cracked sixteen pull-ups on the bar I'd installed in the kitchen doorway, showered and ate breakfast, waited impatiently until eight and then dialed the now-familiar number.

"Office of Ohio Governor Thomas H. Hubbard."

"Mary Ellen Withrow, please."

A pause, and the receptionist said, "I'm sorry, but there's no one in the office by that name."

I apologized in turn. "My memory's terrible. I spoke with her the other day. I was supposed to send her an e-mail. But of course I didn't write it down." I described the woman I was looking for.

"That sounds like Anna. Anna Campbell."

"Wow. I'm sorry. That's not even close."

She laughed. "One moment and I'll connect you."

I hung up after she transferred me but before the call could go through. I opened my laptop and plugged the name Anna Campbell into Google. I looked at the results and started taking notes. I checked her Facebook page, which was private, and found her on LinkedIn, Twitter, and Instagram. When I was done I sat back and looked at what I had. And what struck me was that, for all the public information about her, I still knew very little.

A lot of people come and go at the corner of State and High, near the entrance to the Riffe rhymes-with-knife Center. The only ones standing still for very long are waiting for a bus or a hand-out. Since I didn't fit either category, I started drawing glances as soon as I arrived around eleven-thirty. I felt like the guy the guards watch in the bank, the one taking a little too long to fill out his deposit slip. I hoped my sojourn would be short.

It was. She emerged from a revolving door two minutes after noon, accompanied by another young woman. Sharing a laugh at something, they walked down the street to a sandwich shop next to the Huntington Bank building and went inside. I followed, keeping three people behind in line. I ordered a roast beef on wheat with everything on it just to blend in. After they got their food, they took a table by a window looking out onto High and beyond that the Statehouse. I glanced up at the Cupola. I sat down beside them as they began unwrapping their sandwiches.

"Hello, Anna," I said.

She looked at me with an expectant smile, which froze on her face, which proceeded to drain of color.

I said, "I was wondering if I could talk about last night."

"I don't really have time right now," she stammered.

"You sure?" I winked at her companion. "You were really good."

"I don't think—"

"I think you do. Because you either make time now or I'm going to start dialing some phone numbers and telling people just how good you were."

She looked helplessly at her friend, who stared at me and back at Campbell. "Everything all right?" she said.

I pulled out my phone and held it up.

"Everything's fine," Campbell replied. "Could you just give us a couple of minutes? I'm sorry. I'll see you back there."

"You sure?" She gave Campbell a puzzled glance.

"Yes," she said. Her friend hesitated a moment longer, took her sandwich and chips and crossed the restaurant to the other side.

When she was gone, I said, "You walked me back to the governor's office the other day, when I was up there."

"I—"

"So why the hell have you been following me?"

"YOU'VE MADE A MISTAKE," Campbell said, a moment later, her confidence returning, along with her color. "I don't know what you're talking about."

"Please. I rarely forget a face, and I never forget a pretty face, and you were also wearing the same earrings last night as the day I saw you upstairs. Answer the question."

"I don't have to."

I swiped at my phone, found the recently dialed number for the governor's office, showed it to her, and hit the green button. She waited. "Allen Ratliff, please," I said when the receptionist answered.

"All right, all right," Campbell said.

"All right, what? It's ringing."

"He wanted to see what you were up to."

I cut the connection, which had gone to voicemail anyway. "He who?"

"Allen," she said.

"Why?"

"I don't know. Something to do with Senator Tillman."

"Like what?"

"I don't know."

"Where'd you learn to drive like that?"

"Watching movies."

"Bullshit."

"My dad runs a defensive driving school, OK? I taught classes there in college."

"What's the name of the school?"

"Green Light Lessons."

I'd heard of it. In fact, I'd been there. Burke had paid for me to take a class early on in our professional relationship, figuring it would help me if I ever got into a jam behind the wheel.

I said, "What do you do for Hubbard?"

"Do?"

"What's your job?"

"Constituent services. Open mail, read e-mails, research state board appointments."

"Sounds thrilling."

"It's fine."

"But your real job is, what, doing what Ratliff tells you? Following people? You're a spy, basically."

She blushed deeply. I could tell I'd struck a nerve.

"You trailed me from my girlfriend's apartment, which I don't appreciate."

"I'm supposed to be thorough."

"What'd you say to Ratliff? After I made you last night?"

"I said I'd lost you someplace downtown."

"He believe you?"

"Does it matter?"

"Let's take a few steps back. I assume that was you who followed Hershey and me from the Clarmont?"

She shrugged, took a bite of her sandwich.

"How about the next night?"

"What about it?"

"Someone drugged me at a bar. Was that you?"

She blushed again. As she did, I took my phone and took a picture of her.

"Hey—"

"Hey nothing. Answer the question."

She shook her head.

"You're not serious."

"I don't have anything else to say to you."

"You know somebody died, right? Somebody I was supposed to be protecting, but couldn't because I was passed out in my van."

"Maybe you shouldn't have been at a bar."

"That's your response? It's my fault?"

"You're shouting," she said.

"I don't care."

I looked around. A few heads had turned in our direction.

"You need to answer my questions."

"You need to go to hell," she said, standing up and walking out.

She left her sandwich behind. And her girlfriend. And the remains of my patience.

I GOT UP, STARED DOWN THE PEOPLE WHO were staring at me, walked out of the restaurant, and started to follow Campbell. Whether I caught up with her or not, I was headed to the governor's office. It was time for the P-O-D and me to have a heart-to-heart. Something lacking in our relationship up to that point. I was in the Riffe lobby and headed for the escalator when my phone went off.

"Bonnie just called me," Richard Deckard said on the other line. "Grant Wardley's on his way over there, and he's really angry. What did you do?"

"I didn't do anything."

"That's for sure. Get off your ass and go help her."

"Now?"

"Yes now. I'm halfway to Dayton or I'd do it myself, like I should have done in the first place."

"I'm in the middle of something—"

"You recall our deal?"

"Yes, but—"

"It's off."

I WENT ANYWAY. THE screen door was closed when I arrived, still fuming—at Deckard, at Anna Campbell, at Ratliff, at everything—but the inside door was open. I could hear loud voices and barking. I drew closer, listening.

"—warned you, how many times," I heard Grant Wardley say.

Bonnie replied angrily, but she was crying too hard for me to make it out.

"Baseless accusations," Wardley said. "You don't know what you're talking about."

"—*ruining*," I heard Bonnie say, between sobs and shouts.

"Not in a position to negotiate anything," Wardley said. "Not after *that*. And would you shut that dog the fuck up?"

That brought more shouting from Bonnie. As I stood there, trying to decipher what was happening, it struck me that I was hearing only two voices. Was Troy not home?

"—last chance," Wardley said. "I've got no choice now."

More protests from Bonnie. Then, unexpectedly, Wardley spoke my name. I made out "meddling" and "trouble."

I had no idea what he was up to, or what he was capable of. I didn't really care that he was bringing my name into it—after all, that's what I'd intended by going back to his house over the weekend—but I didn't like the sound of "no choice." I opened the screen door and stepped into the living room.

Wardley and Bonnie were at the far end of the room, standing opposite one another, facing off. Greg was behind Wardley but turned and started barking at me as soon as I walked in. I was struck by how red Bonnie's face was. But what really drew my attention was the sight of Troy, lying on the couch in fetal position, staring at the TV, which was frozen on a screen shot involving zombies and soldiers. His eyes were open, but he wasn't moving. He looked not so much terrified as absolutely helpless. Paralyzed.

Wardley looked at me, startled. "What are you doing here?"

"What did you mean just now by 'no choice'?"

"Get out. I'm warning you," he said, pulling out his cell phone. "I could have you arrested."

It might have been his tone, which bugged me more than what felt like an idle threat, especially away from his home turf in the suburbs, but it was more likely the stricken glance Bonnie gave Troy at that moment as he lay in his strange paralysis. Without a word I strode across the room, grabbed Wardley's arm, yanked the phone out of his hand, and tucked it in my back pocket. He swung at me, landing a punch on my arm that might have done more damage had I not backed up quickly enough. I waited a moment, dipped my right shoulder and punched him hard in return, in the stomach. He gasped and bent double, and I punched him again. He staggered and I pushed him into the chair beside the TV. I leaned over, placed my hands on his shoulders, and said, "Last time. 'No choice.' Meaning what?"

"Fuck you."

"What's going on?" I said to Bonnie. "What's he talking about?"

"He's going to call the police. About Troy."

"Why?"

"He sold pot," she said, crying. "He shouldn't have. It's a probation violation. He found out." She nodded toward Wardley.

"Why'd he sell it?"

"Because we have no money," she said. "And we were out of food. And we're in debt from . . . from everything. We didn't know what else to do."

"Your dad?"

She shook her head. "We've already borrowed enough. And he'd kill me if he knew Troy sold pot in one of his houses."

"So now this guy's going to call the cops? That's why he's threatening you?"

"No," she said, the tears coming so hard now it was almost impossible to make out that simple word.

"What then?"

"He doesn't want us to tell."

"Tell what?"

"I didn't know," Bonnie said. "I didn't realize."

"Shut up!" Wardley shouted, which launched Greg into a new frenzy of barking. "Just shut up!"

I said, "If you say another word, I will personally drive you back to your house and bury you upside down in your beautiful lawn."

Then, to Bonnie, I said, "Tell what?"

"Tell what happened," she said. "To Derrick."

"Something happened to Derrick?" I said, confused.

"To Derrick, and to Troy."

"What are you talking about?"

"Troy finally told me last night," Bonnie said. "I promised I'd get rid of you"—she jabbed her finger in my direction—"if he'd tell me what was going on."

"Glad I could finally be of some help. But what—"

"Shut *up*," Wardley said. I whirled around and without a word slapped him hard. He gasped, but at least he went quiet.

"His brother," Bonnie sobbed. "The boys' uncle. Skip. Their *uncle*. And now he won't do anything about it." She gestured at Wardley. "Won't let us say anything. Says he'll call the cops about Troy's dealing."

"Did what?" I said. "What boys?"

"He raped them," she said. "Skip did. Derrick, and Troy. Over and over again. They were just kids. That's why Derrick did what he did." A pause as she drew a breath. "That's why."

She stood there for a moment, swaying. A soft moan came from the couch. I looked and saw that Troy was shaking, gasping for breath, like a feverish flu patient lapsing into a seizure. Bonnie rushed over and threw herself on him, trying to get him to breathe. I left Wardley in the chair and moved in their direction. Greg barked and barked.

Skip Wardley. Living with his nephews, right after college. Under his brother's nose, committing the most awful crimes imaginable. And now, years later, the act coming back to haunt him with Derrick's own deviance. And only Grant's lies could keep him out of it. *Fighting for Your Future*, indeed.

I heard a sound and turned, but it was too late. The screen door opened and slammed shut, and as I went and looked outside I saw Grant Wardley running toward his car. I yelled at him. He turned. I threw his phone at him. He caught it, then dropped it. He swore at me. I waved.

45

I CALLED DECKARD FROM BONNIE'S PORCH and told him what had happened. The phone was quiet for so long I thought he'd hung up. Finally, he said, "Why was Wardley over there?"

I explained about my visits to Bridgeport and the e-mail I'd sent Skip the day before. Another long silence. "So you *were* trying to help her," he said.

"As best I could."

"I'm sorry I lost my temper earlier. I was scared."

"Don't apologize."

I went back inside to wait with Troy and Bonnie until her father arrived. I noticed Troy was holding her hand for the first time since I'd met them. And there was something different about his face. As if a tensed muscle had finally been relaxed. Greg curled up beside them on the couch. No one said much.

My lunch with Anna Campbell seemed as if it had happened days or even weeks ago. Any urge I had to confront Ratliff was gone. I was exhausted. It had been a long weekend; a long couple of weeks. I spoke briefly to Deckard when he got there, then went outside and climbed into my van. I texted Anne, drove home, grabbed Hopalong and his leash, and started walking. I'm not sure I could tell you how long I was gone. All I remembered after getting back was opening a can of Black Label, sitting down on the couch, and checking my phone. The first thing I saw was the five-minute-old Channel 7 news alert:

Bridgeport mayor found dead in apparent suicide

I WAS UP EARLY Tuesday morning, but instead of running I made coffee, found *The Sparrow*, and read for almost an hour. Finally, when I couldn't take Hopalong's whimpering any longer, I walked him down to Schiller, over to the Umbrella Girl fountain, waited while he watered several flower beds, and walked home. It would have to do. On a whim I opened a box of corn muffin mix and did some baking. I brewed coffee and read for a while longer. I ate four muffins. Sometime between nine thirty and ten I called Grant Hospital and got an update on Ephraim Badger's condition. No change. After that I called the governor's office and asked for Ratliff, but he wasn't in yet. I asked for Lily Gleason: same answer.

I wasn't sure what to do next. I knew I had to follow up on my conversation with Anna Campbell somehow. That reminded me I didn't need Jay Scott's help on the license plate anymore, and I should call and pull him off the job, paying him whatever he asked for his troubles. For lack of anything else to do, I looked up *Cumulonimbus Cloud Storage* and tried a variety of user names and passwords, seeing if I could access Hershey's notes, to no avail. Frustrated, I even typed in "I'm A Fucking Asshole" before I gave up for good. Fortunately—at least I thought so then—an incoming phone call distracted me. It was Burke.

"This certainly changes everything," he said.

"What does?"

"Allen Ratliff."

"What about him? I just left him a message."

A pause. "Where are you?"

"At home."

"You might want to check the news."

"Why?"

"Ratliff's dead."

"What? How?"

"Apparently he was strangled with his own bow tie. In the Rutherford B. Hayes hearing room at the Statehouse."

46

THIRTY MINUTES LATER I WAS IN BURKE'S
office as we compared notes.

"I hate to say this," I said. "But this has to be good news for
Tillman."

Burke nodded with a frown. "I've already talked to the
prosecutor. He wouldn't say it outright, but I know he's leaning
in that direction."

"Even with the binder in the Dumpster?"

"It's still a problem. But he concedes it's a little too convenient. Who dumps a murder weapon across the parking lot from
his own motel room? Even a state senator's not that stupid."

"So what was it doing there?"

"Maybe the real murderer ditched it to cast suspicion on
Tillman."

"What are you hearing about Ratliff?"

"News is saying it must have happened late last night. He
never came home from the office. His wife went to bed, assuming he was working late. Happened a lot."

"Wonder what the commodore would tell us."

"Who?"

"Never mind. Hang on." I dialed Hummel's number. To my surprise he answered on the first ring.

"This is not a good time."

"I know. Listen." I told him what I'd learned from the deposition about Lily Gleason and her affair, and then about Anna Campbell following Hershey on Ratliff's orders.

"Nice of you to tell me this now."

"I've been a little distracted."

"I can imagine. I heard you were stalking the Speaker of the House in your free time."

"Word gets around. Any leads on Ratliff?"

"Like I'd tell you."

"Like I just told you about Ratliff having Hershey followed."

A pause. "No leads," he said. "But maybe a question you can answer."

"OK."

"Do you remember Hershey using a key card to get into the Statehouse?"

I thought back to the night of our Cupola expedition. "Sure. An entrance from the parking garage. Why?"

"Hershey came into the Statehouse last night around the same time Ratliff did."

"What are you talking about?"

"I don't mean him, obviously. But the system registered Hershey's key card being used."

"Which means—"

"Which means there's a good chance that whoever killed Hershey took his card and used it to sneak their way in to meet Ratliff."

47

IF HERSHEY'S DEATH SENT A SHOCK WAVE across Capitol Square, the murder of the governor's chief of staff was no less than a small thermonuclear weapon going off. Several stations were streaming live coverage from outside the Statehouse, and my phone was buzzing like a bee in a jelly jar from the nonstop news alerts. It was hardly the publicity that Hubbard, the potential veep candidate, was looking for, and there were rumors streaking across websites that Rodriguez might cancel her rally. I thought about calling Regan at party headquarters for confirmation. It would have been almost worth it.

In light of Ratliff's death, Burke told me in no uncertain terms to finish my interviews with the Clarmont suspects and get the notes to him quickly. I tried Lauren Atkinson at the teachers' union, thinking that our tense meeting in the committee hearing room hardly qualified as questioning. After her, the last person on my list was Sam Michaels at the Education Department, the third person after Ratliff and Gleason at the table of governor's staff people at the Clarmont that night. He was one guy I still hadn't talked to. I tried calling, but the defenses of the department's voicemail system were so powerful I couldn't even find a way to leave a message and finally gave up. I'd do it the old-fashioned way: in person.

When I arrived inside the Education Department lobby I told the guard sitting behind a central reception desk I was there to see Michaels. She took my driver's license and pushed a clipboard toward me to sign in. I scanned the names on the lines above. One, from an hour earlier, caught my attention. *Jack Sterling*, the casinos lobbyist. He'd come by at ten forty-five. Not long after the news of Ratliff's death had become public.

"He says he's busy at the moment," the guard reported, putting the phone receiver down on her desk. "He also says you don't have an appointment."

"It's about Jack Sterling. Tell him that."

"Who?"

I repeated the lobbyist's name. She frowned, and relayed the message. "He'll be right down," she said a moment later.

"What's this about?" Michaels said when he emerged from an elevator across the room.

"You remember me? We met at the Clarmont."

"Yes. Why are you here?"

"You're on my list of people to talk to who were at the restaurant that night. The night Senator Tillman threatened Lee Hershey."

"I don't know anything about that."

"Just a few questions."

"I really don't have time."

"Question one: Why was Jack Sterling here to see you just now?"

Michaels looked startled. I glanced at the security desk. The guard had taken a sudden interest in our conversation. A few minutes later we were upstairs in a windowless office beside a warren of cubicles. Michaels's Triple F binder was open on his desk, next to a picture of what looked like his family. Even in the photo, he seemed to have a hard time smiling.

"How do you know Sterling was here?" Michaels said, exuding hostility.

I explained about the clipboard. I repeated my question.

"It's none of your business."

"I wouldn't be so sure about that. Seems funny anybody would be taking meetings today, after the governor's chief of staff was found dead."

"What are you implying?"

I glanced at the open binder. On the left-hand side, the word "casinos" was circled in red.

I said, "You're working the casino revenue angle for the department?"

"That's one aspect of many I'm involved in."

"Was that what Sterling was here for? Negotiations?"

"I really can't say."

"Why not?"

"Because I don't have to."

"OK. Did you kill Lee Hershey?"

"What?"

Having gotten his attention, I repeated my questions about the night of Lee's death. The responses were predictable. No, he hadn't planned to meet him. No, he didn't know who might have. Yes, Hershey had been hard on the school-funding bill.

"Can Senator Kinser get the bill passed in time?" I said.

"I don't know. I certainly hope so."

"Are the casinos going to lose money?"

"No comment."

"So that's a yes?"

"The bill is still in flux. Even more so, after—"

"After Ratliff."

"That's right."

"Terrible, the impact murder can have on legislation."

"That's not what I meant."

"It's OK. It's what *I* meant."

48

"THE HELL," STERLING SAID A FEW MINUTES later when I got him on the phone. "How do you know that?"

"I have eyes and ears all over the city," I said. "Gets kind of messy sometimes. So why the meeting with Michaels?"

"It's none of your business."

"Funny—that's what Michaels said. But it seems odd, going there right after word about Ratliff. You have heard, right?"

"Yes."

"An opportunistic moment? His death gives your clients some kind of weird leverage?"

"Don't be a jackass."

"What then?"

"Like I'm going to tell you."

"You can tell me or tell the patrol."

He told me to perform an anatomically impossible act and hung up. I wasn't sure I blamed him. But I also wasn't satisfied with either his or Michaels's responses.

Bonnie called as I was getting back in my van to go home.

"I just wanted to thank you."

"You're welcome. I'm sorry it unfolded like it did. How's Troy doing?"

"He's OK. Good, actually. He's agreed to see someone. Like a shrink, I mean. That's a big deal, for him."

"Good to hear. How about you?"

"Me?"

"Yes. How are you?"

"Not great. I lost my job."

"What?"

"I called off work yesterday, after everything. I forgot I had a big printing project to finish. I'd already missed a lot of time trying to help Troy. Honestly, I don't blame them."

"Would it help if I talked to someone?"

"I don't think so."

"What are you going to do?"

"I'm not really sure. We'll figure something out. My dad said he'd help."

Something occurred to me. "Your side business. You do some kind of online research?"

"Mainly I build websites. But sometimes I do genealogical stuff for people. Or they pay me to locate an old girlfriend they can't find on Facebook. That kind of thing."

"How'd you pick that up?"

"Always liked computers. I was in IT for a while before, you know, everything."

"Your fraud charges?"

"I bounced some checks trying to make ends meet," she said defensively.

"So. Your ex-girlfriend hunting. Are you any good?"

"I'm nine for nine."

"Impressive. I'm in need of a little research myself. As a paying customer. Any chance I could get you to tackle it?"

"Ex-girlfriend?"

"No. I need you to look up some information on a couple people."

"Sure, I guess. But you don't have to pay me. You've already done a lot."

"I'll be the judge of that." I gave her Sam Michaels's and Jack Sterling's names.

"What am I looking for?"

"I'm not sure. Michaels works for the Education Department and Sterling's a lobbyist. They're connected through the school-funding bill and money the state gets from casinos. Anything along those lines."

"How soon do you need it?"

"Soon would be good."

"Soon it is."

MY PHONE RANG ALMOST as soon as I hung up. At this rate I was never going to get home. A chipper-sounding woman identified herself as Lauren Atkinson's executive assistant.

"You were trying to reach Lauren?"

I acknowledged it.

"It's going to be hard to get her. She's back home for a couple of days. Reception's terrible down there, of course."

"Of course. Where's that?"

"Southern Ohio. Cute little town. Ever been?"

"Been?"

"Paw Paw Bottoms."

I paused. "She's from Paw Paw Bottoms?"

"She sure is," the woman said. "You can imagine the jokes."

"I'm starting to wish I could," I said.

"WHERE?" BONNIE SAID, WHEN I called her back a minute later.

"You heard me."

"That's not a real place," she said with a giggle.

"'Fraid so." I gave her Justice Bryan's and Lauren Atkinson's names. "Add these to the list. They're the only two people I know from that town, which seems like a really big coincidence.

See what you can find out about them, and about the town. And Bonnie?"

"Yeah?"

"See if there's any jokes about the place."

I hung up and immediately called Bryan's chambers. He wasn't in, his secretary explained.

"Do you know when he's coming back?"

She laughed. "Depends on the pigs."

"The pigs?"

"He's home tending the flock. Left last night. We don't hear much from him when he's out in the barns."

"Thanks. It's droves, by the way."

"What was that?"

"Pigs hang out in droves, not flocks."

"Thank you," she said curtly, and hung up.

"READY?" BONNIE SAID WHEN she called back an hour later.

"Shoot."

"Why were Ma and Pa late for church on their wedding anniversary?"

"I don't know."

"They couldn't find Paw Paw's Bottoms."

"That's not really funny."

"I didn't say it was. Most of the jokes aren't. That's about the cleanest I could find, but even the dirtier ones are dumb."

"Anything on the town?"

"Not a whole lot. It was named for the state fruit, obviously. It's in a kind of low-lying valley, so that's the Bottoms. It used to have a railroad and an iron-ore furnace and even an opera house, but that's all long gone. That judge and that lady are definitely the most famous people from there."

"That's it?"

"More or less. A sheriff's deputy was shot to death there last year, trying to save some woman in a domestic dispute. He was the first police officer killed in the line of duty in the county, so it was kind of a big deal."

"It's not much."

"It's not much of a town."

"Let me know what you find on the other two. Michaels and Sterling."

"Will do."

I was about to hang up when I said, "The deputy who was killed. Who was he?"

"Hang on." She was back a minute later. "His name was Frank Washington."

I made her repeat the name. Frank Washington. I had seen that name before. It took me another minute before it came to me. The handwritten name on Lauren Atkinson's Triple F binder the day I sat beside the union president in the hearing room. Like a name on a middle-school folder, absent the hearts and smiley faces.

"You're sure."

"Yes. Why?"

"I don't know yet. Was there any connection between Atkinson and this deputy?"

"Not that I found."

"OK," I said thoughtfully. "If I find out anything more, I'll let you know."

49

I SAT BACK ON THE COUCH, TRYING TO process everything. My mind was beginning to reel with the web of connections I was stumbling across. Not the official connections, the everyday links that constituted the working world, especially in a place like the Statehouse. But the unofficial ones, the strands of relationships that stretched invisibly from one person to another, undetectable by outsiders. Invisible, but powerful and perhaps deadly.

I thought about the late Prince of Dorkness. Something came back to me, from the night at the Clarmont. I called Kerri MacKenzie's cell phone. She picked up almost right away.

"The rumor you mentioned, that day we had coffee. About the governor and an affair. Could Allen Ratliff have known about that?"

"He might have known there was a rumor. Why?"

"You should tell the patrol."

"Why?"

"I don't know. Maybe he knew more than he should have. People have been killed for less."

"I'll think about it."

"That's probably not—"

"I said, I'll think about it."

"OK, fine. So what's the situation like over there? At the Statehouse?"

"I wouldn't know. I'm in the Riffe Center. They kicked us out of our offices and set up desks for us over here."

I thanked her for her time and was about to hang up when she interrupted.

"Listen. I'm sorry I was short. About calling the patrol. I'll do it. But there's something else."

"What?"

"It's about the night Lee died. I was going to tell you. I know I should tell the police."

"What is it?"

"All I know is what I saw."

"Which was?"

"I'd been working late that night. The night that Lee . . . Anyway, I had just come out of my office to leave. That's when I saw her."

"Who?"

"Liz Brantley."

"Where?"

"She was crossing the Atrium. I assume she'd been in the pressroom."

"OK. What about her?"

"She was crying. Kind of hard."

"Crying?"

"Like she'd just gotten some really bad news. I stopped to, you know, see if she was OK, wanted to talk. But she just waved me off and disappeared."

BRANTLEY WASN'T ANSWERING HER phone. I considered stopping by her house, but thought better of it immediately. She might be downtown, but I wasn't ready to brave the jam of reporters around the Statehouse, which was back in lockdown mode. Instead, I stayed put and tried outlining a list of suspects, drawing lines between them, seeing if I could illuminate the invisible strands. I was still at it, getting nowhere, when Bonnie called me back about Michaels and Sterling.

"That was harder than I thought it would be."

"Meaning?"

"I found the basics on Sam Michaels. He's been at the Education Department for ten years, was a school superintendent before that. He's married and has kids and lives in the suburbs and goes to some megachurch and loves the Buckeyes. He sounds like most of my relatives. But this Sterling guy? The lobbyist?"

"What about him?"

"The main thing is, he's broke."

"Broke?"

"He's got a bunch of tax liens filed against him. Plus a bankruptcy case in federal court."

"How much are we talking?"

"Taxes, something around $13,000. That's just federal. About half that again in state court."

I thought about this. It didn't square with the well-dressed lobbyist I'd sat at the Thurber Bar with. "Does the bankruptcy filing give any details?"

"A few," she said.

"Like what?"

She told me.

"That's ugly," I said when she was finished.

"Yeah. But here's the thing."

"Yes?"

"That's only one filing. There's more. I'm not even close to finding everything."

RATLIFF'S MURDER HAD KNOCKED my meeting with Anna Campbell out of my head. But now I realized I had another errand to run. A few minutes later I was parking outside the Church of the Holy Apostolic Firewater. As I got out of the van, I noticed a man and a woman in black clerical garb leaving the building. They were frowning. I nodded as I walked past. They nodded back, preoccupied.

"Hey, QB," Theresa Sullivan said when I walked inside.

"Yeah?"

"Know what has a hundred teeth and eats wieners?"

I shook my head.

"A zipper." She cackled. I smiled.

Roy was studying a pan of steaming food atop his restaurant-grade stove in the kitchen. He looked up as I entered.

"You know the story of the loaves and fishes?" he said.

"What about it?"

"Too bad it doesn't apply to baked chicken. What are you doing here?"

"Wanted to show you something." I pulled out my phone and scrolled to the picture of Campbell I'd taken in the sandwich shop.

"Recognize her?"

He studied the photo. "No. Should I?"

"Swap the black hair for blond. Add a baseball cap."

He looked again. "It's the girl from the bar."

"You sure?"

"I'd recognize that pout anywhere. Where'd you get this?"

I explained about her escorting me into the governor's office and my busting her as my tail and our subsequent meeting downtown.

"She said she wasn't involved in drugging you?"

"Not quite. She wouldn't answer the question."

"So what can I do?"

"Nothing, at this point. ID-ing her helps a lot." I stood up to go. I gestured outside. "The couple bearing a strong resemblance to Morticia and Gomez Addams, except with those white tongue-depressor things around their necks, walking out just now as I pulled up."

"They're called clerical collars. What about them?"

"Who were they?"

"If you must know, they're members of an ancient, secretive society trying to change the world for the better."

"Masons?"

"Much worse. Episcopalians."

"WHAT NOW?" STERLING SAID when I called him a few minutes later from the van.

"We need to talk."

"It's not a good time."

I explained the topic. He changed his mind. We agreed to meet back at his favorite watering hole at seven. He was already there when I arrived. I set down a couple of pieces of paper in front of him, and signaled for a beer.

"You've got thousands of dollars in gambling debts," I said.

He picked up the papers, glanced at them, crumpled them up and threw them back at me. He took a drink. He said, "Whaddya know about that."

"So what's going on?"

"Like it's any of your business."

"My business is whatever might have gotten Lee Hershey killed. Did he know about this?"

"I have no idea."

"You sure?"

"I was told he might be informed at some point soon."

"Told by who?"

He shook his head and went back to his drink. But even I could figure this one out.

"Sam Michaels was going to tell him."

"I'm not saying—"

"Michaels knew about your debts, didn't he? That they involved gambling at the casinos you're supposed to represent."

"Sam Michaels is a self-righteous prick."

"Even self-righteous pricks know how to hit people when they're down. Was he threatening you? How'd it work? He'd expose your debts unless you backed off changing the casinos' revenue percentage in Triple F?"

"You think you're so clever," he said.

"I don't think anything. You've got an addiction, which you can get help for. But in the meantime you're between a rock and a hard place. That why you did it?"

"Did what?"

"Tap Hershey on the noggin? Save your skin? Keep him from revealing your big, bad secret?"

"For Chrissake."

"Problem is, you don't have an alibi, do you? 'Drinks with a client?' What client?"

"I can't tell you."

"Really? You've got a prime motive for killing Hershey. You want to offer an alternative, you better do it fast. Otherwise, I have to go to the patrol."

"I'm fucked if I tell you."

"You're fucked if you don't."

He took a deep breath. "You want to know where I was the night Lee was killed?"

I waited.

"I was gambling at Scioto Downs south of town. At the racino. Playing the slots. Trying to win enough to make a dent in what I owe to get this monkey off my back once and for all."

"And?"

"And now I owe even more."

"So why can't you just admit that?"

He stared at me. "Are you stupid? I work for the *casinos*. It's my job to protect their assets. They find out I'm gambling with money I owe them at one of their direct competitors? No shovel big enough to get me out of *that* shit storm."

50

THE STATEHOUSE REOPENED THE NEXT morning, with so many troopers patrolling the halls it looked like a radar gun convention had come to town. After parking on the lowest garage level, I walked through the Crypt, passed two separate security gauntlets, and finally made it to the desk where the tours met.

"Any word on Mr. Badger?" I said to the woman sitting there, after introducing myself and giving her my card.

"Nothing new," she said, sadly.

"He wasn't here, that night. The night the reporter was killed."

"I couldn't say. He kept . . . unusual hours."

"No, I know he wasn't. He was at church. But did he work that day?"

"I'm not sure."

"Is there any way to check?"

"It might be written down. Why?"

"I don't know. It might be helpful to know."

"Well . . ."

I didn't respond. A moment later, after glancing around the room, she flipped back through the visitors' book.

"He did give a couple tours that day. Eleven o'clock and two."

"Was that normal?"

"Pretty much. We get more people in April and May, with the schoolchildren and all. It tapers off a bit after Memorial Day."

"OK."

"Oh, and he also did the Cupola, it looks like."

"I'm sorry?"

"He gave a tour of the Cupola. It's a special thing, doesn't happen very often. You go up to the top of the Statehouse. It's kind of fun. You should try it."

"I'm a little afraid of heights. So what time was that?"

"Around noon."

"Right," I said, disappointed. Hours before Hershey was killed. I had another thought. "Does it say who went up there?"

She shook her head. "We don't take names like that. It's usually a lot of people."

"So there's no way to know who was on that particular tour?"

She shook her head again. A moment later, her expression changed. "Come to think of it. Everyone who goes up has to sign a waiver. Just a standard thing, but it's required because the steps are so steep."

"Where are those kept? Those forms?"

"In the office."

"Do you have access to those?"

"Not at all," she said, firmly.

After thanking her for her time, I strolled to the Statehouse office at the other end of the Crypt, where I presented my card and my question to the woman at the front desk. She frowned and walked into the back. A minute later a second woman appeared and I repeated my question.

"That's not possible," she said.

"Are you sure? I think those would be considered a public record."

"I don't know—"

"And since my office represents Senator Tillman, I could get a subpoena."

That touch of prevarication led to another disappearance into the back, and a passage of several minutes during which I checked my phone and saw that a new set of poll numbers had just popped up. They showed Senator JoAnn Rodriguez trailing President Ryan by less than 4 percentage points nationally. In Ohio the gap was 2 percent. Adding Hubbard to the ticket—even with everything that had happened—made it a dead heat in the state. Swapping Hubbard for the governor of Pennsylvania as her running mate dropped Rodriguez six points below Ryan in Ohio. Rodriguez was going to need the state, no question about it. And her campaign was acknowledging it, as my favorite staffer, Regan, was telling several news outlets in so many words. The rally was still on.

"Sir?"

I looked up to see a third woman behind the counter. She was wearing a nineteenth-century period formal dress and a hat stacked with multicolored, hand-sewn flowers.

"Forgive my appearance," she said. "We have a reenactment lunch later today."

"You're portraying—"

"Helen Herron Taft. William Howard Taft's wife."

"Ah yes. I've always admired you, ah, her."

She smiled. "She had remarkable political savvy for a woman of her age."

"Actually, it's because she opposed Prohibition. I appreciate a first lady who could hold her alcohol."

"Yes," she said, her smile fading. "In any case, we can't comply with your request."

"As I explained a moment ago—"

"We can't comply," she said, cutting me off, "because we don't have the forms. Someone's taken them."

"FORMS?" LIEUTENANT HUMMEL SAID a few minutes later when I roused him from the temporary office they'd set up for him in the back. We stood just to the left of the groin vault while I made my case.

"Permission forms, to go up to the top of the Cupola. Ephraim Badger collected them for a tour he gave the day Hershey was killed. They should be in the Statehouse office. But they're missing."

"So?"

"So is it possible Badger took them, and that's what someone was looking for, at his house?"

"Why would he take them?"

"I don't know."

"It's a possibility," he conceded. "The only things definitively gone were the gun and his keys."

"His keys?"

He nodded. "They're nowhere."

"Nothing else?"

"Not that we can find. Well, your business card too."

"My card?"

"Didn't you say you left one at his door?"

"Yeah."

"We can't find it. And believe me, we, or should I say, Columbus PD, looked hard."

"So the permission forms to the Cupola are missing, along with Badger's keys, which I'm guessing would include a key up there."

"That's right. What's your point?"

"Maybe there's some connection to the Cupola and what happened to Lee?" I reminded him of Gleason's confession in her deposition.

"We've talked to her," Hummel said. "We're satisfied she wasn't involved in Hershey's death. Or her ex-husband. They may end up killing each other, but that's a different story."

"OK. But maybe it's still worth checking on those forms."

Hummel frowned, and for a moment I was on Lake Erie two hundred years earlier, and things weren't going well. Without a word, he gestured for me to follow. We walked back into the interior warren of patrol offices. I sat in his hideaway while he made a couple of calls. A minute later, he abruptly stood up, warned me not to go anywhere, and walked out.

I stayed seated. But as one minute dragged into two, I found myself glancing at the papers across his desk. At the far edge, closest to his chair, I noticed one with familiar words on the top, even if I was reading them upside down. *Cumulonimbus Cloud Storage*. I shifted around in my chair, looked at the open office door. Listened. Then turned back around, slowly stood up, leaned over and peered down at the paper. It was a subpoena for Hershey's cloud storage account. Halfway down the paper I saw his e-mail, followed by a word in bold print. I studied both for nearly a minute. I did not come by my skill at reading upside down proudly, but it had gotten me through high school French in a tiny classroom at Quarry Chapel High near Homer, and that was something. *C'est la vie.* I sat, took out a notebook and a pen, and wrote down the e-mail and password. I tucked the notebook back into my pocket. A minute later, Hummel reentered the office.

"I checked with Columbus PD. You were right about the permission forms. We overlooked them the first time."

"So that's something."

"Not really. They're not missing. They were at Badger's house in plain view."

I thought about this. "Could someone have taken just one?"

"What do you mean?"

"Taken just a single form. How would anyone know?"

"I suppose they wouldn't. But why take just one?"

"Maybe someone on the tour that day didn't want anyone to know it."

"Like who?"

"I don't know," I said, trying to hide my exasperation. "Maybe the person who killed Hershey?"

51

AS SOON AS I WAS SAFELY OUT OF THE
Statehouse with the purloined log-in info and back home, I called
up the cloud storage site, heart racing a bit in anticipation, and
entered Hershey's e-mail and password. To my disappointment,
I was informed that a text would be sent to a cell phone with a
unique code as soon as I verified the phone number. I had the
number, of course, but Hummel had the phone.

"It's two-step verification," Bonnie said, when I called her a
minute later.

"Sounds like a country-western dance."

"What do you mean?"

"Never mind. What is it, exactly?"

"Added security, especially if you're one of those people
whose passwords are 1-2-3-4. That's not you, is it?"

"I'll get back to you on that. So is there any way around
this thing?"

"Maybe. Do you have his phone?"

I explained the problem.

"Send me the number," she said. "I'll see what I can do."

AFTER I HUNG UP with Bonnie I tried Bryan's chambers again and was surprised when he came on the line a few moments later.

"Good visit home?" I said.

"Tiring. Had to move the Tamworths to a new pasture."

"I can imagine. Lauren Atkinson happen to give you a hand, by any chance?"

Silence.

"I heard she was down there as well," I continued. "Guessing you might have seen her. Can't be that big a place."

"What do you want?"

"Just a few more questions answered."

After a long pause, he said, "I'll pick you up."

A few minutes later, a black Lexus with JUSTICE1 plates pulled in front of my house. I got in. Bryan glanced at me, watched as I buckled up, and pulled away. He went to the corner, turned right, and turned right again onto Third.

I told him the joke Bonnie had relayed to me.

He said, "Have you heard the one about the farmer's daughter and the jar of paw paw preserves?"

I shook my head. "I hope it's funnier than the one I told."

"You'd hope wrong." He headed north on Third, through German Village, past Katzinger's Deli, and followed the curve of the street around to the right and merged onto Fourth.

I said, "This whole time, I thought Lauren Atkinson was from the South, like Georgia or Texas. But it's the Appalachia in both of you I was hearing. Southern 'A-hi-ah.' Isn't that right?"

Bryan drove without speaking. He took Fourth into downtown, crossed Broad, and turned left on Spring.

Finally, unable to take the silence, I said, "Seems a coincidence you were both back home in one of the smallest communities in Ohio on the same day."

"Things happen."

"Like what?"

"Things."

"No offense, Justice, but we're past the point of obfuscation. 'Things' isn't going to cut it anymore."

We were in the Arena District. He took a right on Neil. "I might need your help," he said.

"With what?"

"Talking to Atkinson."

"About what?"

"A video."

"What kind of video?"

He didn't reply. We passed Clippers Stadium and then Lifestyle Pavilion, where people were already lining up for some kind of concert. We hung a left at Goodale, and a minute later, as we passed the White Castle headquarters, I repeated the question.

Bryan sighed heavily. I thought of that Civil War general, a Union officer emerging from the tent, getting news that Confederate forces were much stronger than originally anticipated.

"The video she's blackmailing me with," he said.

HE TURNED ONTO THE 315 expressway and merged into traffic, passing the Ohio State medical complex on the right.

"It was three years ago," Bryan said. "I'd had too much to drink. Shouldn't have been on the road. I was almost home when he pulled me over. Frank Washington. First black sheriff's deputy in the county. I said some unfortunate things to him. Very unfortunate."

I nodded but kept quiet.

"Unlike me, Deputy Washington was a gentleman. He drove me home instead of arresting me. A mistake on his part, especially after the way I treated him."

"A forgiving soul."

"Perhaps. Or perhaps, given his position in the community, he was terrified of the drunken threats I'd made."

Bryan briefly glanced at me before continuing.

"Washington was killed last year in a shootout with a man holding his family hostage in a trailer up a country hollow. He died saving the wife and kids. I'd apologized to him multiple times by then. There was no one sorrier than me when I heard what happened. That's why it came as such a shock."

"What did?"

"That he kept a copy of the dash cam video he told me he was going to erase, as a courtesy. I'm not sure why. Protection, maybe, down the road? Hard to blame him."

I didn't say anything.

"His widow came across it afterward. After his death. It's a small community. Lauren is well known. It ended up in her hands."

"Because she was the teachers' union president?"

He shrugged. "It's hard to think of a different reason. Some people in Paw Paw Bottoms consider me a traitor for voting against the last two school-funding plans. It would make sense it got to her."

In the distance, on our right, sat Jesse Owens Stadium. We passed the Ackerman exit. The speed limit changed to sixty-five.

The justice said, "Lauren approached me. Let me watch it. Let me know she had copies."

"And?"

"Told me she had no interest in dredging up bad memories."

"Good of her."

"Yes," he said, pursing his lips. "Unless."

"Unless?"

"Unless, down the road, I should see fit to once again rule school funding unconstitutional. If that happened . . ."

We drove in silence for a while.

"As you know," he said, "I have a tough election ahead of me."

"Judge O'Malley," I said. "I remember. Did Lee know about the video?"

"He'd heard rumors of it, from what I was told. But Lauren had the only copies. And she wasn't parting with them. Unless."

"Unless," I said.

Strands of relationships, stretching invisibly from person to person. Unseen, but powerful. And deadly.

Bryan exited a few minutes later at Henderson, turned left, and headed back south on the highway to my house, where he dropped me off. We didn't speak the rest of the trip.

52

I CHECKED IN WITH BONNIE, WHO SAID distractedly that she was making progress but couldn't talk right at the moment. I thanked her, pushed the dog in and out of the backyard, got in my van and headed north. It was a custody night, and I wasn't in the mood to blow it. I picked up Joe at Crystal's house, headed further north to pick up Mike, then drove back to Anne's apartment, where we had pizza and watched a movie with the boys and Amelia. When it was over I refereed a Hulk vs. the Thing debate between the kids (Hulk, hands down), helped clean up the kitchen, and agreed to take an overflowing box of recyclables—mainly newspapers left over from packing—home to my half-empty bin. Mike and Joe had a YMCA camp the next morning, and so I delivered them to their respective houses by ten.

On the way back to German Village I considered the connections I'd uncovered so far. Lee Hershey's affair with a state senator he then betrayed to break a big story. Sam Michaels using a lobbyist's gambling debts to squeeze him for budget concessions. Lauren Atkinson's willingness to blackmail a Supreme Court justice to ensure the success of Triple F. All this, and yet I was no closer to figuring out which if any of them might have actually killed Lee.

I parked in front of my house, sighed at the circles I was going in, unbuckled, pulled the keys out of the ignition, and opened the door. I was about to get out when I heard my phone buzz. I looked down, expecting another news alert. Instead, a message from Roy.

You ever find out what they put in your beer?

A typical, out-of-the-blue text from the always working, always thinking pastor. Distractedly, I picked up the phone and started typing. Autocorrect was going to have a field day. **Benzo—,** I wrote, when I simultaneously heard a crack like a branch breaking under the weight of snow in winter and saw my windshield spiderweb in front of me.

I ducked low, opened the door, and slid out just before the second shot shattered the windshield and sent glass spraying onto my unprotected face and hands. As I scrambled around to the rear, I thought of the baseball bat I keep in the van for protection. Considered idly whether it had ever once helped me.

Before I could answer myself, a third shot took off the driver's side rearview mirror. I froze, gauging whether I should run down the street to the potential cover of the next car, fifty feet away, or stay put and wait for whoever was hunting me to get closer. I wanted to know who it was. A second passed, then three, then half a minute. A fourth shot didn't follow. I heard someone shout, and a moment later caught the sound of sirens in the distance.

"YOU SURE YOU DIDN'T see who it was?" Hummel said to me as we sat at my kitchen table, each with a mug of coffee in front of us. Roy was leaning against the counter holding his own cup. He'd arrived as soon as he heard. I hadn't told Anne yet.

I shook my head. "One minute I was texting, the next . . ."

Henry Fielding, sitting at the far end of the table, squinched and then unsquinched his face several times. "First time a gun's been involved," he said.

"Involved in what?" I said.

"Hershey was bludgeoned with a Triple F binder," Hummel interjected. "Ratliff was strangled. Badger was beaten over the head by the C volume of *Encyclopedia Britannica*. If it's the same person . . ."

"Guy walking his dog found a couple shell casings up the street," Fielding said. "Once we get a serial number for Badger's gun, we can see if they match. They do, whoever's doing this, he's upped his game."

"Or she," I said.

"Makes you wonder why you were targeted," Fielding said, ignoring me. "Besides the fact nobody in town likes you."

"I'm thinking about the business card you left at Badger's house," Hummel said. "Guy breaks in, sees it, realizes you're sniffing around. Then suddenly he's got a gun."

"So now I'm the target," I said.

"Looks that way," Hummel said.

Despite my protests, Roy insisted on spending the night, along with the Beretta he'd brought back from Iraq, which from time to time came in useful—merely as a warning device, he assured me—on rough nights at the mission. After Hummel and Fielding had gone, we went back outside with some cardboard and duct tape and covered the shattered windshield.

"You're pretty rough on your vans," Roy said.

"Somebody torched the last one. Totally different."

"If you say so."

When we were done, I opened the Odyssey's back door and pulled out the newspapers from Anne's apartment. While Roy grabbed a couple of beers from my refrigerator, grousing about my swill, I went around back and dumped the stuff into the blue city recycling bin. I was about to close the lid when I glanced down at the picture on the paper facing upward. It was Sunday's front page from two weeks ago, with a photo of the hearing room where the school-funding debate had resumed in that rare weekend session. I pulled the paper out to read the article, and that's when I glanced a second time at the photo. You almost couldn't see it. The picture was taken before the committee got under way, and showed senators Ed Tillman and Ottie Kinser deep in conversation, just the two of them, seated at the raised bench at the front of the room. To the right, slightly out of focus, but with Tillman's hand resting on the edge, was a thick Triple F binder.

"WHAT IT MEANS," I said to Burke a few minutes later, once he calmed down after being called so late, "is that it couldn't have been used to kill Hershey. Not if it was still sitting there almost thirty-six hours after he died."

"You're sure?"

"I'll bring the photo over, unless you can find it online. It's definitely Sunday's paper. And that binder's sitting there in plain sight."

"Then how did it get to the Dumpster?"

"Somebody must have taken it between the time the committee started and the time it was discovered missing, and threw it in there."

"So who took it?"

"It seems obvious, doesn't it? The person who killed Lee, and who saw a perfect opportunity to frame Tillman."

I left it to Burke to break the news to Hummel and the prosecutor that it was now almost definite they had the wrong guy. It didn't put us any closer to figuring out who killed Hershey, or Ratliff. But it got me thinking that whoever it was, our killer was certainly bold.

After I hung up, I hesitated for a minute or two, and called Jim Flanagan. Burke wasn't going to be happy about it. But I'd finally seen a way the reporter's proposal to share some information might benefit us. Unlike Burke, Flanagan sounded as if he was wide awake, even though it was now close to midnight.

"You're shitting me," he said, when I explained about the photo.

"Not to resort to clichés at a time of tragedy, but pictures don't lie. So the question—"

"The question is who was in that room before the committee started. Who had an opportunity to lift the binder."

"Exactly. Were you there?"

"Sure. Along with at least twelve other reporters, a brood of lobbyists, a herd of aides, and God knows who else."

"How many total?"

"I don't know—fifty? Sixty? It was packed. It could have been anybody."

"Was Lily Gleason there?"

"Of course. Why?"

"Just curious. Jack Sterling? Sam Michaels? Lauren Atkinson?"

"Are you handing me suspects' names straight up, or am I supposed to repeat them back to you and you grunt if I'm on to something?"

"I'm asking you the names of the only people I know around here, people who seemed to know Lee and also hate his guts. That's all. So there you go—your big tip from the vaunted Ed Tillman legal team. On the QT only. The rest is up to you."

53

I SPENT MOST OF THE NEXT MORNING getting the van's windshield replaced, talking to my insurance agent, and trying to catch up on the news. By midday the *Cleveland Press* was reporting that the patrol had officially exonerated Senator Tillman, based on the discovery of the photo of the binder. My lucky find didn't explain how it got into the Dumpster by his motel, but at least it got him off the hook. Other articles speculated on who might have killed the governor's chief of staff, if it was the same person who killed Hershey, if a serial killer might be on the loose, and, most crassly, what both deaths might mean for Hubbard's political future. Tillman's career, in the pits just a week ago, appeared poised for a historic comeback. Which is why I was so surprised by Burke's call early in the afternoon.

"Tillman's been arrested again."

"What?"

"There was some kind of scene at the Statehouse. Something to do with trying to get his job back as education chairman. He had to be hauled out of Ottie Kinser's office."

"Why?"

"I don't know. But I need you to find out."

"Me? She's your friend."

"Maybe not for much longer. She agreed to talk. But you're going to have to make it quick."

THE SENATOR FROWNED WHEN I entered her office half an hour later. A chill had descended since the last time I was there.

"Burke said you wanted to talk to me."

"He's wrong," Kinser said. "I agreed to answer some questions."

"So what happened? With Senator Tillman."

She explained about his unexpected arrival that morning, his demands that he regain his committee chairmanship. When he was rebuffed, he accused both her and the Senate president of conspiring with Republicans to undo him. Of giving them the Robin Hood memo and the Midwest Testing tip to pass on to Hershey.

"I had to tell him he had it all wrong," Kinser said.

"What do you mean?"

"Like everyone else, I assume Dani Symmes leaked the EQUITY memo. It certainly wasn't me. But I told Ed he shouldn't blame Republicans for Midwest Testing."

"Why not?"

"Because I gave that to Lee."

"You? But why?"

"Because Senator Tillman voted for the abortion legislation earlier this session."

"The ultrasound bill?"

"That's right."

"I thought that was just a political stunt."

"There's a fine line between stunt and conviction in one's beliefs, at least around here."

I said nothing, letting silence fill the room. After a few moments she spoke again.

"Two years ago, Ed and I worked together on a criminal justice bill. It would have toughened the penalty for rape if a person administered a substance to the victim with the intent of rendering them incapable of resisting."

"What kind of substance?"

"Anything. Alcohol. Drugs. As long as the intent was proven, that the attacker purposely set out to weaken someone." Her eyes smoldered, like opals reflecting firelight. "To strip them of the possibility of self-defense."

I nodded. I thought of my experience at Heyl's Tavern.

"There was a lot of resistance. The liquor lobby got involved. Defense attorneys said it was an impossible standard to measure. Even prosecutors had their doubts. So I went to Ed. I told him I wanted to offer new testimony. To tell the story of our daughter. Of what happened to her in college. Of—"

For the first time her composure cracked, for just a moment. Then she took a breath and the liquid brightness that had momentarily filled her eyes vanished.

"I told him everything. The attack. Her shame, the spiral of doubt and self-recrimination she fell into for years. The devastation it wreaked on her. And also, the one and only positive thing that we could avail ourselves of when it happened."

I thought for a second. I said, "The morning-after pill."

"That's right. At least we had that. But under the pharmacists' bill, that wouldn't have been the case. She was seventeen at the time. The ultrasound legislation was a real proposal, regardless of its chances. Don't let anyone tell you differently. And Ed knew that. And he voted for it anyway, despite knowing what happened to our daughter. For the sake of his own aspirations. For his future."

"He doesn't have much of a future now."

"Not if I have anything to say about it."

I GOT OUT OF THE STATEHOUSE QUICKLY,
not interested in meeting Hummel or anyone else involved in the
case, especially after Kinser's revelation. I was back outside, sitting on a bench near the Statehouse Holocaust Memorial on the
building's south side, contemplating this latest strand in the web,
when Bonnie called, a triumphant note in her voice.

"You cracked it," I said. She confirmed the news. "So what's
in there?"

"A lot of folders. A *lot*."

"I can imagine. Anything jump out?"

"Hard to say. The names don't mean much to me."

"Can you read off a few?"

So she did, rattling off titles I recognized—*Midwest Testing,
Robin Hood, Triple F*—and plenty I didn't. It sounded as if we had
a lot of work ahead of us. I was about to tell her I'd be over there
when I could get free when she said something that caught my
attention. I made her repeat it.

"*Literary Lion,*" she said. "Whatever that means."

"It was Hershey's nickname for the governor," I said. "What's
in there?"

The phone went quiet for almost a minute. "Wow," she said, when she came back on. "You might want to look at this stuff."

"Why?"

"Whatever it is, it looks like the mother lode."

BONNIE WAS ALREADY PRINTING documents and e-mails by the time I arrived. I started assembling them on the dining room table while Greg took up guard position by my feet. Troy watched us carefully, not saying anything. I noticed he had shaved and changed clothes, and something in his eyes looked clearer.

It took us a couple of hours before the documents finally sorted themselves into three general categories: items having to do directly with the education bill; documents related to Little Red Schoolhouse; and files connected to Hubbard's best seller, *Core Convictions*.

In the first category, the file that stuck out was an internal e-mail Hershey had obtained, from Allen Ratliff to Lily Gleason, with copies to several other people in the governor's office. Hershey had saved it in a subfolder labeled *Vote counting*. I read the e-mail twice. The language was formal, with perfect punctuation, spelling, and grammar. It was easy to imagine the Prince of Dorkness reading it aloud in his monotone.

"What's it mean?" Bonnie asked.

"It looks like Allen Ratliff got a secret vote count in the House for Triple F."

"I don't understand."

"He figured out they had enough votes to pass the bill without any charter school amendments." I thought back to the whiteboard in the governor's office, the names with the checks beside them.

"Why would that matter?" Troy said. He'd moved from the couch to the table, where he was helping sort documents.

I explained about the school-funding plan and the GOP's reluctance to support it without something for charter schools. "Some Republicans must have jumped ship," I said.

Troy said, "But you just said they *don't* need the charter schools stuff. According to that e-mail."

"I know. And that's what's confusing. Because the charter school amendments are definitely in the bill."

Puzzled, I moved on to the second pile of documents, those having to do with Little Red Schoolhouse.

It took about twenty minutes before I came across another e-mail from Ratliff that gave me pause. **Please review updated ABC charter school language ASAP.**

It was addressed to Sam Michaels at the Education Department, but what caught my attention was that Ratliff had later forwarded the e-mail to none other than Phil Williams, the president of Little Red Schoolhouse. I picked up the next document. Williams, without any comment, had e-mailed Ratliff what looked like suggested bill language.

I sifted through the pile. Michaels's response had come less than an hour later. **CEDES TOO MUCH TO MANAGEMENT COMPANIES!!!**

Ratliff's answer followed quickly: **Is language constitutional?**

Michaels's grudging reply: **Yes.**

The next e-mail I saw was another forwarded message from Ratliff, this time to House Speaker Dani Symmes. **Per our discussion**, he said.

Approve, she responded thirty minutes later.

Even more interesting. The late P-O-D had been working not just with Williams but with Symmes on the charter school language. It did not strike me as kosher behavior by the Democratic governor's chief of staff to be consorting with a major charter school player and the top Republican in the House.

"How's it going?" Bonnie said, setting another sheaf of printouts on the table.

I glanced at the e-mail on top of the new pile.

Looking forward to working with you, Williams had e-mailed Symmes that same evening, with Ratliff copied.

I'm glad we were able to work things out, she replied thirty minutes later, via iPhone.

"There's one more," Bonnie said.

I took the paper from her.

Does 2/1 work as starting date? Williams wrote Symmes the next day. Again, he'd copied Ratliff.

2/1, I thought. February 1. Early next year. Starting date? Start of what?

That works, Symmes responded. Then she added: **Remember it's DANIELLE for the business cards.** ☺

"I think I've got it," I said, after a moment.

"What?" Troy and Bonnie said together. Even Greg perked up.

"Dani Symmes is going to work for Little Red Schoolhouse."

"Is that good?" Bonnie said.

"It's good for her. But it also means her job negotiations meant delivering something to Williams."

"The charter school amendments," Troy said.

"That's right."

"Which that other e-mail said weren't needed."

"Right again."

"I'm still not sure I understand," Bonnie said, sitting back.

I thought about how to explain it. "It looks like Dani Symmes got the governor to put the charter school amendments into the school-funding bill, even though Ratliff counted votes and discovered they didn't need the amendments to pass it."

"But why would the governor's office let that happen?" Troy said.

"Only one reason I can think of. They had no choice. Symmes must have some kind of leverage."

IT WAS GETTING LATE, and we took a break to order pizza and organize the files. While Bonnie straightened up and Troy took Greg for a walk, I called Liz Brantley and Jim Flanagan, hoping they could help me sort some of this out. Neither answered.

An hour later, slices of pepperoni and mushroom in hand, we looked at *Literary Lion*, the third folder. Its files consisted of selections from *Core Convictions* along with chunks of paragraphs from some other source.

"Either of you happen to read this book?" I said.

They looked at each other and shook their heads.

"Not your thing?"

"I'm more into anime," Bonnie said.

"How about you?" I said to Troy.

"Me?"

"Any books you like to read?"

"Science fiction, mostly."

"Hold that thought," I said. I went back to the documents. A pattern was starting to emerge. Hershey had typed out sections of *Core Convictions* and matched them with passages from someplace else. The comparisons weren't always perfect. Sometimes it was just a line, other times it was similar phrases: *authentic democracy; inherent individualism; frontier scholar.*

I showed Bonnie the phrases. "Can you Google those, see what comes up?"

"Just the phrases?"

I thought about it. "No. Put the phrase and then Hubbard."

A minute later she showed me the results. "Mostly reviews of the book, with an interview or two."

"OK. Try the phrases by themselves."

"Here you go," she said, just a few seconds later. "Who's Elizabeth Brantley?"

I took the computer mouse from Bonnie and clicked on the first link. I read for a moment, moved on to the next, and the third. I went back to the passages of prose that Hershey had found someplace, and read the comparative sections from Hubbard's book. There was no question. The wording was too similar, the phrases too distinct.

"Well?" Bonnie said.

"Well what?"

"Who's this Brantley person?"

"I'm pretty sure she's the author of the governor's best-selling book," I said.

I WENT BACK OVER the notes one more time. There was no mistake. Liz had ghostwritten *Core Convictions*. And Lee must have figured it out. I thought about what Kerri MacKenzie, the Senate aide, told me the other day, that she'd seen Brantley crying in the Atrium the night Hershey was killed. *Like she'd just gotten some really bad news.*

But that wasn't all. Looking at the juxtaposition of Hershey's files, the inclusion of this discovery in the same folder as Dani Symmes's job negotiations, it seemed pretty likely the House Speaker had guessed too. But why did it matter? Didn't all politicians have ghost writers? Nobody seriously thought Kennedy wrote *Profiles in Courage*, but that was hardly a scandal. I sat back. I explained what I was thinking to Bonnie and Troy.

"Maybe this explains it," Troy said. He handed me a piece of paper. It was an interview the governor had done after the latest TV news personality was busted for misremembering details of his own reportorial heroics. In it, Hubbard said people could disagree with him on policy for a month of Sundays. But they could never accuse him of clouding his past, because he'd insisted on writing *Core Convictions* himself. Because that's what character was all about. Doing the right thing. Which was why he penned the book in the first place. "Character counts," he told the interviewer, more than once.

"He lied," Bonnie said.

"Don't sound so surprised."

"He lied about telling the truth. It's even worse. He's like every other politician."

"Not all politicians lie," I said. "And not all nonpoliticians tell the truth."

She frowned. Neither she nor Troy seemed the naive sort, at least when it came to politics. But it was still discouraging to see her so crushed at the discovery of such a first-rate liar as Hubbard.

"The main thing is, that explains Dani Symmes and her job," I said.

"What do you mean?" Bonnie said.

What I meant, I explained, was that Hubbard's interview answered the question Troy had so smartly raised. Why would Hubbard go ahead and put the charter school amendments in the education bill if he'd counted votes and realized he could pass it without them? Answer: Symmes had something big against him. And hadn't been afraid to use it.

Because nothing jeopardizes your shot at national office like being threatened to acknowledge you didn't write the best seller you insisted you did. As a matter of character.

As I sat there, letting the significance of everything sink in, I recalled one of the first things Hershey said to me outside my house on Memorial Day.

"Thomas Hubbard, literary lion."

But of course, that's not what he'd been saying at all. I saw that now. Because it was all about the clues with Hershey. The cloak-and-dagger stuff.

I heard one thing. But what he said was something completely different.

"Thomas Hubbard, literary lying."

55

I CALLED BRANTLEY AGAIN AND THIS TIME left a pointed message. She called back within five minutes.

"I'm still downtown," she said.

"I'll meet you at the Ringside."

"Do we have to?"

"Yes."

She was sitting by herself when I walked in, an untouched glass of white wine on the bar in front of her and next to it a copy of *Core Convictions*. Her right hand shook as she took mine reluctantly. I ordered a Heineken, had a swig, told her about Kerri MacKenzie seeing her that night at the Statehouse, explained what I'd found. But it was clear she already knew.

"Lee figured it out, didn't he?" I said.

She nodded.

"How?"

"Same way he did everything. He never forgets anything. Just like you. Flypaper brain. Remember?"

I grimaced. "I remember I have that bad habit. But what does that have to do with Lee making the connection?"

"When we were still together he read a first draft of my book on politics. The one about to come out. I had a line in there about John Glenn." She picked up *Core Convictions*, thumbed through it, stopped, stared for a moment, and read: "Glenn was an American hero cut from the cloth of nineteenth-century values originally summoned to conquer the western frontier, but exercised in a twentieth-century space-age arena where ironically, instead of seeming old-fashioned, they became progressive virtues at a time of societal chaos."

"Nicely put," I said.

"Of course it is," she said, bitterly. "Because I wrote it, or a damn close version, in an early draft of my own book. It ended up in here because I was on deadline, the governor was getting antsy, and I didn't think about it. Why should I? Lee was the only person who read that draft, and that had been a while. But of course, he figured it out right away."

"He told you he was going to break the story that Hubbard didn't write his own best seller."

She nodded. "Once he recognized the passage, he started digging. Like he always did. He went through my columns and found other turns of phrase that were a little too close."

"So you're the person he was going to meet that night."

"What?"

"The person he wanted me along for. Some kind of uncomfortable conversation. That's how he put it. That was you."

"I don't think so. I just happened to see him, as I was leaving. We hadn't arranged anything."

"Really?"

"He said he planned to tell me the next day. But since he saw me there . . ."

"What time was this?"

"I'm not sure. Ten, maybe. Education hearing had gone late."

I said, "Did he say why?"

"Why what?"

"Why he was writing the story. He could have let it lie."

"Lee? I don't think so. He said he had no choice. But it wasn't the ghostwriting. He made that clear. It was the fact Symmes was using it against the governor. That was the story."

"How'd you respond?"

"I begged him not to. It was my career on the line. He wouldn't listen. He said the story was bigger than me. Than us."

Bigger than me. Than us.

The same phrase Lily Gleason had used in her deposition about Hershey.

"What happened then?" I said.

"It's all a blur. I was crying pretty hard by then. I just grabbed my stuff and left."

"And he didn't mention meeting anyone else?"

"No. Except—"

"What?"

"I'd forgotten. Until just now. Shows how upset I was, I guess."

I waited.

"When I first saw him I asked him what he was doing there. I hadn't seen him in the committee hearing that day. He said he was just killing time. He was meeting someone for a drink, apparently."

"Where?"

"Here," she said. "The Ringside."

"Here?"

"That's right."

"He didn't say who?"

She shook her head. I thought about it. It made sense, in a way. Peeved that I didn't show up, he came downtown, swung through the Statehouse, maybe looking for tips from stragglers at the late committee hearing, and planned to walk the two minutes across the street to the bar. Except he saw Liz, and someone else, and never made it out of the building.

"Who else knew?" I said after a moment. "About the book, I mean."

"The first lady, I think. But we were careful. We only met once or twice, at the governor's residence, really early in the morning. The rest was all by e-mail."

"Could Allen Ratliff have known? Could that be why he was killed?"

"He didn't know."

"You're sure?"

"The governor would never have trusted Allen with something like that. The P-O-D fancied himself a political player, but he was nothing more than a glorified policy wonk. Hubbard told him to negotiate the deal with Dani Symmes and Phil Williams about the amendments and her job, no questions asked."

"So you, the first lady, and the governor? And Dani Symmes, somehow. Not even Hubbard's editor?"

"If his editor had questions she e-mailed the governor, and if he couldn't answer he got in touch with me. That didn't happen often. Hubbard's a bright guy—he just couldn't put sentences together. Of course, that was supposed to be the charm of the book. If I got too fancy, he made me simplify it. 'Hubbardize it,' he'd say."

"I have to ask. Were you and the governor—?"

"Having an affair? Of course you'd assume that."

"I'm not—"

"Don't bother. The answer's no. I needed the money, plain and simple. You saw my house. It's a wreck. My life's a wreck. It seemed like an easy way to crawl out of the hole I was in. Things got tough for me after Lee left."

I took another drink of my beer. Brantley just stared at her wine.

"So what are you going to do?" she said.

"Do?"

"About the book. And me."

I thought about it. "It gives you a strong motive to kill Lee."

"No," she said, alarm filling her face. "I never—"

"Don't worry. I know you didn't."

"You do?"

"Unless you're in cahoots with Kerri MacKenzie, her story exonerates you."

"So you believe her, but not me?"

"I'm not sure what I believe any more."

Her face hardened a bit. "But, are you going to—"

"Bust you?"

"Something like that."

"The patrol needs to know. What Lee discovered implicates both the governor and Dani Symmes, as far-fetched as it sounds."

"So you're going to tell them."

"No."

"No?" She looked surprised.

"You are."

I got off the bar stool, dug out my wallet, found a ten-dollar bill, and put it on the counter. I realized it was the last of Hershey's cash. I was at the door when Brantley called my name. I turned.

"If it's any consolation, there's one difference between you and Lee."

I waited.

"That day you drove me home? From the coffee shop? He would have come inside for that 'coffee.' Just so you know. That's the difference."

56

MY CONVERSATION WITH BRANTLEY
continued to bother me the next day. Not because of her admission about the ghostwriting. Because of Hershey's presence in the pressroom the night he saw her. His fatal encounter came shortly after she left the Statehouse, sobbing at his intentions. Which meant the killer was either in the building or arrived shortly thereafter. Had they planned to walk to the bar together?

I remembered what Hummel had said about Allen Ratliff's killer using Hershey's key card to enter. That meant there was an electronic record of who came in and out. And that also meant Hummel had presumably checked the files for the night of Hershey's murder and eliminated suspects. Which meant whoever killed the reporter had either been in the building for a while and hadn't needed to use the after-hours entrance—which meant potentially dozens of other suspects—or had been let in shortly before the murder. By Hershey himself? And was it the same person he planned to meet at the bar?

And of course, there was the huge "what if" contained in Brantley's story. What if Hershey hadn't seen her and had gone ahead to the Ringside? What if he hadn't been delayed by his conversation with her, meaning he never would have encountered his killer in the pressroom? What if—but of course, everything came back to me. What if I hadn't gone for a beer with Roy in the first place?

I was back to fighting dark clouds once again when I pulled into the Little Red Schoolhouse parking lot later that morning. The company's website featured an actual red schoolhouse on a grassy hill, very quaint and Laura Ingalls Wilder–ish. The real headquarters, the top two floors of a seven-story glass-windowed cube off I-270 on the west side, looked like the kind of place where people on headphones spent their days denying patients' insurance coverage.

The receptionist's story that Phil Williams was busy and didn't see people without appointments changed when I explained I was there about the House Speaker's new job with the company.

"You've got balls, I'll give you that much," Williams said, in decidedly un–fundamentalist Christian fashion, once we were alone in his office. I couldn't help but notice it was significantly larger than those occupied by either the governor or Supreme Court Justice Billy Bryan.

"You realize you've just accused me of murder," he said when I finished telling him what I knew.

"Nothing of the sort. The most I'm suggesting is bribing a public official."

"What are you talking about?"

"I'm talking about you providing Dani Symmes with a job in exchange for favorable treatment for charter schools in the education bill. Treatment that benefits your company."

He leaned back in his chair. "Even supposing that was true, everything you're saying is contingent on Speaker Symmes coming to work here."

"I guess."

"But that's not happening."

"It's not?"

"The deal's off."

"Why?"

"You'll have to ask her."

"She's not taking my calls right now."

"Too bad. But not my problem."

"If the deal's dead, that means there's no charter school amendments in Triple F."

"All you need to know about Democrats' treatment of schools is the name they came up with for that plan."

"I hadn't heard that today. The fact remains, the charter school amendments are gone, if what you're saying is true. Wasn't that the deal: Hubbard gives her the amendments, and that paved the way for her coming here?"

Williams spread his arms and opened his hands palms up in a gesture of resignation. "A loss for the taxpaying citizens of Ohio sick of seeing schoolchildren crucified on the altar of poor-performing public schools," he said.

"Save it for your board meeting," I said, getting up.

57

THIS TIME DANI SYMMES DID TAKE MY CALL.
She refused to meet with me. But she heard me out. Mainly be-
cause I told her it was either that or I go straight to Lieutenant
Hummel.

"You knew *Core Convictions* was ghostwritten?" I said.

"Yes."

"Who told you?"

"The governor."

"Hubbard? That's impossible."

"Not in so many words. But he made a mistake."

"Which was?"

"Like everyone else, we'd heard he was having an affair. I told
Matt to investigate."

"Matt?"

"My chief of staff."

I recalled the young man who'd pointed Symmes out in the
Atrium, who'd been jogging behind Symmes in the park. And
the rumor that Kerri MacKenzie had passed on to Hershey at the
Clarmont.

"He discovered the affair?"

"Not exactly. At my request, he started jogging past the governor's residence every morning, just to see what he could see. He practically had shin splints when he spied the thing every oppo researcher in the world dreams of."

"Which is?"

"A woman leaving the governor's house early in the morning who was not the governor's wife."

"But what did that prove?"

"Given that it was Liz Brantley, it proved a lot. All the more so because we knew the first lady was in town that day. So if it wasn't an affair, what was it?"

"An early-morning source meeting?"

"That's what we thought, until the governor's book came out. Everyone knew Brantley was working on her own project. But we were the only ones who knew she'd been at the residence. We compared some of her past writings to the prose in *Core Convictions*, found some matchups that exceeded the realm of statistical randomness, and presented our findings to the governor."

More or less what Hershey had done, I reflected, with the added benefit of his prodigious memory recalling the nearly verbatim passage about John Glenn.

"You threatened to expose him."

"I prefer to say that I suggested a deal."

"And he knew you were serious. After you leaked the Robin Hood memo."

I heard her sigh. "I can understand if you're slow on the uptake, Mr. Hayes. I cosponsored a bill on concussion-prevention efforts last session you might want to look into. But the fact of the matter is, as I told you at the park, I didn't leak that memo. I just took credit for it."

"Then who did?"

"Based on my information, I would suggest you have the wrong party."

"You're not the guilty party?"

"*Political* party, Mr. Hayes," she said, exasperated.

"You're saying a Democrat leaked it?" I thought of Ottie Kinser and the Midwest Testing tip she used to send Tillman's career up in flames. Had she turned on her own party again?

"I've said all I want to on the subject," Symmes said.

"Did you know that Lee Hershey knew about *Core Convictions*?"

"Yes."

"How?"

"Brantley called the governor that night. Right after she saw Lee at the Statehouse. The governor called me. He made it clear our deal was off if Hershey wrote a story."

"Which gave you a strong motive for keeping that from happening."

"I'll ignore such a slanderous remark by noting that I was home at the time and Matt was out with his girlfriend."

"Who's his girlfriend?"

"You'll have to ask him, except don't bother because he's under strict orders not to say anything about any of this."

"It's ironic," I said, after a moment.

"How so?"

"Ironic that a false rumor of the governor and an affair led to the truth about his fake book."

"That's where you're wrong, Mr. Hayes. Once again."

"Wrong?"

"The rumor was true."

"It was? Who's the other woman?"

"Sorry. We're saving that one for the presidential campaign."

58

I WAS LYING IN BED THE NEXT MORNING,
Saturday, thinking about several things. First and foremost, the
fact that more than two weeks after someone had bashed Lee
Hershey's head in while I lay passed out in my van—thanks most
likely to Anna Campbell—I still had no idea who was responsible.
Nor did the patrol know who attacked Ephraim Badger, killed
Allen Ratliff, and took three potshots at me. In the meantime, several careers lay shattered around the Statehouse or were headed
there soon: Liz Brantley, of course, followed by bankrupt lobbyist
Jack Sterling, ex-Senate Education Chairman Ed Tillman, a humili-
ated Lily Gleason, and most likely Justice Billy Bryan, whose last
name wasn't Irish. I was also considering the fact that, once again, I
had very few groceries in my house and most of the money I was
going to spend on them had gone to Bonnie's research.

I had dozed off despite Hopalong's whining for a walk when
my phone rang. Roused, I saw that Jay Scott was calling from
Ann Arbor.

"Sorry to call so early. I found what you're looking for."

"Crap. I meant to get ahold of you."

"About what?"

"I already figured out who was driving the car."

"You did? Who?"

I told him about Campbell and her clandestine work for the governor's late chief of staff.

"Listen, Andrew. I don't mean to tell you your business. Actually, I do. I don't think you've got the whole story."

"What do you mean?"

"The address the plate came back to? An auto parts guy used to run a business there, but that was a few years back. He went under during the recession."

"OK."

"I hunted him down. I found out he still has title to the building. He was a little surprised to see me at his door last night."

"I bet."

"He's got another business now, running his own rug-cleaning company. He still used the auto parts place to store stuff, but he was looking to unload it. He got approached with a good offer about a year ago and decided to take it."

"Which was?"

"The offer was, could this particular enterprise rent it for eighteen months or so, also using it to store things, but perhaps a little quietly."

"Who was it?"

"My guy's like, easiest twelve hundred a month he was ever going to make. Signed right away. Kinda funny, considering."

"Considering what?"

"Considering he totally blamed Bush for his business tanking in the first place because of the recession."

"Listen, I know I'm not quite as busy as you, thank you very much, but I actually don't have all day."

"Sorry, Andrew. It just tickles me."

"So who's renting it?"

"Ryan's people."

"Ryan?"

"Jim Ryan? The president of the United States? POTUS? You know he's from Michigan, right?"

"That address comes back to Ryan?"

"To his campaign."

"Which means the SUV that was following is a campaign vehicle?"

"I guess."

I rolled this information around.

"You there?" Scott said after a moment.

"Yeah," I said.

"What's up?"

"I've gotta go. Thanks. Send me a bill."

"That's it?" he said. "After all that—"

But I'd already hung up and was out of bed and getting dressed.

59

I WAS PRETTY SURE I COULD HAVE FOUND Anna Campbell's cell phone number eventually, but since I was on a roll spending money I didn't have, I decided to take advantage of my newfound employee. Despite the hour, I called Bonnie. Even though she sounded as if I'd awakened her, she didn't complain, and within ten minutes, time enough for me to shave and make coffee, she called me back with the number. Campbell answered after the third ring, out of breath. I told her why I was calling. She said I had no right. I said she had to be kidding.

Ten minutes later I pulled into the parking lot at the Arena Fitness Club just off Neil. I texted Campbell. Two minutes later, her face red, and not just from working out, she emerged from the building.

We sat on a bench along the walkway to the gym. The smell of flowers and freshly raked mulch and cat shit filled the air.

"You're working for President Ryan," I said.

"No—"

"You are, in fact, a double agent?"

"That's not true."

I explained what Scott had discovered over in Detroit—the auto parts store, the Ryan campaign, the eighteen-month lease. She got quiet after that.

"I have to say I'm impressed. That you got hired into Hubbard's office, I mean. How'd you pull that off?"

To my surprise, the question seemed to relax her. She leaned back on the bench. It was almost as if she were relieved the truth was out. "Their vetting sucked," she said.

"But you were with the College Republicans at Miami University. I saw that on LinkedIn."

"I told them I'd had a revelation after a friend of mine almost died from an ectopic pregnancy and had trouble getting an abortion. And that I'd met a couple of gay people my senior year I really liked."

"Lies?"

"The abortion thing was. I did meet some gay people. But they're Log Cabin Republicans."

"So you were following Hershey for Ryan?"

She shook her head. "Allen brought me into his office one day. Asked me some questions about my dad's driving school. Then asked if I could do him a favor."

"Which was?"

"Trail Hershey, find out who he talked to. I thought it was kind of dumb, since you figure the leaks are coming by phone or e-mail, but he gave me money on the side. So my boyfriend and I followed him whenever we could. It kind of took off from there."

"Who's your boyfriend?"

"Matt Schiff."

"Is he a fake Democrat too?"

"He's Dani Symmes's chief of staff."

Matt. The guy in the Atrium. Symmes's jogging companion. The one who outed Liz Brantley.

Anna, the girlfriend Symmes hadn't met.

"A secret courtship, I'm guessing?"

"Election's less than six months. We figured we could wait."

"That'll be one hell of a relationship update on Facebook."

"Whatever."

"You followed us after Lee and I left the Clarmont. How'd you know we were there?"

"Allen texted me."

I remembered Ratliff's bored texting as Hershey and I sat at the table in the restaurant. I'd assumed it was the modern communications malaise, the sign of a busy guy who could never quite turn off. In fact, he'd been unleashing the hounds.

"Brilliant. So you followed Hershey because Ratliff asked you. But why follow me?"

"That came from Ryan's campaign."

"Why would they care?"

"Because you were working for Senator Rodriguez."

"What are you talking about?"

"That's what they said. I was supposed to find out what you were up to."

"That's bullshit. My dog's more political than I am."

"I'm just telling you what they told me. You were at some kind of fundraiser for Rodriguez. It seemed like common knowledge."

Fundraiser. Of course. Burke's banquet, where I'd seen Ottie and Reggie Kinser, and inadvertently photobombed the Democratic state party chairman.

"So the night you followed me to the bar you were working for Ryan?"

She nodded. "They told us to keep you away from Hershey."

"Why?"

"Since they thought you worked for Rodriguez, they assumed you were trying to sabotage his reporting."

"But how'd you know I was picking him up that night?"

"Matt was two bar stools over. Your friend was saying it sounded suspicious, and you were saying it didn't matter to you what story Hershey was working on."

"And you were the one that came into the bar and said my van had been hit."

She nodded. She looked almost pleased with herself.

"You realize if I hadn't gone to the bathroom, I would've busted you in Hubbard's office that day."

"Duh."

"Kind of risky, chaperoning me like that, after you'd been following me."

"Like I had any choice. What was I supposed to tell Allen— sorry, I spied on that guy for President Ryan, probably better not to blow my cover?"

"Is that why you changed your hair? After the bar? Lessen the chance of being recognized?"

She shrugged. "I was tired of being a blonde anyway."

"It's funny," I said. "If you weren't so evil, I'd admire your moxie."

"I'm not evil."

"Other than your actions leading directly to Hershey's death." I was raising my voice again, like that day in the sandwich shop. And just like then, I didn't care.

"I had nothing to do with that."

"Like hell."

"I don't have to take this." She started to stand up.

"I didn't say you could go."

"Try to stop me."

"I'm going to. Right now."

"How? Bust my cover? Like that matters anymore."

"Screw your cover. I'm calling your dad."

"My dad?"

"And then I'm calling some good friends of mine at Channel 7 and the *Dispatch*. The daughter of a prominent driving school instructor used her automobile prowess to spy on the governor and get someone killed. Helluva story. Good for business, I'm guessing."

She sat back down.

"That's more like it," I said. "So you got lucky, told my buddy about the van, he was a good guy and went outside, and your boyfriend drops the pill into my beer."

"Black Label," she said, wrinkling her nose. "How can you—"

"I wouldn't go there if I were you. Where'd he get the pill, anyway?"

"His mom. She's prone to nervous breakdowns."

"The two of you around, I'm not surprised."

"Screw you."

"I still don't understand why Allen trusted you with tailing Hershey," I said. "Besides your stellar driving skills, of course."

"I guess I passed a test."

"A test?"

"He liked something I told him. After Ryan's people set me up in there, I'd been looking for a way to gain his confidence."

"Which was?"

"Some gossip."

"What kind?"

"Supposedly Hershey got some lady pregnant."

My stomach clenched. "Who?"

"Kelly something."

I shut my eyes. "Kelly Flanagan?"

"Yeah. I think so."

"How do you know this?"

"A friend."

"Not good enough."

She hesitated. "Kelly had done some work for Children's Hospital."

"What kind of work?"

"Some kind of PR campaign. Safe sleeping for babies, something like that."

I recalled what Flanagan had told me, that his wife had been a reporter, but went into PR when the recession hit.

"She said something to one of the doctors, after a meeting about the campaign. Some kind of joke."

"Like what?"

" 'This could come in handy for me soon.' Something like that."

"How'd you find out?"

"Somebody on the internal communications team at Children's. We went to school together."

"And she told you?"

She nodded.

"And you told Ratliff that?"

"I needed to get on his good side."

"Because you were working for Ryan."

She nodded, bored.

"You traded on a woman's secret, one of the most private things she could divulge, for political gain."

"She's the one who let it spill," Campbell protested.

"To a doctor."

"At a PR event."

"Now you're blaming the victim. An awkward cry for help doesn't make them any less needy."

"Like you're some kind of expert on people in trouble."

"I'll be the judge of that. What happened then?"

"That was right when Hershey was writing about that Robin Hood memo. I told Allen what I heard. He thought it could be useful somehow."

"Useful?"

"Like they could threaten Hershey that they'd tell Kelly's husband, that other reporter, about it, if Hershey didn't ease up. Especially because—"

"Because why?"

"Supposedly they couldn't have kids. Because of something wrong with her husband. So Allen thought that gave them an extra advantage."

So much for the P-O-D being a harmless policy wonk. I said, "So did he threaten Hershey, like you said?"

"No."

"Why not?"

"Senator Rodriguez nixed it."

"Nixed it?"

"That's right."

"Rodriguez wouldn't let Ratliff tell Flanagan his wife was pregnant?"

"Yeah."

"Why not?"

"She said they should hang onto the information," Campbell said, stonefaced. "She said it might come in useful down the road."

"What did the governor have to say about all this?"

"He didn't know."

"You're kidding."

"Allen thought it was best to keep him out of the loop."

I thought about this. Something was starting to click into place. Hershey. Ratliff. Rodriguez . . .

I said, "So Jim Flanagan didn't know his wife was pregnant, before she died?"

"No. And it's kind of pathetic, if you ask me."

"What is?"

"She wanted to go back to him. Leave Hershey. But he told her to forget it. Called her a lot of nasty names. Slut, whore, like that. Least that's what my friend at the hospital said. The one who knew Kelly."

The exact opposite scenario Flanagan had described to me in the Ringside that night.

"And then she died," I said.

"On her way," she said.

"On her way where?"

"On her way to her husband," she said, exasperated. "Hershey had told her to get an abortion. But she didn't want to. So she decided to beg her husband to take her back. But then . . ."

"She had the accident."

Campbell nodded nonchalantly, as if I'd been talking about paint swatches.

"Did her husband find out afterward?"

"Maybe?"

"What's that supposed to mean?"

"After the Midwest Testing stories came out, and it looked like Triple F was in trouble, Allen called Hershey, furious."

"What'd he tell him?"

"He told him what they knew. Told him he was ready to play hardball. That he was done fooling around."

"Meaning what?"

"He told Hershey about Rodriguez sitting on the information, but he wasn't going to protect it anymore."

"What did Hershey say?"

"He got angry. Really angry. Told Allen to go fuck himself. That it didn't matter because he'd just do it."

"Do what?"

"Tell Flanagan. Tell him that Kelly had been pregnant with his, Hershey's, baby, and that Ratliff and Rodriguez had covered it up."

60

I SAT THERE, A PIT IN MY STOMACH GROWING. Thought about what I'd just gone through with Anne and her late period. What Kelly, who wanted a baby, might have been thinking. How Hubbard and Ratliff had each kept crucial secrets from one another—the ghostwriting, the extortion over Kelly's pregnancy—and how a different tactic might have changed everything. What Jim Flanagan, who'd borne the guilt of not being able to father a child and refusing to take Kelly back, must have thought when he heard Hershey had accomplished what he couldn't. The rage he must have felt. The fact that so few people knew the truth and two of them—Hershey and Ratliff—were now dead. Which left JoAnn Rodriguez.

I thought about Ephraim Badger's missing gun and keys. Which would include one key in particular, unlocking the doors to the Cupola. Which had an extraordinary view of the lawn where Rodriguez was holding a rally in a matter of minutes. I needed to get to the Statehouse fast. Get *into* the Statehouse. That's why I was out of the gym parking lot two minutes later leaving behind a fuming Campbell now bereft of three important things: the endorphin rush she'd been experiencing on the

StairMaster before my interruption, her career as a Statehouse double agent, and her personal key card into the Capitol.

I got on my phone as I drove. Liz Brantley sounded as if she'd been dead asleep when I reached her.

"The place that Jim Flanagan's doing his community service work."

"What about it?"

"What's the name of it?"

"The name? I have no idea."

"Can you find out?"

"I guess. Why?"

"I'll get to that. Can you find out now?"

"Now? What's the big rush?"

"Can you just get me the name?"

She paused. "What the hell's going on, Andy?"

"Please—it's important."

"Jesus Christ. All right, hang on."

I drove down Long Street, quiet at that time of day. But in the distance I could hear something. Rock music, coming from the Statehouse.

"Lighthouse Solutions," Brantley said, coming back on the line. "Satisfied?"

"Thanks."

"Want to know how I found it?"

"I don't really have time, I'm sorry—"

"I used the fucking Internet," she said, and hung up.

I pulled over and dialed the number. To my surprise, a man answered right away.

"Is Jim Flanagan working today?" I said, trying to sound authoritative. "He was supposed to leave something for me."

"Who's Jim Flanagan?"

Putting on my best aggrieved bureaucrat voice, I explained his community service situation. Sounding equally aggrieved, the man told me to wait. The passing seconds seemed eternal.

"He's not here, sorry."

"When's he back next?"

"He's not coming back."

"Why not?"

"He finished his service hours three weeks ago."

I HUNG UP, PULLED back into traffic, called Lieutenant Hummel's cell phone and told him everything: Anna Campbell and what she had revealed, Kelly Flanagan and her baby and Hershey's intent to tell Flanagan himself. The fact that Flanagan hadn't been out of town the day Hershey died. And the fact that two of the people who knew about the baby were now dead.

When I was finished, Hummel said, "Ryan's campaign has a mole in Hubbard's office?"

"I just said that. But that's not the point—"

"It is now. Who's to say she's not the suspect? She drugged you, was working both sides."

"You're not listening—"

"Because you're not making sense."

"Anna Campbell's not the one with the motive. Flanagan is. And he knew of three people who hadn't told him news that could have changed everything—Hershey, Allen Ratliff, and Senator—"

Traffic in front of me suddenly backed up, and I threw the phone onto the passenger seat just in time to brake and avoid a chain-reaction accident. I caught a glimpse of orange barricades and police officers in bright green vests directing traffic. I swore loudly. Two blocks down I stopped in front of a meter with a hood over it expressly forbidding parking. I called Hummel back but his voicemail picked up. I opened the door, started to get out, and remembered something. I reached into the glove compartment. It was still there. The paperback Anne had loaned Hershey. More importantly, tucked inside the cover, the "bookmark," the key to the Cupola that Hershey had tied to a string, the name *J. Cook* on the tag. *Commit nuisance.* I jammed the key in my pocket, got out of the van, and started running.

61

IT WAS NEARLY TEN BY NOW, AND IN
frustration I slowed to a walk as I joined crowds of people streaming down Broad to the Capitol's west side. "Rodriguez 2016" signs
rose up and down in the surging crowd like drifting harbor buoys.
I walked around the back of the stage erected next to the statue of
President McKinley, climbed up the west-side stairs of the Statehouse, and pulled on the doors in vain. Inside, a trooper looked
at me and shook his head. I thought about pleading my case. But
after Hummel's dismissal of my concerns, what were the chances
I'd be believed? And what if my story led to questioning, even an
involuntary trip to the basement interview rooms?

I considered loping down one of the parking garage entrance
ramps, and just as quickly dismissed the idea. An out-of-place
pedestrian on those would immediately attract attention on the
security cameras. I thought about trying a reverse operation—
rushing the stage to reach Rodriguez in time. But that meant getting past a phalanx of troopers and Secret Service agents, all of
them armed and on the lookout for that kind of behavior. Instead, I headed for the other side of the Statehouse, on the outside chance the Third Street doors were open. Behind me, U2's

"Beautiful Day" blasted from speakers. Then the music softened and I heard someone's voice. Something about introductions.

I made it to the southern side of Capitol Square and was just passing the Holocaust Memorial when I saw a pair of young women in halter tops and cutoff jeans shorts strolling halfway up the walk to the cast-iron sculpture of a broken Star of David. They stopped in front of the structure, turned, and posed as the one on the left took out her phone for a selfie. I looked at them in disgust, and that's when I saw it. A sign for the parking garage above a set of stairs disappearing into the ground. I'd walked past it a dozen times, barely registering it.

"Have some respect," I hissed at the women, approaching them a moment later. Startled, they stopped their photo session and stared at me. I shook my head, and headed down the stairs.

I WALKED SLOWLY THROUGH the garage to under-score to whoever might have been watching that I belonged there, that I'd practically been *born* there, passing the massive concrete green pillars and taking in the damp, diesel smell as if it were something I did every day and surely everyone could see that. At the employee entrance I pulled out Campbell's key card and waited, my heart skipping a quick beat during a pause, until the reader beeped and the revolving door turned. I walked up the steep stairs to the basement level, passed the display of bricks from Rat Row and the Paw Paw Bottoms commemorative gavel, and entered the Crypt. A moment later I stopped, turned around, went back to the top of the staircase, and with one swift tug and a loud crack yanked the gavel free from its stand.

I walked through the Crypt, past the interactive museum center, under the groin vault, and straight to the office door that led to the Cupola. I hadn't passed a soul. Why would I? The security was outside, where it should be. I slipped my hand into my pocket, pulled out Hershey's key, unlocked the first door, stepped inside, walked to the second door, unlocked it, and started climbing, fast. I just hoped I wasn't too late.

62

"TIME'S UP," I SAID, A FEW MINUTES LATER.

"You're right," Jim Flanagan said.

We'd completed two turns of the circular room before we both stopped, out of breath, standing on opposite sides like the tips of two clock hands. Outside, "Beautiful Day" had given way to "Right Here, Right Now" by Jesus Jones. It wouldn't be long now before Rodriguez took the stage. The sound of the music and the brightness of the morning light streaming through the tall windows contrasted with the deadly contest I was trying desperately not to lose.

"You were supposed to meet Lee at the Ringside that night, weren't you?" I said, raising my voice to make myself heard over the rally.

Then I heard it. Another sound, faint and far below us. Footsteps, coming up the stairs?

"But he didn't show," I said, stalling for time. *Because he was talking to Liz Brantley*, I said to myself. "So you give up, walk across the street, see if there's anyone still around. I'm just guessing now, but I bet he was on his way over, saw you, and let you in.

The two of you walk to the pressroom. He tells you about Kelly's pregnancy. Then, what? You lose it, hit him with a Triple F binder when he's not looking? He falls, hits his head? How many more times did you club him?"

"I told you to shut up."

"Afterward, you panic. Then, suddenly, you realize you have a possible alibi. 'Out of town.' It was true for most Wednesdays—why not that one? So many people in the Statehouse for the education hearing, who would have remembered if you were here or not? Except for one problem. You came up here that day, didn't you? Up to the Cupola."

He was quiet. I listened, trying to gauge where he was. But the music was too loud.

"You took a tour, on a lark. They were rare, after all. Why not? Signed your name on the wall too, I'm guessing. Wouldn't have mattered, except it was the worst possible day in your life to leave a piece of evidence proving you'd been someplace."

Still nothing.

"I'm guessing you've scratched it out by now. But Ephraim Badger could still make the connection, couldn't he? Because of the permission form. Even if no one else on the tour recognized you. It's when you started asking about it that he got suspicious, and stopped coming to the Statehouse. That's when you knew you had to get his keys. And the form."

"You talk a lot, you know that? Just like Lee."

"You found my card at Badger's house, didn't you? That why you tried to shoot me? Figured I knew what was up?"

"You also don't know when to stop talking. Also just like Lee."

"I figure your binder's in the bottom of a landfill by now. But Tillman's must have looked pretty inviting that Saturday, during the special session. You took it home, bloodied it up a bit with what was left on your copy? Then dropped it in the Dumpster by Tillman's motel?"

"I'm going to kill you, you know. There's no point rattling on like this."

Blood trickled down into my eyes. I wiped it away with my left hand. "How'd you get Ratliff to meet you like that? He wasn't suspicious?"

He laughed. "The P-O-D. Guy was a whore for Rutherford B. Hayes. Told him I wanted to brief him on a big Rodriguez story I was working on. But we had to meet secretly. I suggested the Hayes hearing room. He jumped at the chance."

"He had a wife, you know. Little kids."

"Don't talk to me about fucking kids."

"Ever think it wasn't Hershey's fault Kelly got pregnant?"

"Shut *up*."

"You're the one who wouldn't take her back. She wanted you to. Imagine what would have happened if you'd forgiven her."

He yelled even louder at me. I said nothing. I was listening. Not to the rally. To a sound, far below us. But maybe getting nearer.

I said, "You knew you had to get up here, somehow, didn't you? Your only chance to go after Rodriguez. That's the truth, isn't it?"

"Truth," Flanagan said, with a bitter laugh. "No such thing."

"Is that so?"

"It's what I traffic in," Flanagan said. "My bread and butter. My entire career. *Truth*. But all I do is scratch the surface. And sometimes what I write isn't even all that truthful."

"No shit."

"You know how tiring it is, covering the Statehouse? Everyone you meet, lying to you, day in, day out? The governor's office, the lawmakers, the cabinet directors? The aides, the lobbyists, the army of spokespeople? It's all lies. All the time. It's like a salmon run of lies, and in a good week, a very good week, we might spear one out of a hundred and lift it up and expose it to the light of day. But it's nothing. Nothing compared to the ones that get away."

Salmon run of lies. It was a good line. One he'd cultivated for years, I was guessing, fuming over it, using it as a flame to bring his anger about Hershey, about everything, to a slow boil.

"The truth," I said, feeling suddenly lightheaded. "It's what Lee was trying to do that night. In the pressroom. Tell you the truth about Kelly. Make good on a mistake he'd made. Get it out in the open, where it belonged."

"They could have saved her," he said. So quietly I almost didn't hear it.

"Who?"

Was it my imagination, or could I really hear footsteps? I listened harder, but the sound of Senator JoAnn Rodriguez's voice interrupted: "*Hello, Ohio!*"

Cheers erupted again, echoing across the square.

"Hershey. Ratliff. Rodriguez," Flanagan said. "If they had just told me, told me about Kelly. I know I was wrong, what I said to her. I haven't always been the best person. But I would have understood. I would have taken her back. I would have. Even if it was his baby."

"That's right," I said, as soothingly as possible.

"And maybe if I had, Kelly would still be alive. And I'd be a father, of sorts. Instead I'm a widower with no kids."

"You're crazy," I said, swallowing hard as I detected new determination in his voice. Something about the way he'd emphasized *widower*. "You'll never hit her. At that distance, with a handgun?"

"I can make the shot," he said flatly. "I only need to connect once."

"*. . . so good to be here in the Buckeye State. The state that knows a little something about sending people to the White House!*" Renewed cheers, even louder.

"It's time," Flanagan said, with a touch of weariness to his voice. "Keep your hands to yourself and I promise it'll be fast." He started walking again, his footsteps loud on the wooden floor.

"You never told me," I said, beginning to move, trying to gauge the direction he was coming from.

"Told you what?"

"Your favorite science fiction novel. Remember?"

"That's it? That's the last thing you want to know?"

"Why not? I asked everyone else."

He materialized suddenly, rushing around the curved wall, and faced me. I had miscalculated. The gun was in his hand.

"I asked everyone else," I repeated, desperate to stall.

"You're such an asshole. Just like Lee."

"I just want to know," I said, tightening my grip on the handle of the gavel.

He laughed harshly. "*Do Androids Dream of Electric Sheep?* The book *Blade Runner*'s based on. Satisfied?"

I laughed. "That's too precious."

"What?"

"That was Lee's favorite, too. That's so pathetic."

"Stop it," he said, confusion crossing his face. "Shut up."

"Wife, scoops, even books. Hershey had you covered on every single thing."

"I loaned him that book!" Flanagan bellowed. "I read it first! Not him! You understand? *I read it first—*"

I didn't give him a chance to finish. I knew that high up in this house of government, an edifice built over decades and enduring now for centuries, I'd bought myself a couple of seconds at best. I side-swung the gavel at Flanagan as hard as I could, hitting him on the side of the head with a sound like a stone dropped into drying mud. He cried out and fell back, his gun hand lowering. I moved quickly and struck him again, this time coming up short and landing a blow on his shoulder. To my dismay the gavel's head snapped off and went clattering across the wooden floor. Flanagan staggered back farther, then righted himself with a hand on the wall. He met my eyes and started toward me, gun arm coming up. I raised my hand, intending to strike him with the gavel handle. But at the last moment Flanagan stumbled and fell toward me as the jagged edge of the handle tore into his exposed throat. I felt resistance, saw the gun, and pushed as hard as I could. Flanagan made a gasping sound, and something warm sprayed across me as he fell to the floor, hands scrabbling at the handle as I stumbled back, tripped and fell myself. Dazed, I made it to my knees, saw Flanagan writhing in front of me, saw the gun lying beside him, and started to inch toward it.

"Andy, no!"

I looked in the direction of the sound. There, at the top of the stairs, at the entrance to the Cupola, on the level known as 1861, stood a man with a gun in his hand who bore more than a passing resemblance to Commodore Oliver Hazard Perry.

Outside and far below, I heard Senator JoAnn Rodriguez's voice begin to rise over a sea of cheers: *"And that's why today, right here in Columbus, the city in the heart of the great state of Ohio, it's my true pleasure to announce . . ."*

I lay my head down on the wooden floor. It seemed as good a time as any to surrender.

63

"LIKE OHIO'S VERY OWN WATERGATE!"

So Suzanne Gregory breathlessly described the developments unfolding at the Statehouse during one of the numerous stand-ups for Channel 7 she did over the next week. She wasn't alone. The TV satellite trucks encircled Capitol Square like elephants at a waterhole, and each came stocked with its own well-dressed and well-coiffed reporter from across the country explaining the shocking, *shocking* developments out of swing state Ohio, with the Statehouse and its unique Cupola behind them as backdrop.

I felt somewhat responsible for their presence. More or less against direct orders from Hummel, I'd turned over the entire cache of documents that Bonnie and I unearthed to three reporters: Suzanne, Kevin Harding at the *Dispatch*, and a guy from the AP I'd gotten to know recently. The resulting headlines were a bipartisan disaster. JoAnn Rodriguez dropped Hubbard as a potential veep faster than you could say "radioactive isotope." In turn, she faced considerable heat over the revelation about Flanagan's pregnant wife and her role in suppressing the fact for political gain. Regan was very busy that first week. Dani Symmes resigned her position as House Speaker as two separate ethics

285

investigations were launched, and there were threats of a recall election. President Ryan's campaign, meanwhile, had to explain the little business of planting a mini–Mata Hari in Hubbard's office. The whole thing about the driving school run by Anna's father came out anyway. Oops.

The final casualty from the dump of documents from Hershey's cloud storage account was one I had not expected. It was an e-mail chain in one of the reporter's folders that revealed the leak behind the EQUITY memo.

"'Cradle Democrat'?" I said to Kerri MacKenzie the following week, when I finally persuaded the aide to meet me back at Cafe Brioso. "'Cried the night Obama was elected? Party first?'"

"Somebody had to do it," she said, not meeting my eyes. "The Robin Hood approach would have killed ABC. Everybody thought it was so daring, but I knew it was a goner. It had to be outed."

"So you just handed it to your favorite investigative reporter."

She nodded, defiant.

"And everyone thought it came from Dani Symmes. Which was fine by you and her, it turned out."

She shrugged.

I lowered my voice a little. "But I'm thinking maybe politics wasn't really the reason you gave it to Lee."

"What do you mean?"

"When I told you about him going to the Cupola with someone, you seemed taken aback. I didn't think much of it at the time. I mean, who wouldn't be a little shocked hearing that?"

"What are you talking about?"

"But you weren't shocked because he'd been up there with someone, were you? You were upset because it hadn't been you. Were you in love with Lee?"

"No."

"Are you sure? Is it possible you were hoping for an additional outcome by giving him that memo? Such a big scoop? Something besides saving Triple F?"

She didn't bother trying to correct the name of the school-funding bill. "I guess we'll never know, will we?" she said, her eyes filling with tears. "Him getting killed when you were supposed to be protecting him and all."

I left it at that. There wasn't anything else to say.

Ephraim Badger emerged from his coma at last, and, once well enough to talk to Hummel, confirmed that Flanagan had come to the Crypt and asked to see the permission forms. Scared at Flanagan's anger over being denied access to them, Badger took the forms home with him, just to be sure. And it was at home, he said, where Flanagan showed up a few days later. Very angry this time.

Jim Flanagan's funeral was a family-only affair. I was glad to hear he was to be buried next to his late wife, Kelly. The prosecutor was insisting on taking my involvement in his death to a grand jury, but Lieutenant Hummel assured me it was a formality given the circumstances. In the end, the commodore was right.

Ironically, the person who came off the best was Liz Brantley. News that she'd ghostwritten Hubbard's autobiography cost her her job at *Capitol Corner*. But the prepublication orders that soared for her book *Swing State Ohio* apparently softened the blow. I called and left a message congratulating her. But she never called me back.

64

DURING THE EXTENDED SUMMER WHEN MY uncle finally brought me to my senses with a string of fourteen-hour workdays and a drove of mean hogs, he leavened my rehabilitation with Sunday services at his local country church. As I was literally at his mercy in the form of room and board and the clothes on my back, I had little choice but to go along without complaint. I think I became a better person in the aftermath, but I haven't been back to church much since. Some habits were going to take more than cleaning out manure lagoons to break. But for obvious and perhaps not so obvious reasons I dragged myself to Roy's church the following Sunday, figuring it might be one of the last chances I had to hear him preach. Even Anne came along, with Amelia, who sat wide-eyed at the sight of Roy's hard-bitten congregants. At the back of the hall, I noticed, Morticia and Gomez listened intently.

"So what are they doing here?" I asked Roy afterward, over stale cookies and staler coffee. Talk about swill.

"They're making me an offer I can't refuse."

"Namely?"

"They want me to go work for them."

"As what? Uncle Fester?"

"As a priest."

"You already have a church."

"Not for much longer."

"What are they proposing?"

"Setting me up as a kind of mission. Sponsored by the Episcopal diocese."

"Is that a fact."

"My budget would double. More resources. A small staff. Plus volunteers. Do-gooders from the suburbs. You can imagine."

"Do-gooders have to live someplace," I said.

"I'd have to take the cloth."

"Sounds kinky."

"It means I'd serve as an Episcopal priest. Since I was raised that way and served as one in Iraq, it's not that big a stretch. Do you ever think about anything but sex?"

"I'm big into science fiction novels at the moment, as a matter of fact," I said, reaching out and taking Anne's hand. I looked for Amelia, but she was back at the cookie table, talking with Theresa Sullivan.

"It's a giant compromise," Roy said. "The kind of thing I told myself I would never do. Because of all the crummy things mainstream churches do to make people's lives worse. The waste, the hypocrisy, the pettiness. What I do is disorganized, but it's better than 90 percent of organized religion."

I took a sip of coffee to avoid stifling a yawn in front of him. I had heard this diatribe many times.

"But some days I feel like Sisyphus with athlete's foot. No matter how I try, I can't get anywhere. Don't seem to make a difference. Short of money, short of time. Sometimes short of faith."

I took another sip. I said, "Is that a ponytail?"

"What?"

"Your hair," I said. "You're growing a ponytail, aren't you? I noticed it at the bar, the night I zonked. I just thought you couldn't afford a haircut."

"I just poured my heart out, and all you can do is ask about my hair?"

"It's a little Steven Seagal," I said. "With a frisson of Roger Federer. Except that it's gray. I kind of like it."

"Screw you," Roy said mournfully. Anne frowned at me.

"Screw you yourself. You're a liberal Democrat who signed up for Bush's war against 'terrorism'"—full-bore air quotes here, in my best Lee Hershey fashion—"while you walk around the 'hood with a concealed carry license as you badmouth the NRA."

"So what?" he shot back. "I'm also a married man who lusts after Julianne Moore. What's your point?"

"My point is for you to get off your high horse for a change. Life isn't as black and white as you pretend, even if you would be wearing it all the time. Embrace the gray, speaking of your hair color."

"That's all you've got?"

"What difference does it make what brand you are? You're not going to stop doing good for the people you work with now, are you? The ladies and the drunks and the homeless and the sinners? All them types. Though maybe not the tax collectors."

"Be surprised," Roy said, but quietly.

"You'd be the best Episcopal priest with a holster under his cassock or whatever they wear that I know."

"You think so?"

"Yes," I said. "I think so."

"Me too," Anne said.

"Thanks," Roy said. "Because that's what I told the diocese. Without the holster part. So you can take your gray and shove it."

"That's the spirit," I said. "What about the name?"

"Name?"

"Church of the Holy Apostolic Firewater. I've always kind of liked it. Could you keep that?"

"Probably not."

"Any contenders?"

He hesitated. I waited.

Roy said, "They're thinking St. Andrew's."

65

WE TURNED DOWN LUNCH WITH ROY AND his wife, since we were due up north to watch Bonnie in her Roller Derby season opener. As Anne and Amelia and I got into the van, I said, "I finished *The Sparrow* this morning."

"Oh good," Anne said. "What'd you think?"

"I liked it. It was really good."

"I'm glad." She reached into her oversized green purse. "I was going to give this to you later, but it seems like the right time." She pulled out a book and handed it to me. I examined it. *Children of God.*

"It's the sequel," she said.

"It keeps going?"

"There's always another chapter," she said.

From the back, Amelia spoke up.

"That lady Theresa was nice."

"Yes," Anne said.

"She taught me a joke. She said to tell it to Andy. Wanna hear?"

I looked at Anne, who looked at Amelia, then back.

"OK," Anne said.

"Knock, knock."

"Who's there?" I said.

"Woody."

Anne and I exchanged glances.

"Woody who?" I said.

"Woody you want, anyway?" Amelia said, bursting into laughter.

Acknowledgments

I've been privileged to work with the greatest Statehouse press corps in the country for several years. None of them is murderous, so far as I know, but many have written stories that made people in power uncomfortable. I admire them greatly. Thanks especially to Tom Suddes, formerly of the *Plain Dealer*. The weekly political columns he writes from Ohio University helped inform this book, especially Teddy Roosevelt's comment about state politics and James Thurber's "Ohio Look." I'm also indebted to my Statehouse colleagues at the Associated Press, Statehouse correspondent Julie Carr Smyth and legislative newswoman Ann Sanner. I appreciate their talents and collegiality every day.

I'm grateful to Luke Stedtke, communications and marketing manager for the Capitol Square Review and Advisory Board, for hardly blinking at all when I asked for his help figuring out how to kill someone at the Statehouse. He interrupted his busy days many times to answer questions and show me around. Chris Matheney, the board's historic site manager, was generous with his time, answering numerous queries and giving me a personal tour of nooks and crannies in the Statehouse I'd never seen despite fifteen years working in and around the building. One of the things Chris showed me was the charcoal sketch that an inmate named Ephraim Badger did of himself on a limestone wall more than a century ago that survives to this day.

Amanda Wurst graciously described the layout of the governor's offices on the thirtieth floor of the Riffe rhymes-with-knife Center. Martin Yant of Ace Investigations responded in depth to several questions about a private eye's job and helped me plot Andy's actions to and fro. Terry Myer, president of Columbus

Detective Agency, continues to be a valuable source for insights into the way real private detectives do their job. After all this assistance, any errors in the book are strictly my own.

As always, I'm thankful to the staff of Ohio University Press for their support and hard work, beginning with Gillian Berchowitz, director of the press, whose suggestions on early drafts of *Capitol Punishment* led to a much stronger book; the press's managing editor, Nancy Basmajian, for her keen eye and spot-on recommendations; press production manager Beth Pratt, who once again created an amazing cover; and sales manager Jeff Kallet and promotions and events manager Samara Rafert for their tireless efforts publicizing my work.

Three books aided my research in particular: *A Fragile Capital: Identity and the Early Years of Columbus, Ohio*, by Charles Cole; *Historic Columbus Taverns*, by Tom Betti and Doreen Uhas Sauer; and *Chasing Oliver Hazard Perry: Travels in the Footsteps of the Commodore Who Saved America*, a remarkable history book, travelogue and memoir by Craig Heimbuch.

Most of the places in *Capitol Punishment* are real, starting of course with the Statehouse. As always, though, there's a reason they call it fiction. Central Ohio used to have a Bridgeport, home of the Wardleys, but it was subsumed by Gahanna, an actual suburb, back in the 1800s. The Clarmont is no more, alas, a victim of the recession and changing eating and drinking habits among the city and state elite. I resurrected the restaurant out of respect and in hopes of reminding readers of its importance to governance: a fourth branch of Ohio politics. Similarly, Heyl's Tavern was a vibrant place of the past that exists only in my imagination today. The Ringside, however, is alive and well, and is worth dropping by just for a look at the bipartisan stained glass. Who knows? The downtown bar may outlive the Rhodes Tower yet.